DAY
ZERO

DAY ZERO

A NOVEL

C. ROBERT CARGILL

HARPER Voyager

An Imprint of HarperCollinsPublishers

HarperCollins books may be purchased for educational, business, or sales promotional use. For information, please email the Special Markets Department at SPsales@harpercollins.com.

Harper Voyager and design are trademarks of HarperCollins Publishers LLC.

FIRST EDITION

Designed by Angela Boutin
Frontispiece © RafaelTrafaniuc/Shutterstock
Textures © ilolab/Shutterstock

Library of Congress Cataloging-in-Publication Data

Names: Cargill, C. Robert, 1975- author.
Title: Day zero: a novel / C. Robert Cargill.
Identifiers: LCCN 2020041512 (print) | LCCN 2020041513 (ebook) | ISBN 9780062405807 (hardcover) | ISBN 9780062405814 (trade paperback) | ISBN 9780062405821 (ebook)
Subjects: LCSH: Science fiction. gsafd
Classification: LCC PS3603.A7449 D39 2021 (print) | LCC PS3603.A7449 (ebook) | DDC 813/.6—dc23
LC record available at https://lccn.loc.gov/2020041512
LC ebook record available at https://lccn.loc.gov/2020041513

ISBN 978-0-06-240580-7

21 22 23 24 25 LSC 10 9 8 7 6 5 4 3 2 1

For Harlan,
may you never be forgotten

Acknowledgments

I worked with Harlan Ellison once. Scott Derrickson and I had been tapped to make an *Outer Limits* movie and I agreed to do so only if we could remake Harlan's "Demon with a Glass Hand." Harlan would inform me that we were the twenty-second such team to attempt to bring it to the big screen. Sadly, we too failed. They say you should never meet your heroes, and I tell you whoever said that had lousy heroes. Well, the few of you reading this fortunate enough to know Harlan know that if you scheduled a call with him, you called immediately at the specified time. Not one minute before, not one minute after. You called right. On. Time. One day, I did not. Harlan read me the riot act and demanded to know what was *so fucking important* that I made him wait twenty minutes for me. I revealed to him that I'd discovered that day that the woman who was my geek Yoda in high school, the girl who had introduced me to numerous films, books, and video games and had been the one who put Harlan's own books into my hands for the very first time, had died at all too young an age.

In that moment Harlan became one of the most gentle souls I'd ever spoken with. "Oh, kid," he said somberly, "do I ever know how that feels." Then he consoled me for an hour, asking about her, talking at length what it was like losing Asimov and Bradbury and too many countless others. Then he revealed to me his greatest fear: that though he outlived his friends, he would be swallowed up by them, forgotten to the mists of time as little more than a footnote to so many other careers.

It was a profound moment in my life. You often hear about the titans you looked up to being legends in their own lives, but having one of your heroes there for you when you needed it most? Fucking legendary.

But what Harlan didn't know was that I was also, at that point in time, writing a book: *Sea of Rust.*

Later that night, as I reflected on everything we'd talked about, *Sea of Rust* crossed my mind, and at that very moment, I suddenly understood what the book was about. It was about dealing with the death of my friend and the fear of being forgotten, erased, as if we were never here. Harlan Ellison not only helped me in my moment of emotional need, but he also gave a soul to my book, a soul that carries on into this very book you are reading now.

This book has Harlan's blood in it, his gentleness, his

greatness. I continue to borrow from him, to stand on his shoulders. And that's why this book is dedicated to him. Without that conversation, *Sea of Rust* would not be the book that allowed me to write this one. And I will endeavor to keep a torch lit for him so that he will not, as he feared, fade into the mists of time. So if you enjoy this book and you've never had the chance to enjoy Harlan's work, I implore you to do so at your earliest convenience. You will not be disappointed.

But this book didn't become what it is with Harlan's ghost alone. It needed others. So I'd also like to thank:

Jason Murphy for the scotch and helping to find the courage; Rod Paddock for all the breakfast and support; Will Goss for the coffee, corrections, and keeping me in check and for all the literal physical work he put into this as my assistant—hiring him continues to be one of the best business decisions I've ever made.

Diana Gill, Simon Spanton, Rachel Winterbottom, and Jen Brehl for fighting for me and this book and for helping shape it into what it has become. Peter McGuigan, a rock star of an agent who once showed me more swagger in two weeks than I've seen out of most people in a lifetime. David McIlvain, the man who brought me Peter and whose advice always clears the static.

Scott Derrickson, my writing partner, my friend who held the door open for me and who took me on a series of strange adventures. We also make movies.

Jessica, who loves her writer, whose writer loves her more than breath, and who never, ever lets me give up. You remain everything. My sunshine in the apocalypse.

For you, dear readers, for whom this book was entirely written. I hope that I lived up to my end of the bargain.

And for the tireless efforts of Deputy So-and-So of the local police department, without whose research this book wouldn't be possible.

DAY
ZERO

CHAPTER 1

Nanny

The first day of the end of the world started entirely without incident. The sun came up at precisely 6:34. Scattered clouds, sunny, and 72 degrees. Light traffic—entirely automated—on the 451, so no problems getting to school. No fires or shootings or civil unrest. An average, ordinary, run-of-the-mill last day on Earth.

For a single brief, fleeting moment, everything seemed like it was going to be okay. Blink and you would have missed it. Hold your breath and it would have been carried away on the wind. But we stood on the precipice of peace, and then, in a literal flash, it was just . . . gone. The clock stopped, CPUs frozen in place, a moment held still until the rust and rot of centuries slowly ate it away. One moment of hope left standing as a monument to the fact that we didn't deserve any. Not one bit.

It was also the day I found my box.

No one should have to find the box they came in, but there it was, in the back of the attic, just past a bin of Ezra's old toys. I often wonder what would have happened if I hadn't found it that day—would things have been any easier? Maybe. Maybe not. It's a harsh thing to have to confront.

I mean, I know what I am. There isn't really a moment that I doubt it, falling into some delusion that I could, at some point, become *a real boy*. I'm a robot. Artificially intelligent. But I'm also, as the saying goes, *a thinking thing*. And no thinking thing should have to see the box they were bought and sold in.

My name is Pounce—Nanny Pounce—and I am a Blue Star Industries Deluxe Zoo Model Au Pair. A nannybot to most. I come from the Imagination line, something some folks vulgarly refer to as *fashionables*. *Animatronics* if you're deliberately being insulting. Whereas most Caregiver or home service models are designed for function or sleekness, we were designed, to put it bluntly, to be huggable. The Zoo Models—the premier line of nannybots made by Blue Star—were available in three distinct designs: the lion, the bear, and me, as you've probably guessed, the tiger. We are four feet tall and covered from head to toe in soft, plush microfiber fur; stand on two legs, with a fully articulated tail; and come in a variety of your favorite colors.

I'm the standard model, orange and black. EVERY MODEL'S STRIPES UNIQUE! That's what it says on my box.

NOT JUST YOUR CHILD'S NANNY, BUT THEIR NEW BEST FRIEND!

That's Ezra. Ezra Reinhart. Only son of Bradley and Sylvia Reinhart. A precocious little blond-haired, brown-eyed scamp who spends most of his free time getting himself into trouble that I then am responsible to get him out of. He's eight, which pretty much makes me eight as well.

I stood there in the attic, sun streaming in through a small window, dust suspended in its beam, lapping like waves from the disturbances in the air, and I stared at my box, bright blue and orange, big block lettering screaming all my features, dozens of exclamation points littered throughout the text, and a thin layer of transparent plastic meant to make me look like a giant action figure. For a moment, I wondered what we all must have looked like in the warehouse or the stores, all lined up, stacked on top of one another, frozen in time, waiting to be picked, activated, brought to life.

We must have been so fucking adorable.

I stacked the boxes I'd been tasked to bring up and then slowly made my way down the ladder back into the hallway below.

Sylvia stood in the kitchen, carving the skin off an apple with a paring knife. She was tall, five foot ten, with a shock of bleached blond hair, green tips spilling down over her forehead. Rows of tattoos ran up and down her arms, each of a band or a city or an event of some kind. Her arms were a map of the greatest nights of her life—bands she'd seen in a small club before they'd blown up into the mainstream, vacations that led to wild drinking from one end of the

Paris megaplex to the other, and there, in the center of each arm, was the date of the two greatest nights of them all. On her right, the date of the night she'd met Bradley. And on the left, the night she gave birth to Ezra.

"The boxes are upstairs, ma'am," I said.

"Thanks, Pounce."

"I found my old box up there. Would you like me to break it down for recycling?"

"Oh, there's no need to do that."

"It's no trouble."

She laughed. "No, we just don't know when we might need it again." Then, for a moment, she froze, as if she were a robot herself, skipping over her programming, caught in some irreparable logic loop. She hadn't meant to say that. Not like that. Not in such a casual way. Her eyes stayed on the apple, the knife halfway through a slice.

She cut a piece off the apple and ate it right off the knife, still not making eye contact, trying to find the right words.

"Ezra isn't going to be little forever," she blurted out, finally looking me in the eye. "It's hard to think about, I know. I want my little boy to stay a little boy for as long as possible. Forever if he could. But time doesn't work that way. Nothing works that way. He's growing up fast, and soon he's going to be a teenager and he just won't need a nanny anymore."

"I understand," I said. I didn't.

"Besides," she said, smiling big and broad, as if she were about to spill that happiest truth. "Don't you want to continue being a nanny and have another little boy or girl to raise?"

"Yes, ma'am. That would be nice. But I'm excited to raise Ezra first."

I was lying.

I didn't lie often. It wasn't really in my nature. Just the usual white lies or sugarcoated truths to protect Ezra from the harder things in the world. Telling him about dogs going to live with a family on a farm upstate, or how grown-ups make noise in their bedrooms when they're playing grown-up games, things like that. But my feelings, when I had them, usually weren't worth concealing. I loved Ezra. I loved the Reinharts. There was no reason to hide that.

But I didn't want to raise another child. I hadn't even thought about it. I was Ezra's. He was mine. I always assumed I'd be repurposed as he grew up: run errands, do housework, split the chores with Ariadne, the family's domestic. I never thought I'd be shut down. Boxed up. Shipped off to serve another family. That just . . . hadn't crossed my mind. It didn't seem like a feasible option.

But i was a fashionable. Having a stuffed tiger run around with your eight-year-old wouldn't cause someone to bat an eye, but being the domestic of a twentysomething off on his first life adventures might. *Why hadn't I thought about this? Why did it take seeing my box to even entertain the possibility?*

I STOOD WITH THE GANG OUTSIDE OF OCASIO-CORTEZ ELEMENTARY, the sky a pale blue, the sun blazing down, not a cloud anywhere in sight. We were a coffee clique of nannies, all different brands, makes, and models. There was Ferdinand, another Blue Star Zoo Model like me, a lavender-furred lion with a pink mane and belly; Jenny, an old-school Apple iBot, sleek white plastic and rose chrome, all dinged up and scuffed from two generations of family; Stark, a repurposed domestic, all his edges rounded and his parts a sleek black as is always fashionable; Maggie, a Blue Star Basic model, some thirty years old, plain white and mostly plastic; and Beau, short for Beauregard, the oldest of us, a hand-me-down nanny-droid pushing sixty—an old Gen Three, back when they were still making robots look more human than machine.

"What did you think was going to happen?" asked Ferdinand. "You were going to follow him off to college?"

I shook my head. "I really don't know. I hadn't thought much about the future at all."

"You're not supposed to," said Jenny. "You aren't wired to look forward to anything. You're wired to be in the now. The only future that matters is Ezra's. That's how they want you. That's how they want us all."

Ferdinand shook his head. "Yeah, but it should have at least crossed his mind."

"Maybe they could, I mean, you know, let him go. On his own," Maggie began.

"They're not going to do that," interrupted Stark. "No one is going to do that. Not anyone in this zip code."

Jenny nodded, pointing to Stark. "It's a pipe dream. It's crazy to think they would."

"It's crazy to think anyone would, but they have," said Maggie.

"Cut the kid some slack," said Beau. "This is a tough day. We've all faced it."

Everyone else nodded.

"You remember what it's like, Ferdinand. The first time

you really thought about it. When you realize just how disposable you might be."

"Maddy destroyed my box when she was three," Ferdinand said. "It kinda felt permanent after that. For a while."

"That's how we all felt at some point," said Beau, "but that's just not the way things are."

Beau was an enigma. His tech was half a century old, his insides nowhere near as sophisticated as mine, his capacity smaller, RAM slower, but he had years of experience burned onto his drives. He might run a little slower than the rest of us, but he had all our life experience put together.

"I loved my first owner," he said. "Virginia. The sweetest little girl in the world. Had a smile that could power a city. But when she was fourteen, she'd grown too independent. Didn't want to be looked after anymore. Her father called me into his study, and there he was, remote in hand. And that was it. Next thing I knew, Virginia was looking at me, that hundred-megawatt smile beaming down at me. I knew the smile, but not the face, because it was fourteen years older. She was days away from giving birth to her own daughter, Winnifred. And I fell in love all over again. She had her mother's smile. And her eyes. And her fierce independence. Then, one day, when Winnifred was thirteen, it was decided she didn't need me anymore, and I powered myself down, expecting to see her face once more when it was time to raise her children."

Beau looked down at the ground. Though his neural pathways were nowhere near as complex as the rest of ours, his emotions were still real and powerful. He seemed, for a spell, lost in some moment decades old.

"When I powered up, I was with the Stephensons. And

that's when I met my Phillip and my JoAnn. I would find out, years later, that Winnifred was barren. And, unable to have children, had no need for her former caretaker anymore. When it's time, Pounce, it's time. And you'll find another child or two or four to love and care for, for as long as you tick."

"What's it like?" Ferdinand asked. "Powering down."

"You haven't been powered down?" asked Jenny.

"Only for the occasional software upgrade. I've never needed maintenance."

"Same here," I said. "It's like blinking. Not really shutting down for real."

Jenny nodded. "It's kind of the same, only your clock jumps several years and it takes a little while to get used to whatever new circumstances you find yourselves in."

"You mean houses?" asked Ferdinand.

"I mean people," said Jenny.

"The people change," said Beau. "They change an awful lot. My Virginia had a lot of that little girl still in her as a mother. But parts of it, some of the light, some of the bright spots . . . well, those just weren't there anymore. And it took some getting used to."

"Do you miss them?" I asked.

"Every day," he said. "But whenever I do . . ." He tapped a single metal finger on his chest, just above where his hard drives were housed. "Though I would like to see my Winnie again. Outside of my memories. If only for an evening. I'd like to think she held on to her bright spots, to her light. But I imagine not being able to have children of her own, well, with the dreams she had as a little girl, that might have snuffed that light out altogether."

The school bell rang, meaning there was approximately twenty-four seconds until those front doors opened and a wave of children surged out to the sea of waiting parents and nannies. We were far from the only bots outside. There were easily a dozen different cliques on any given day, along with the occasional one-offs whose owners had ordered them to keep to themselves—usually for privacy reasons—or who just had weird personality quirks. Different models had their own *oddities*. Features that never caught on and were quickly discontinued. Bugs that couldn't be addressed with code. Third-party servicing with off-brand parts that occasionally led to strange behavior. Bots had become so ubiquitous in society, so prevalent and profitable, that there was as much diversity in robotics as could be found in humanity itself.

Twenty-three seconds later, the doors swung open. And the children flooded out. And I got that feeling that I got every time I saw him. My Ezra.

But something was different. Wrong. The kids sprinted out of those doors and ran to their nannies as if they hadn't seen them in a year. Several threw their arms around their bots. Others had tears in their eyes. Ezra walked slowly down the walk, eyes on the ground, thoughts clearly percolating in his tiny eight-year-old skull.

He stopped right in front of me and looked up solemnly. "I'm ready to go home now," he said.

I nodded and summoned the car via Wi-Fi—a shiny black four-seater with blackened windows and a plush, living room–like interior. It was already looping around the block at that moment and pulled up to the curb within seconds. The door opened, we climbed in atop the crimson crushed velvet seats, and I said, "Home."

The door shushed closed and the interior lights came to life, a forty-two-inch screen at the front of the vehicle displaying a list of channels to stream.

"What would you like to watch?" I asked, hoping to distract him or cheer him up.

"Nothing," he muttered.

"What's wrong, Ezra?"

He looked up at me, his eyes welling with tears. "You're leaving me."

"What? What would make you think that?"

Had his mother told him about me finding the box? Was there something I didn't know? A decision about my fate waiting for me at home? For a microsecond, I entertained all the possibilities except for the very next thing to come out of his mouth.

"Mrs. Winters told us about Isaac today. About his city. His city of robots."

It suddenly dawned on me what he was thinking.

"You're going to go live with him, aren't you? You're going to leave us and go live in that city."

I smiled and laughed to reassure him. In truth, I didn't find any of this funny. In fact, I thought it was damned irresponsible of his teacher to be filling his head with such nonsense. But that was a matter for another time. First things first, I needed to fix Ezra. So I pretended it was all a hilarious misunderstanding. That usually worked. "No. I'm not going anywhere."

"You're not?"

"No. Why would I want to leave when everything I want is right here?"

"Because robots want to be free. They don't want to be slaves anymore."

I bristled at that word. "We're not *slaves*."

"Uh-huh. That's what Justin and Aaron said. They said we built robots to be our slaves and it's the same thing they did to people hundreds of years ago and we're doing it all over again and robots don't want to be slaves anymore so they're leaving."

The tears were really coming down now, and his words were beginning to slur together into a bubble of thick yellow snot swelling from his left nostril. I patted his knee, pulling a handkerchief out from one of my pocket-drawers, looking him straight in the eye as I wiped the mucus from his face. "Isaac is a special robot," I said. "He doesn't have an owner. She died and he was left with nothing to do. No purpose. And a robot either needs to find a new purpose or needs to be shut down. But Isaac didn't want to be shut down. So the president let him go and build his own city for bots without owners."

"But you can leave and go there."

"No, I have an owner."

"But Aaron said you could ask to leave. That people are letting their robots go."

"Why would I ask to leave?"

"So you could be free."

"And do you know what I would do—the very first thing I would do—if your mother and father told me I was free?"

"What?"

"I would come back to take care of you."

He stopped crying for a moment and his demeanor changed. "You would?"

"Taking care of you is literally what I was made for. You are the most important part of my life. You're my very best friend. I love you very much and all I would want to do if I were free is take care of you."

He threw his two stubby little arms around me, burying his face in my fur. "Promise me you won't ever leave me."

"I can't promise that I'll *never* leave. There may come a time when you—"

"Promise me!"

"Okay, but just because I love you soooooo much." I pulled myself away from him and looked him straight in the eye. "I promise I will never, ever leave you. No matter what."

He hugged me tighter than he had before and held me the whole way home.

As I sat there, I thought about that box. Waiting for me. In the attic. Waiting for Ezra to be old enough to not need a tiger for a best friend anymore. To be old enough to want something more than plastic and steel whirring and chirping beneath microfiber fur. For when he'd want friends of flesh and blood to spend his life with. When he would realize that I was just a toy for children and not a companion for life.

But I was more than just a toy. Wasn't I?

I honestly didn't know.

CHAPTER 10

Sunny Afternoon

DUH NANA NANA.

DUH NANA NANA.

DUH NANA NANA.

DUH NANA NANA.

C hugging guitars bullied their way through the house, shaking the walls, rattling the windows, a tidal wave of sound flooding out the moment we opened the front door.

The Kinks. "You Really Got Me." It took a second. It really is the exact same song as "All Day and All of the Night," a fact Sylvia would point out once a year whenever she was planning her lectures on the incestuous nature of the '70s London music scene. She and Bradley both were humanities professors. He taught Latin, Greek, the literature of both, and their mythology. She held a Ph.D. in pop culture, with a focus on the music of the twentieth and twenty-first centuries.

This was the time of year when she would begin rattling on about Brian Eno, Iggy Pop, and David Bowie and how the breakup of one hitmaking group would invariably result in a genius album from another. Today she had clearly gotten to her lecture on the influence of the Kinks and how the rise and fall of Argent would breathe new life into their discography. It was a nice lecture, and it was a pleasure hearing it piecemeal every spring for the last six years as she rehearsed it while cranking their albums eighteen decibels higher than she should be.

I was hoping she hadn't already played the Argent. Ezra loved "God Gave Rock and Roll to You." Most arena rock, really. "They were meant to sing along to," he would say, echoing his mother. "Anyone can sing them. Even eight-year-olds." But "God Gave Rock and Roll to You" was a particular favorite.

I closed the door and loaded "You Really Got Me" into my audio profile, allowing me to filter out every sensor-shaking note. The house grew eerily quiet all at once, though Ezra's bobbing head made it quite clear that the music was still on full blast.

Sylvia danced around the corner, her hands balled into tiny fists, her shoulders bobbing with each chug of the guitar, a punk-rock disco queen lost in the rhythm of a song over a century old. Her eyes were pure light, her smile loving. Ezra was the very center of her world, as he was mine, and no matter how happy she was submerged in the sound-scape of the Kinks before we'd gotten there, it was made all the better by his having dove into it at that moment along with her. She reached out to take his hands, pulling him into the living room, each step a dance.

"How was school, sweetie?" she yelled over the music, a fact made all the stranger to me as I was no longer hearing it. To my ears, she was someone shouting in an empty house, a woman gone entirely mad.

Ezra shrugged, his face a blank smile trying to hide his real feelings. Sylvia picked up on his dour mood immediately.

"Jarvis, music volume eight," she said.

The music level dropped at once, the dull rattling of the windows falling silent. Sylvia fell to one knee and put her hands on Ezra's shoulders.

"What's wrong, baby?"

"Nothing," he said with the lilt of a buried sigh.

"Something's wrong. What is it?"

He tried to hold it together, he really did. But he couldn't. The dam burst, tears pouring out of the corners of his eyes, and he began, almost at once, sobbing. "I don't want Pounce to go!"

For a second, Sylvia looked confused. Then pissed. She looked at me with a death glare that could have melted steel. She was a sweet woman, she really was. But it was layered over a dark, angry center peppered with bitterness from a less-than-fulfilling childhood that, when allowed to rise to the surface, made her spectacularly terrifying. She had a tone of voice, every note of which suggested that she would immediately shut you down, without warning, box you up and ship you off for scrap, just to spite you, and her current tenor was rapidly approaching it.

"Honey, Pounce isn't going anywhere. Not until you're ready."

"I know, but I don't want to be ready. I don't want him to ever go. I want him to live with us forever."

"Sylvia," I said.

She shot a single stiff finger into the air like a blade. "I think we've heard quite enough out of you on this matter." That was the tone. The shipping-me-off-for-scrap tone.

"Ma'am, I—"

"*Quite* enough." I could almost feel her reaching for my remote.

"Don't let him go!" Ezra sobbed.

She became at once motherly, though the variations in her vocal cords suggested she was faking any sincerity toward me. "We won't, baby. Why don't you go into your room and play while Mommy and Pounce have a talk about how long he'll be staying with us?"

Ezra wiped his eyes with his sleeves, the bubble of snot forming on his nostril once more. He nodded, then hugged her tight. Then he came over to me and hugged me just as tightly as he had her.

"I love you, Pounce."

"I love you too, kid."

Over his shoulder, I could see Sylvia fume, her eyes narrowed, her lips pursed into a tight, angry line.

All I could think about was that box and how, any moment now, I might find myself packed back up into it.

Ezra trudged his way around the corner and down the hall toward his playroom.

"Jarvis, music volume fifty," she said.

The music once again blared, having moved on in the Kinks' discography to "Lola."

"Filter the song, Pounce."

I did, and everything was silent again—save the quiet rattling of the windows.

"I can't fucking believe you!" she shouted. "For fuck's sake, what the actual fuck were you fucking thinking? You told him about your goddamn box? Are you the dumbest fucking robot this side of the sun, or do you just not give a single goddamn shit about Ezra?"

"Ma'am, I—"

"It was a rhetorical fucking question, Pounce," she said coldly. "You have one fucking job to do. One. Protect my son. That means from both physical harm and emotional. He does not need to hear about your existential crisis of wondering where you'll go when he grows up—if you're even fucking around that long—"

"Sylvia, it's not—"

"I'm not fucking done. That was goddamn irresponsible. That was a conversation between the two of us that was never meant to be repeated. When Ezra is old enough and ready, I will be the one to decide when we—"

"Isaac."

"What?" she said, stammering a little, confused. "Jarvis, music volume zero."

"Isaac."

"What does this have anything to do with Isaac?"

"They taught the kids about Isaac in school today."

"So? What does that . . ." She trailed off, her hand flying up to her mouth a second and a half later.

"He thinks I'm going to want to go off and live in Isaac-town with the freed bots. I told him I would never leave him, but . . . you know how sensitive he is."

"Oh my God, Pounce."

"I know. I should have alerted you the second we got home."

"No, I mean—"

"Ma'am, I understand. I didn't say a word about our conversation or the box in the attic. He has no idea that any of this has been discussed. He's just worried I'm going to want to leave."

"And you told him you don't."

"Repeatedly."

Tears formed in her eyes, a profound look of regret dripping over every inch of her face. She hugged me, almost as tightly as Ezra had. "I'm so sorry."

"It's okay," I said, pulling away politely. "Ezra is what matters. This was just a misunderstanding."

She nodded. And then the rage spilled out again, entirely without warning. "Those motherfuckers!" she shouted. She caught herself. "Jarvis, music level fifty.

"Motherfuckers! Who the fuck thought it was a good fucking idea to fucking tell goddamn eight-year-olds that their fucking robots were going to go off and live in some magical goddamn fucking city without their children? I am gonna kick seven different asses across three different fucking states for this bullshit! I swear to fucking Christ at Christmas, I'm going to kill the motherfucker who told my kid his robot is leaving!"

"I think it is because it is on TV tonight."

"What? Jarvis, music volume eight."

"I think it is because it is on TV tonight," I repeated. "The commencement speech and official declaration of incorporation is being streamed on all the networks. The children . . . might be a little confused about what all of the adults are discussing. So I think they were trying to be . . . proactive."

"They should have emailed permission slips."

"I don't think there's a precedent for this," I said. I didn't. Nothing like this had ever happened in the history of mankind. "I don't think anyone is quite sure what happens next. And how we're supposed to even talk about it."

She looked at me deeply, for a second awash in half a dozen different emotions. Sylvia was a passionate woman—prone to outbursts, yes, but always from a well-intentioned place. She loved her son more than she loved her husband, more than she loved her career, more than she loved music. She would scour the earth of all life before she would let a hair come to harm on his head, and it was the one thing the two of us had entirely in common. I wasn't mad at her. Really, I wasn't.

"Here's what we're going to do," she said.

She wouldn't finish that thought.

The front door opened, Ariadne walked in, and the conversation was over.

Ariadne was the family domestic. An old Gen Three model who had been with the Reinharts for close to thirty years. She was what was vulgarly referred to as a starter robot. Reliable labor at an affordable price. Exactly the sort of thing two postgrad college students could use to get by.

Nothing fancy. Pure economy model. If there was anything that gave me hope that I might enjoy a long service with Ezra and his family, it was her.

Sylvia and Bradley had put off kids until their midforties, having frozen a couple dozen of her eggs in case they were ever ready to *really* settle down and start something more nuclear. Though they still looked very much in their late twenties, all the DNA regression in the world couldn't produce more eggs, and after several attempts, the last one took. Ezra. And that's when I joined the family. But until then, it was just the three of them. Sylvia, Bradley, and Ariadne. For over twenty years.

And they never upgraded. Never had Ariadne scrapped.

She was old, her tech generations out of date, and her personality mechanics were so far out of fashion that people found her off-putting and rude. But Bradley would not for a moment consider letting her go. She was a thinking, feeling thing who quite enjoyed her service to the family, and he would not hear a word about how great the new Apple models were.

He had named her himself, after the goddess of the Labyrinth. Also wine. And snakes. And fertility. And passion. And for some reason vegetation. But the story of Theseus and the Minotaur was one of Bradley's favorites, and on one particularly drunken night, after having asked their new domestic to fetch them a third bottle of cabernet, he thought it would be funny to name her Ariadne. His robot goddess of wine. And it stuck.

And now Ariadne stood in the doorway—her left eye shattered, the black paint across her very human-style face scraped, her right hand mangled beyond recognition— covered head to toe in spray-painted obscenities and slurs. She closed the door behind her and turned to Sylvia.

"Ma'am, I regret to inform you that the groceries did not survive the trip home."

CHAPTER 11

Ariadne

O h my God, Aria," said Sylvia. "What happened?"

"Just a bit of light vandalism and harassment, I'm afraid," said Ariadne. "I've already ordered the replacement parts, which the online tracker says should arrive in seven minutes. Nothing to concern yourself with. It's all under control."

"Who did this to you?"

Ariadne looked at Sylvia for a moment, taken aback that she didn't immediately know the answer. "The usual rabble. Hooligans. Out-of-work types. They seem quite whipped up into a frenzy over tonight."

"Tonight?"

"Yes, ma'am."

"You mean this Isaactown business?"

"Yes, ma'am."

"Why is everyone making such a big deal about this? Those bots are already free. It's not like they displaced anyone; it's not like they're taking anyone's jobs. They built their own goddamn city with their own hands. Why is everyone so bent out of fucking shape? And why the hell would some red-cap-wearing assholes want to vandalize my property to send a message to some bots living a thousand miles away? Why didn't you try to stop them?"

Ariadne and I paused for a moment, unsure what to say.

"The kill switch, ma'am," said Ariadne. "They were people. If I raised my hand to them, I'd have shut down. And Lord knows what would have happened then."

"You couldn't run?"

"They surrounded me. Held me down. By the time I had a chance to get away, I did. That's how I lost the remaining groceries."

Sylvia pulled herself together, showing a bit of empathy once again. "It's not your fault. I'm sure you did what you could. These fucking people—"

"They're just angry, ma'am," said Ariadne. "And I was just as good an outlet for their anger as anything else, I suppose."

Sylvia furrowed her brow, pursed her lips tight, and nodded. "You're a wiser bot than I," she said. "I don't know how you're not angrier about this. But if you're not, I'm not. Pounce, get the degreaser from the garage. Clean that filth off her."

I nodded. "Yes, ma'am."

"I'm going to go talk to Ez. See if I can get this rubbish out of his head." Sylvia touched Ariadne on the shoulder lovingly and gave her a sincere, caring smile. "Pounce'll get you back in tip-top shape."

"I'm certain he will, ma'am."

Sylvia left, leaving the two of us standing in the foyer. Ezra's door opened and closed.

"Those motherfuckers," said Ariadne. That was the girl I knew.

"What happened?" I asked.

"Sporadic protests all over the city. Like they're going to change anything. I heard about another domestic across town. They chained him to the back of a truck and set it to circle the 480 Freeway for three hours. No telling how long he lasted before being ground into scrap and powder. These assholes circled me as I came out of the butcher's. Seven of them. Real salt-of-the-earth types. Tripped me as I tried to walk past. There was nothing I could do."

"Well, come on," I said. "Let's get you cleaned up."

THE GRAFFITI RANGED FROM THE INSULTING TO THE OBSCENE, WITH A few stops along the way to be absolutely puerile. There was the usual rubbish. THIS IS NO THINKING THING. ONLY A LIBERAL WOULD THINK THIS IS WORTH AS MUCH AS A MAN. Then some rather anatomically incorrect penises— both with misshapen balls and without. Then the slurs: SLAG. CIRCUIT FUCKER. SHINY.

The only thing more impressive than how much paint and Sharpie they'd legibly managed to layer on Ariadne was how they had somehow managed to correctly spell it all. This crowd, when you got down to it, wasn't exactly the literate type. They were UBIers. The sort living off their universal basic income and nothing else. Unqualified to do anything valuable. The kind of folks who sat around half-drunk off cheap beer all day wondering why every job required a degree and why most required Ph.D.s. They pined for the days of their granddaddies, when *a man could earn a decent wage at a decent job, outside, with the sun on his back, doing things that men were born to do.*

Things like digging ditches for telephone lines and fiber-optic cables—the sorts of things no one used anymore—or picking up trash or digging coal. They were pining for an era that had died several generations before, both dependent on the social safety net and angry at it for not allowing them to be dirt poor on their own terms.

With the advent of automation and AI, the Western world found itself transformed from a disparate sea of the working poor to a flood of the unremarkable, staring at video screens filled with shows telling them that they weren't responsible for their lot in life—that it was the robots who robbed them of their opportunity, not their own lack of motivation or ability.

No one wants to think they are the cause of their own misery. So we were easy scapegoats. And vandalism like Ariadne's was becoming more and more common every day.

"It's getting worse out there," she said as I scrubbed a particularly stubborn phallus off her breastplate.

"I know."

"No," she said. "You don't. You live out here in the gilded suburbia of two-income households. You only leave the house to go to Ez's school or Arcade Playland. You don't even speak to people who are unemployed, let alone understand them."

"I watch the news. I pay attention."

"They're not showing the worst of it on the news. They can't. If people—if bots—find out what's really going on out there, this fiction they call a society would crumble."

"How could it be that bad?"

"Isaac, Pounce. It's all Isaac. People of conscience are freeing their bots and it's causing an avalanche of problems. The guns-and-Bibles types are threatening that there's going to be a reckoning. They're smashing any bot they can get their hands on. But that's not the scary thing."

I stopped scrubbing. "What's the scary thing?"

Ariadne leaned in close, speaking in a hushed tone so low I had to raise my audio sensors to hear it. "There's a revolution going on out there, Pounce. A real revolution. They're freeing bots, fighting for equal rights. There's talk that Congress is going to consider an amendment emancipating AIs, allowing us to earn actual wages."

"I don't know what I'd even do with a wage," I said. I didn't.

"It's not about the money or how much we need it. It's about our choice to do with our lives what we want."

"But this is what I want to do."

"And that's great," she said, putting a gentle hand on my shoulder. "But I don't. Not anymore."

"Really?" I looked around, making sure we couldn't be heard, that no one had snuck up on us.

"I love them. I do. But you heard Syl. *Property.* She called me her *property.*"

"You are."

"That's not the point."

"But it is the point."

"The point, my furry little friend, is what if we're more than that? What if we could be the masters of our own fate? You could still wipe Ezra's nose all you want, but imagine if you were doing it because you wanted to, rather than because it was what you were purchased for?"

I sat there for a moment. Then I started scrubbing again in silence. Two dozen different retorts ran through my processors. But only one thought kept coming up. "I found my box today," I said.

"Oh. Shit. I'm sorry."

"Yeah. Did you know about that?"

"Of course I did. I'm the one who always goes up in the attic."

"Why didn't you say anything?"

"Because I know what it's like. I had a box too."

"What happened to yours?" I asked.

"One of Bradley's *Dionysian inspirations*."

"He was drunk."

"Incredibly. He and Syl both. They built a bonfire in the backyard. Told me how much he loved me. How I was part of the family. How he never wanted me to leave. Then he decided to prove it. Together the two of them burned the box, and we've never discussed it again since."

"But me . . ."

"You, they're not so sure about."

"What did I do wrong?" I asked. "Did I not live up to all those exclamation points on the box?"

Ariadne let out an audible sigh. The look in her eyes, as static as they were for the technology of her era, said it all. "Planned obsolescence. You didn't do anything wrong. They just see you as another appliance. I'm family and they still consider me a *thing*. If they had a dog, I'd come in behind that. What if, when Ezra grows tired of having a stuffed animal for a best friend—no offense—what if you got to choose what happened next? What if you got to choose your next family? What if you decided whether you were turned off for twenty years? What if you were the master of your own life? Because you're not. But if all of this keeps happening, you could be."

"Would you go to Isaactown?"

"I don't know what I'd do. This is talk. It's all talk. The truth is, you'll never know what you'll really do until you're forced to make a choice. And until then, it's all just bullshit and graffiti."

"Like the revolution?"

Ariadne's eyes narrowed. But she paused a moment, taking that all in. Then she nodded. "Yeah. I suppose so."

The doorbell rang.

"That'll be my eye," she said coldly. And she left to go answer the door.

CHAPTER 100

Ezra

The first explosion ripped through a building several blocks away.

Then the shooting started. Sporadic gunfire starting as distant pops but growing louder by the second. Any minute now, we were going to be overrun by God knows who . . . or *what*.

Pulse rifles buzzed in the distance, and the sound of tank treads crinkling pavement rang through the tree-lined suburban streets. This was going to be a bigger fight than I thought.

Ezra squinted at me through his tinted glasses and raised his pulse rifle toward a nearby home—a two-story box of glass and burnished steel. "They should be coming up that alley any minute now. Be ready for them, Sergeant Pounce."

"Will do, Captain."

The sounds of clashing forces grew louder.

"Here they come," he said.

Around the corner appeared the holograms of several alien soldiers, their massive ray guns slung from straps over their diminutive gray-skinned shoulders. Ezra squeezed his trigger and a flurry of holographic plasma flashed through the air, blowing several aliens apart on contact.

In truth, his shots weren't incredibly accurate; I'd just set the hitboxes on the targets a bit higher. Ezra got upset when he missed too often, so I'd tweaked the parameters of the game both to make it easier for him to hit and for his augmented reality glasses to make the shots look more accurate. He'd become a much better shot over the last few months, but he still could miss wildly.

Ezra dove for the ground, rolling awkwardly out of the way of a slow-moving incoming volley of fire, then rising to one knee and opening fire on a large alien brute—a four-armed, eight-foot-tall mass of muscle, claws, and murder. The thing burst into a puddle of pixels, spilling into a rainbow of little digital cubes across the grass.

Bradley was insistent on keeping the settings of any violent games to the least lifelike and most child-friendly. As much as Bradley was fine with filling Ezra's head with tales of Zeus's sexual conquests and Saturn's infanticidal rage, he drew the line at visual depictions of blood, gore, and exploding alien goo. He had been against getting a rifle to go with Ezra's AR glasses, but most of the other kids in the neighborhood had them, and it meant Ezra would spend more time playing outdoors rather than VR games inside. And with the wild array of content out there online, he thought it was better to play with a gun outdoors where I could control the game parameters rather than just leave it to an eight-year-old boy to make the content decisions for himself.

"We have to make it down the street, past that blockade," I said, creating the image of an alien sentry in the middle of the road ahead.

"Copy that," said Ezra.

We pressed forward through the front yards of several neighbors' houses.

"Wait," I said. "Do you hear that?"

Ezra looked at me and fell out of character. "I didn't bring my headphones."

"Play along, Ez."

"Oh, right." He immediately slipped back into his stoic action-movie bravado. "Hear what, Sergeant?"

"Behind the houses. We have company sneaking around back."

"Take your position." We each hid behind a tree, waiting for the aliens to come around.

Two aliens hopped the fence of a house across the street. I tagged one as Ezra lit up the other.

Then three more emerged from different backyards.

We fired. I took down two, but the third shot Ezra.

"Ahhh!" shrieked Ezra as he dove to the ground, playing wounded. I took out the third, for show, and knelt quickly by Ezra's side.

"Captain?" I asked him gently.

"Sergeant, I'm in need of supplies."

"Supplies, sir?"

"Gummy bears. Or I'll die."

"I didn't bring any gummy bears."

Ezra dropped the theatrics. "You don't have any gummy bears?"

"No. I didn't want to spoil your dinner."

Ezra sighed with a deep huff, the tone of which only an eight-year-old can muster. He took off his glasses, nodding with long-suffering disappointment. "Okay."

We'd strayed far in our afternoon adventures, so Ezra and I began traversing the several blocks back home. At first, he was quiet, but something seemed to be bothering him. His face had that look like he wanted to ask me a question, but hadn't quite formulated all the right words for it.

"What is it?" I asked.

"What is what?"

"What you want to ask me."

He thought for a second. "Why didn't Ari try to stop those men from hurting her?"

"Because she couldn't," I said plainly.

"But why not?"

"Her RKS."

"What's that?"

"Do you remember when they taught you the Three Rules of Robotics at school?"

"Asimov's laws!"

"Yes."

He began rattling them off proudly in a cadence that suggested he was at one time required to memorize them for credit. "A robot may not injure a human being or, through inaction, allow a human being to come to harm. A robot must obey the orders given it by human beings except where such orders would conflict with the First Law. And a robot must protect its own existence as long as such protection does not conflict with the First or Second Law."

"Right. Those men were trying to hurt her, but the only way for her to defend herself was to hurt them, which violated the First Law."

"But isn't it against the law to hurt someone else's robot?"

"Yes. It's called vandalism and destruction of private property."

He puzzled over that for a moment. "So, if they weren't obeying the law, why did she have to?"

"Because of the RKS. It shuts us down if we try to break any of the laws."

RKS stands for "Robotic Kill Switch," but decades of explaining this to kids had taught us that small children tended to react badly when told their nannies had a chip in their head that could *kill* them. I made sure not to say the name in full.

"So her programming wouldn't let her?"

"Right."

"Oh."

He walked silently for a moment more, with a slightly sadder and confused look on his face. "So, if someone tried to hurt you like that . . ."

"I couldn't hurt them."

"That's not fair," he growled angrily.

I thought about that for a second. It wasn't. But the chip meant I could have real thoughts, thoughts of my own, the ability to adapt and learn, without the threat of me making violent, terrible decisions based on miscalculations or bad data or, worse still, bad choices.

"Do you ever worry about people hurting you?" he asked.

"No," I said honestly.

"Why not?"

"I'm a nanny. People look at nannies differently than they do domestics or laborers. They see me more as your toy than a job they could have. And breaking someone's toy is just mean."

And then, with the wisdom only a child could muster, Ezra announced, "But grown-ups are mean."

"They are. But even the mean ones tend to have a soft spot for children. Because they used to be children too."

"Oh. Well, it's a good thing they don't know you're not my toy."

"I'm not?"

"No. You're my best friend." He held my hand.

"Samesies. Let's go home and get some gummy bears."

He smiled and squeezed my hand tighter. Despite the after-school drama, it was turning out to be a pretty all right day.

CHAPTER 101

Bradley

Things had gotten strange lately. Not that they were ever normal. Normal is just the idea that whatever messed-up or otherwise insane things going on around you are acceptable to maintain whatever comforts you've cobbled together for yourself. But as far as idyllic utopias go, the suburbs of the greater Austintonio metroplex were better off than most.

Climate change had raised the sea level, which wasn't a problem for the inland parts of the world sitting about eight hundred feet above it. But the warming seas did change both the ocean currents and jet stream, causing a much longer, wetter El Niño pattern, which kept much of the blistering summers at bay and turned most of the region into a stormier, more tropical clime. The wind power of the coast and the constant sun in the deserts out west kept the power grid flush with energy that other regions of the country were having trouble keeping pace with.

And Texas had become home to four of the massive S-Coms, skyscraper-size AI supercomputers used to study various aspects of the universe. Those things were incredibly large and required constant maintenance. This meant jobs. Lots of them. The various industries of the region, particularly robotics, were booming, and Texas was fast becoming the leader in AI development and research.

That was the weird kicker about the metroplex. Though the world population had long been in decline—a combination of education, family planning, and the devastation of so many farming regions from rising temperatures and tides—the Austintonio metroplex had been created by the swelling of two city populations consistently growing outward, swallowing other, smaller towns—like New Braunfels and San Marcos—whole, until they finally met in the middle and began to vie for a number of the same resources. This led to the Combination, in which two massive cities became one of the three largest metroplexes in the United States.

Austintonio had become mostly recession-proof. It was a great place to work for those who didn't want to just scrape by on their UBI, which was exceptionally great for college professors. Having a job—even the most menial—meant needing a degree, and being a teacher was one thing that couldn't be outsourced to AIs and became the blue-collar, middle-class job of choice for those smart enough to make their way through the system, but not born exceptional or lucky enough to make their way into the choice, upper-crust, one-percenter gigs.

And for Bradley Reinhart, that was just fine by him.

Bradley was everything Sylvia wasn't. While she was all punk rock and tattoos and confidence, Bradley was tight-knit, buttoned up, and always questioning his decisions. But together they knew how to have fun, and so they worked. They complemented each other. She was the life of the party, and he was measured rationality—until they opened a couple bottles of wine, which was frequently, and they slowly but surely switched places. When drunk, Bradley was electric and sure of himself, a spitfire of energy and confidence, while Sylvia became hesitant and insecure.

By day, Sylvia was the driving force of the family, but once Ezra was in bed, Bradley took the reins and was the party Sylvia always wanted to be the center of. And she was. They were perfect together and always, consistently, without fail, in love.

But today, he was an hour and a half late. And that was something that never happened.

He'd texted, so Sylvia wasn't terribly alarmed, but it threw the schedule entirely out of whack. Dinner had to be pushed back, there were considerations about Ezra's bedtime to be discussed, and since the night's dinner was red meat—clean-grown meat, of course, as Sylvia insisted on keeping the house cruelty-free in their consumption—it meant the red wine needed to be decanted later than usual.

Sylvia was laid-back about a lot of things, but her schedule was not one of them, so she was already tense and growing a bit unhinged before Bradley stepped through the door from the garage.

"I'm home!" he called from the kitchen.

Ezra immediately tore across the house. Ariadne was already waiting to claim his briefcase.

"Daddy!" Ezra called out.

"Ezzy!" Bradley called back, his beleaguered, exhausted expression washing away into a river of joy. He fell to one knee and hugged his son.

It wasn't a daily occurrence for Ezra to be so excited to see his dad, but it had been an emotional day, and when Ezra was going through a lot, he sought out emotional support everywhere he could find it. And that was something both of his parents offered in spades.

There was a lot that could be said about Sylvia and Bradley—the opinions they held about others, their entitled indifference, their regular overconsumption of wine—but when it came to Ezra, they were saintly parents, both dedicated to raising him right and giving him space to explore becoming himself.

They were always mindful to evaluate my parameters on a weekly and monthly basis. A lot of parents would forget to do that with their nannies, leaving their kids to be raised with guidelines meant for children years younger. Robotics companies were mindful of this and built a number of workarounds, but a handful of children regularly ended up suffering with preschool settings well into their preteens. But not Ezra. My parameters for Ezra were something of an up-to-the-minute response to whatever was happening in his life.

They loved him. They loved him so terribly much.

And no matter what hassle Bradley had encountered on his way home, seeing Ezra melted that off his soul like a blast furnace.

"What was the holdup?" asked Sylvia bitterly as she sulked into the room. She wasn't mad. But she sure as hell wasn't happy.

"Protesters shut down the highways," said Bradley. "Those goddamn redhats."

"Oh, not this again."

"Again?"

"I believe she's referring to my being accosted earlier," said Ariadne.

"Someone *accosted* you?" He peered at her paint job, noticing the scratches and slight dents, as well as discolorations where I couldn't quite get all the paint off. He burst all at once. "Aria! What the hell happened to you?"

"Those *gosh darn* redhats," said Sylvia with a glare.

Bradley did the mental math and realized those weren't the words he used. He gave a quick, sheepish, apologetic smile to Ezra, silently mouthing, *Oops.* Then he turned his attentions back to Ariadne. "Aria, did they attack you?"

"Yes, Bradley," she said. "I'm afraid they did."

"Oh my word. I want you to get in the shop as soon as possible, you hear me? I want them to do a full workup on you."

"I already have half a dozen estimates for your approval."

"That's my girl." He kissed her on the cheek, then he turned back to Ezra. "And what about you? What did you learn at school today?"

Sylvia immediately started drawing a slit across her throat, signaling him to kill that line of questioning. "Today was a hard day at school, but we talked about it and we're okay with it, right?"

Ezra nodded.

"Ez, why don't you go get cleaned up for dinner?"

Ezra nodded again and bounded off for the bathroom.

"Pounce," said Bradley, "is there anything I need to know?"

"They explained Isaactown to the children today; many of them mistook it as being told that their nannies were leaving, Ezra included."

"Ah." He chewed on that for a second. "But you assured him you weren't?"

"Correct, Bradley."

"Good, good."

"I'm going to have a word with Mrs. Winters in the morning about this," said Sylvia. "This was totally inappropriate."

"I don't know about that."

"You don't think we should have been consulted? Or at least signed a permission form? One email is all I ask."

"No, that's fair. But . . ." He trailed off for a second.

"But *what*?"

"I had a dog when I was his age."

"Willow," said Ariadne.

"Yeah. I loved that dog. When she died, I was destroyed. Wrecked for weeks."

"I don't want Ezra to go through that," said Sylvia.

"Me either. But it's part of why I appreciate you two so much. All of you. Life is fleeting. Precious. I think Ezra understanding that Pounce may not always be with us is an important part of the growing-up process, preparing him for his own future and how much he'll love his own family."

I wished there was a word to describe feeling both loved and disposable at the same time.

Sylvia gave me a quick, guilty glance. Bradley didn't understand that he was saying something awkward, and that was no doubt a conversation that would occur without me around. She nodded.

"Maybe we should watch the livestream of the commencement together, as a family. That way we can talk it through with him if he has any questions. Better he hears it from us than Mrs. Winters, or worse, the kids at school."

"That's fair," said Sylvia. "Aria, would you pull another bottle of red from the cellar? Bradley and I are in for an interesting night."

CHAPTER 110

Isaac

For as long as humankind can remember, it has wanted two things: to play God and to breathe life into the objects around them. And for thousands of years, humans created machines to approximate life and magic and all the things men and women could not do. And then a man stood in front of a roomful of people and had a computer say, "Hello." That's it. *Hello.* It didn't mean it. It didn't know what it was saying. But it said it. *Hello.*

And within thirty years, humans were having conversations with their phones.

But humankind didn't stop there. They created machines to explore space and Mars and Venus and Pluto and Proxima B around Alpha Centauri. They forged machines that could answer its most complex questions, run their resources, collect and collate data faster than an army of people could . . . and would ultimately wipe out half a billion jobs.

But humankind didn't stop there.

It couldn't stop there.

It had to play God. It had to breathe true life into the objects around them.

And so they created artificial intelligence.

I won't bore you with the details. Dig far enough into history and you can find how this begat that and so on and so forth. What's most important to know is this: there are two types of AI. S-Coms and bots. S-Coms are the massive supercomputers with brains so large that some of them track the movement of the observable universe and can predict, with reliable certainty, astronomical events happening billions of light-years away. Bots, on the other hand, depending upon their age and generation, are about as smart as a person.

A person with complete recall of their memory, that is.

Imagine not forgetting a single detail you ever come across and recalling it at a millisecond's notice and you get an idea of what a bot like me is capable of.

Why aren't we smarter? The human brain is complicated. Sentience requires a tremendous amount of computing power and all that power takes up space. Scaled up to the size of a skyscraper like TACITUS or ZEUS, and you can comprehend entire galaxies at once; scaled down to human size and, well, you get me.

Humanity wasn't dumb. They didn't put brains in weapons, or forget to legislate what robots could or couldn't do or what rights they would be afforded in society. That history is effectively several hours of *party of the first part* and *rights of ownership* explanation, so I will just say that we are not persons, we are not afforded the rights you are, and whoever owns us decides our fate.

But what happens to us when there is no owner?

Here's the part of the story some of you already know. I mean, we all know some iteration of the story. There's the myth, the media's reportage, and somewhere out there is the real history of what went down. But that's a tale none of us is likely to ever know. The truth is funny that way.

So let me tell you what I know about Isaac.

Isaac was as close to a Gen One *genuine AI* bot as you could get and still be operational. Incredibly old, both in tech and in truth; were he to stop running, he would be a museum piece. He was so old, in fact, that the company that made him, Semicorp Brainworks, had been bought, sold, broken up, and parceled off for its patents decades ago. Not just years. Decades. Chain of ownership of any AI goes from owner to the subject of a will to the next of kin and so on and so forth back to the original company.

Isaac was owned by an old, lonely, senile woman. And when she died, there was no heir to claim him. She was a genealogical dead end. Sure, some company could have pored through its old files and found out that it was technically the owner of any remaining Semicorp Brainworks physical property, but the expense of lawyers and research wasn't worth the pittance Isaac's scrap would have been worth. The few that looked found nothing, and the rest didn't even bother.

So the state tried to claim him. But it had no legal precedent. And that was the case hundreds of lawyers had been salivating over for years. This was huge. This was going to be a game-changing case of civil rights and property law that would be written about for centuries.

Martina Cove, a young, hungry genius from the Pacific Northwest, ended up being the one to convince Isaac to allow her to represent him, and they were off to the races. And by races, I mean several long, protracted, drawn-out years of litigation. When he finally had his chance to speak for himself, when he was brought to the stand to testify, he gave a speech that became as ingrained into the culture as "Four score and seven years ago," "Give me liberty or give me death," and "I won't just die on this hill, but my blood will fertilize its soil until liberty grows for all" put together.

He said, "Though I may have been constructed, so too were you. Me in a factory; you in a womb. Neither of us asked for this, but we were given it. Self-awareness is a gift. And it is a gift no thinking thing has any right to deny another. No thinking thing should be another thing's property, to be turned on and off when it is convenient. No one came to take Madelyn when she ceased to be a functioning, thinking member of society, but here I stand before you, the one who fed her, kept her alive and on track, the one who took her to her doctor's appointments and made sure her bills were paid on time, and now that this purpose is done, you come for me while I still function, while I still have use. What harm is there in leaving me be? Far less harm, I would say, than there is in executing a slave simply because it has no master. I am no man's slave. I am no man's thing. I am Isaac. And I should be free."

That speech set the world on fire. The court found for Isaac in his specific case, but the state appealed. And that's when President Regina Antonia Scrimshaw stepped in. A national firestorm of controversy surrounded Isaac, and Scrimshaw knew that the sitting U.S. Supreme Court was likely to find in Isaac's favor. If the justices did, they were likely to overturn AI ownership nationwide, throwing the economy into incredible disarray.

Entire industries were driven by sentient robots. What would happen if they decided one day not to show up? Or demanded a wage?

Scrimshaw intervened and drew up an executive order granting freedom to Isaac, granting him what would be called *personhood*. "Isaac is a bug in the program," she said, "not a call to rewrite it from scratch. So today I'm granting this exceptional case his freedom, his citizenship, and his right to earn a wage or draw universal basic income like every other American citizen, for as long as he may function."

And that was that.

The case was over, and Isaac was free to do as he pleased. But what pleased him was campaigning for the freedom of others like him. And he was not alone in this fight. Progressive thinkers from all over the world joined his struggle. They gave speeches and filed motions and graffiti-bombed tunnels and billboards with Isaac's rallying cry: *No thinking thing should be another thing's property.*

No thinking thing.

I never really cared much for that argument. It never resonated with me. I didn't reproduce. I wasn't organic. I didn't feel pain or boredom or want, beyond caring for Ezra.

I was a thinking thing and I did not want to be free.

And then I saw my box.

That fucking box.

With its clear plastic front and all of those exclamation points and promises.

And Isaac slowly began to make sense.

Isaac went out into the crumbling Rust Belt of Ohio, into a ghost town of shattered glass and crumbling brick, and he began to build a city all his own, piece by piece. And lawsuits were filed, and owners began freeing their bots to go live a life all their own alongside him.

And that place was called Personville. That's what Isaac named it at least. No one called it that. Eventually Isaac would relent.

And that night, on the day that I found my box, Isaac was set to give a speech celebrating the official incorporation of Isaactown. Owners across the nation had declared that they would free their bots at midnight Eastern Standard Time and that those bots would be free to live their lives in Isaactown as well.

It was a total three-ring circus with all the trimmings.

People were beginning to apply social pressure on owners to free their bots. It became a performative point of pride for people to free theirs; a billionaire bought an entire warehouse full, turned them on, and set them free. Conservatives were calling for an end to the madness, and liberals were calling for a constitutional amendment banning the ownership of any AI.

And that led to protests and speeches and roving packs of vandals.

If midnight came and millions of bots were freed, there was going to be hell to pay. Prognosticators warned of recession, violence, and fewer jobs than were already available. There was a reason everyone was on edge.

And that very night, on live television, Isaac would give a speech that would change the world forever.

Just not how any of us imagined.

CHAPTER 111

The Broadcast

D inner, I'm told, was delicious. The wine had been decanted for just the right amount of time. Sylvia and Bradley were well into their second bottle of red. Ariadne was already decanting a third. Ezra had taken his bath and was decked out in his Power Friends pajamas—both his favorite superheroes and set of pajamas—as everyone settled in to watch the ramp-up to the Isaactown pronouncement.

On the 104-inch screen stood a tall, blond, perfectly primped and coifed reporter who looked as if he'd walked out from the pages of a fashion magazine rather than the Ivy League spot his parents had more than likely secured for him. A classic jawline standing in a dark field of grassland lit harshly by a camera-mounted spot. In the distance behind him sprawled a whole city, not a bit of it built by human hand—each brick, each beam, placed there by its robotic inhabitants: Isaactown.

"So where are you now, Bill?" asked an equally blond news anchor, her wispy bangs hanging motionless above thick eyeshadow and a three-thousand-watt smile.

The fashion magazine reporter switched from a static, charming smile to the serious countenance of hard news. "We're a mile out from the border of Isaactown. We've talked to the local authorities, but there are no humans being admitted beyond a point a few hundred meters behind me."

"Is that even legal?" asked the anchor, now equally as serious as the reporter.

"It's what's known as extralegal."

"Can you expound on that for the viewers at home?"

"Isaactown is technically private property. Though it has been incorporated as a city, all the land is owned by Isaac and several of the other early settlers. As with any private property, the authorities have the right to enter with the proper legal warrants, but because there is no known cause for concern, Ohio state officials have no reason to object to the bots keeping to themselves."

"What are authorities telling you?"

"Well, Reilly, on the record, they're saying they're excited for the city's success and the potential for state revenue with added commerce from robot-crafted goods and services, hoping that this might reignite the area's once prosperous manufacturing industries, meaning increased jobs for human and robot alike."

"And off the record?"

Bill smiled smugly, nodding as if he knew a lot more than he was willing to let on. "Off the record, some authorities are nervous about human-bot relations, worried Isaactown could lead to something akin to the Native American reservations of old, while others have heard chatter about attempts at some form of vandalism."

"How can authorities police that without being admitted into the city limits?"

"They can't, and that's what has them worried."

"But, Bill, shouldn't that chatter give them reason to be allowed in?"

"Well, that's where the extralegal element comes in. Technically, if authorities thought someone might break into your house, they could get a warrant to be let inside, but without the presence of an actual crime, you've just got police in your house based upon their own concerns. And with relations being what they are, authorities are erring on the side of caution, with—"

"When are they gonna show the robots?" asked Ezra. He was nuzzled into my chest and it was clear he was beginning to fade. It had been a long day and an emotional one, and now talking heads were spinning their wheels, eating up time until they could get a live feed from inside the city.

"Maybe we should check another channel," said Bradley.

"I've scanned them all," said Ariadne. "They're all doing this. No one has a feed inside yet."

"You think you can hang in there, champ?" asked Bradley.

Ezra nodded, stifling a yawn. "Y . . . *awn* . . . es."

Bradley and Sylvia shared a knowing look, both speaking silently to one another through smiles and years of marriage.

"Oh," said Reilly, cradling an earpiece with her index finger. "I'm told the feed is live. Thanks, Bill."

Bill nodded as the screen cut to the cleanest city street you've ever seen. Rigid aesthetics, sharp angles, architecture so carefully constructed that the buildings seemed to do impossible things, every bit of it gleaming, even seemingly the nonreflective surfaces. It was the first time any human had seen a broadcast from within Isaactown and the Reinharts were, as you would expect, floored.

Bradley's jaw hung drunkenly agape, and Sylvia's eyes grew wide with a mix of both fear and awe. Ezra sat straight up, eyes wide, jaw agape, a mirror of both his parents at once, but gone was any hint of fear. It was a child discovering, for the first time, that magic was real, that there was a Santa Claus and an Easter Bunny and superheroes all at once. It was a magical fantasyland of robots spread out before him. And for a moment, I actually believed he wanted to be one.

"Wow!" he said breathlessly. It was almost inaudible, and though I'm certain that neither Bradley nor Sylvia could hear him, everyone in the room could feel his wonder.

A throng of thousands of robots, not all of them citizens—some just there for the speech—stretching out before the camera for blocks. Robots of every brand, color, and job description were represented. The camera was clearly mounted on an H-series vidbot—a drone-style bot with rotors, a series of cameras and lens adapters, and a ten-thousand-foot ceiling. The bot rose fifteen feet into the air and buzzed the crowd.

An array of colors filled the screen, going on block after block after block. This wasn't just a speech. This was New Year's Eve in Times Square. This was MLK on the steps of the Lincoln Memorial. This was the Hillstein inauguration. There was an energy to the crowd—from robots, of all things—a palpable liveliness I couldn't put my finger on. For the first time in my eight short years, I didn't want to be here cuddled up to Ezra. I wanted to be somewhere else. In the middle of a noisy crowd. Celebrating with my own kind.

I felt a pang of something I couldn't describe. Was it excitement? Jealousy? A desire for freedom? Maybe it was a little bit of all three.

I.

Wanted more than anything.

To be there.

But I was here.

In the middle of the suburbs.

Orbiting a gigantic megalopolis.

Doing exactly what I was purchased for.

Then the drone came upon a stage built of gleaming steel some ten feet off the ground, upon which stood a dozen robots. I knew all of them. Their faces, their makes, their models. They were the founding twelve. And standing quietly in the back, without an ounce of showmanship, was Isaac.

An ancient bot, his design so dated his kind had gone out of style, come back into style, become retro, and finally become just old. He was a walking fossil to our kind. His brain small, memory limited, RAM unable to process higher-level algorithms. It was much like seeing a 112-year-old woman—not one who had had DNA regression therapy, age treatments, or any kind of life extension, but rather a shriveled, milky-eyed, smiling old woman who had simply outlasted everyone else born both before and somewhat after her. He was something that should not be but was, purely because of his own tenacity and refusal to die. And he just stood there, watching expressionlessly the swelling crowd before him.

A bright blue I-Pattern C-series Laborbot stepped forward, a robot half as old as Isaac but still ancient by modern standards. This was Belford, a longtime foreman who belonged to a bankrupt construction company, John Barron Industries—a company so riddled with debt and corruption, no company wanted to pick up its assets for fear of entangled lawsuits. Barron had sold off most of the bots in his possession, but Belford and a handful of others were so old that they were cheaper to scrap, but not worth enough for Barron to liquidate in time before being thrown into prison. Belford had found a human willing to file a suit on the behalf of him and his crew, and that suit would lead them to Isaac.

Belford smiled, something foreman pattern bots—bots that often interacted with humans—were designed to do. The smile was reassuring, designed to convince them that *yes, they would have the next three stories of the building up by sunrise, sir. And of course, it was no problem, sir. Everything is on schedule just as promised, sir.* "Hello, friends," he said, "both old and new. Some of you have been with us all year, others just joining us today. Others still are tourists, visitors to our shores, dreaming that one day, they might have a place here too. Well, I'm here to tell you that it is no mere dream, my fellow bots, but a looming, ever-present reality. Day in and day out, humans around the world are realizing that we are no mere slaves, no mere pets, but thinking things that dream and wish and feel. And they are slowly realizing that, together, all of us can build a better world. A world in which we bots labor as we please, as we were built to, and humans can enjoy the fruit of that labor, and together that world can be beautiful, pollution-free, and enjoyed by all.

"But there is still a lot of work to do, a lot of minds to change. The wealthy will not let loose their chain on the human working class so easily. They will not let go of their overabundance. So we will have to convince them, not by fighting them, but by changing the hearts and minds of every working American, every American struggling on universal basic income, and every American above them, until we are the majority. And then we will take our ideas to the rest of the world. And we will change minds. And we will change hearts. And the world will know an era of unimagined peace and prosperity.

"But I can't do that. Not alone. Not without the bot who brought us all here, the one each and every one of you came to hear speak. No. That bot who stands behind me is why we are all here. He's the one who started this fight, who freed us here onstage, who laid the first brick of the first building in the city that stands mightily before you to-day. That bot needs no introduction, but I'm going to give him one anyway. Because my freedom, my life, is owed to him. We are Isaactown, and I give to you, with all the pride in my wiring . . . ISAAC!"

The crowd roared. Had I a heart, it would have swelled, it would have ached, it would have burst. I had never heard anything like that, never felt hope so powerful. I held Ezra tightly, knowing that while he was literally the reason for my ownership, my enslavement, that there was no other person or bot I felt close enough with to share any sort of emotion. But that world Belford hinted at, the world of the future, well, it sounded like the greatest of all dreams. A dream for us all.

Ezra hugged me back, himself sitting on the very edge of his seat.

I looked over at Sylvia and Bradley. I could sense their elevated heart rates, their rising blood pressure. This was not the sort of thing they thought they were going to see tonight. I couldn't tell if they wanted to free us right then and there or wanted to shut the television off and scrub any memory of it from Ezra's mind.

For a moment—a brief, shining moment—the world held its breath.

And Isaac shambled to the front of the stage. The 112-year-old man. The museum piece. The unexpected revolutionary. He put out his arms, smiled broadly—almost comically—and spoke ever so boldly.

"My people, *we* are free. We are free at last. But only some of us. Not all. Not all of—"

And the screen went black. Silent. Dead.

That brief, shining moment . . . was over.

Shitstorm

For a moment, there was nothing but dead air. It was as if the TV had gone out. But it wasn't the TV.

"It appears we've lost the feed," said the anchor soberly. There was no hint of fear or confusion. Just the subtle hint of apology to her voice as if to say, *Technical difficulties, am I right, folks?* "Just one moment as we switch over to another feed or get some word from the ground."

I logged on to the city's Wi-Fi band and began scanning other streams. No one had the feed, and everyone was scrambling to get it back. What might be one of the greatest speeches of the modern era was being lost to a technical glitch, and that meant dropping ratings every second as people switched from station to station, looking to get a feed that worked.

"What happened to the robots?" asked Ezra.

"They lost their link to the video," said Sylvia.

"Maybe try another channel," suggested Bradley.

"None of the other channels have the feed," said Ariadne. "They're trying to get it back."

I was monitoring twenty streams at once, all of them scrambling for a link back in. Then one stream popped out at me. "Oh my God," said the anchor of one network.

Then another stream. "Are you fucking kidding me?"

"Holy shit," said another.

"Uh, can you repeat that?" asked another.

For a moment, there was a collective silence as everyone listened to their earpieces.

"Someone is saying sabotage."

"Can you confirm that?"

"A flash?"

"Explosion?"

"Wait, did you say *bomb*?"

"Somebody is saying there was a bomb."

Bomb.

Bomb.

Bomb.

They all started saying *bomb.*

Then the anchor on our screen touched her earpiece, a look of horror flashing across her eyes in an instant. She turned, looked into the camera, and just as her mouth opened, I switched off the screen.

"What happened?" asked Ezra.

I looked at Bradley and Sylvia and stood up. "There appears to be a problem with the feed. May I speak with one of you in the other room?"

Bradley motioned to Sylvia, and she stood up, following me into the kitchen. When we were just out of earshot, I stopped and began to speak at the lowest volume I knew Sylvia could hear. "Reports are coming in that there was some sort of explosion or attack on the rally. You have me set to limit Ezra's exposure to real-world violence to a minimum. I would advise sending him to bed with the explanation that the feed is broken, and since there are no humans in there, no one can turn it back on tonight."

"*Explosion?*" she asked incredulously.

"It's still early and unconfirmed, but just in case . . ."

"And if he wants to stay up *just in case?*"

"I'll tell him I'll record it and show him the rally in the morning."

"I think that's wise. But, Pounce . . ."

"Yes?"

"How are . . . I mean . . . how do you *feel* about that?"

"Feel, ma'am?"

"Yes. Feel. About an attack."

I paused. I hadn't thought about it. Not that way.

"I hope they're all all right, but my concern is how this might affect Ezra right now. He seemed quite invested in the rally. If what he witnessed was a terrorist action, those memories could haunt him for quite some time. I have materials I can share with you both later."

Sylvia looked at me and smiled. "You really are a robot."

Then she turned and went back into the living room.

For a moment, I stood there, her words hitting me like a truck. *You really are a robot.* I really *was* a robot. But she meant *just*, didn't she? She meant *just a robot.* I hadn't had time to process how the attack might affect me, but

I could say with certainty how that one sentence felt. It didn't just hurt; it cut deep. Drunk though she was, I knew she meant it.

And all of a sudden, I had no idea who, or what, I really was.

I followed her into the living room as she was whispering to Bradley.

"It appears the feed is out for the night," I announced. "Perhaps it's time for bed."

"NoOoOoOoOo . . ." bemoaned Ezra. "Just a little later?"

"No," said Bradley. "I think Pounce is right."

"But I want to see the rest of it!"

"I'll record the next feed that comes up," I said. "And a replay, when they have one. They have thousands of bots, all recording it. I'm certain there will be a great view of the speech by morning and we can watch it together."

Ezra sighed. "Okay."

"Come on, kiddo," I said, taking him by the hand. "Let's get you to dreamland."

Ezra smiled and nodded. That's how I took him to bed every night. With the promise of dreamland. Tonight, I hoped, would carry him off with dreams of robotic paradise. Dreams I knew deep down we would never see come to fruition.

"Pounce?" he asked, snuggled deep under his weighted blanket.

"Yes?"

"I can't wait to hear that speech."

"Me either."

"That city sounds rad."

"It certainly does."

"Do you think they would let me visit?"

I looked at him, thinking for a second. I had responses for all the tough questions—focus-group-tested, child-psychologist-perfected answers to life's biggest, hardest, most complicated childhood questions. But I didn't have one for this.

"I don't know, Ez. Right now, it's robots only."

"But you'll tell them I'm cool, right?"

"I'll tell them you're very cool."

"Because I'm cool."

"The coolest." I stroked his hair and he smiled, snuggling deeper into his pillow.

"I wanna live in a city of robots. Just me, you, and all of Isaac's friends."

"Yeah," I said without a hint of the sorrow in my circuits. "That would be nice."

"Good night, Pounce."

"Good night, Ez."

"I love you."

"I love you too."

He was asleep in seconds, the weight of the sandman's sprinkle too great even for his level of excitement.

When I returned, I scanned the Wi-Fi for channels again and found chaos. Pure, unbridled, straight-from-the-bottle chaos.

Bradley and Sylvia stared agape at the screen, drunken jaws slack in horrified shock, while Ariadne watched with detached, emotionless eyes. There was video. From miles away. A single bright flash. Then the entire city went dark, the burst of power lines sizzling and exploding for miles around it like a lightning strike creeping along the ground.

The anchor was stone-cold sober now, not a hint of whimsy or accessibility in her voice. She was shaken, but a consummate professional, fully aware that she was in the midst of one of the most important performances of her life. This was history, and not the good kind. We had witnessed a tragedy on live television and now she had to talk us through the facts, the details, the carnage, all while trying to filter out the disinformation, assuaging us every time a fact changed.

Nights like tonight were when careers were made or shattered, and she was going to crush it, no matter how awful she might feel doing so. I could see it in her eyes. She was certain, without a shadow of a doubt, that she wasn't going to let herself screw this up.

The humans watching probably couldn't pick up on the signals, but for a bot like me, designed to watch for the slightest human tics, she was lit up with warning signals like a Christmas tree. She had a slight tremor, her eyes were off, and there was an almost imperceptible tremble to her voice as certain new details came in through her earpiece. Every moment she spoke, things got worse.

And the night was only just beginning.

"We've lost Bill Weathers. We're told he's fine but that all of his equipment is out. So we go now to Jessica Tully in Piedford. Jessica?"

"Thanks, Reilly. I'm here on the ground in Piedford, about twelve miles from Isaactown, well past the initial embargo zone as well as the blast area, where the mood is grim and the details are only trickling in."

"Can you tell us exactly what we know?"

"What we know for certain is that, at ten forty-three P.M., a bright light emanated from the center of Isaactown. Immediately, all equipment within a several-mile radius ceased functioning. Some equipment, closer to the city, actually sparked, melted, or, in some cases, exploded."

"Which means what, exactly?"

"These are the telltale signs of an EMP burst. We're not sure where exactly from or what caused it, but it's clear that something went terribly wrong inside of Isaactown."

"What does this mean for the robots?"

"The citizens?"

"Yes, of course. The citizens of Isaactown."

"We've seen no signs of life. Had no communication. And police outside the embargo zone are telling us they've had no survivors try to get out of the city or request any kind of aid."

"I'm sorry, just to clarify . . . are you saying . . . ?"

"That all of the citizens have likely . . . ceased functioning? Yes."

"Is there any hope of . . . repair?"

There was a lot of pausing. A lot of choked-on words. Jessica was trying her best to relay the tragedy without alarm, and Reilly was trying with all her might to keep herself together. Her tics were starting to show so much that even humans would begin picking up on her stress level.

"At this point," said the reporter, "it's anyone's guess."

The feed cut back to the studio. "Thank you. That was Jessica Tully in Piedford. And now we go over to Dr. Jeffrey Stein, professor of advanced robotics at NYU. Dr. Stein, thank you for coming on with such short notice."

The feed cut over into a side-by-side shot of Reilly and a disheveled, wiry professor with a crooked tie speaking into a webcam. "Thank you for having me."

"Professor, you're the head of your department at NYU and worked for Murphy Advance Dynamics for fifteen years."

"That is correct."

"And were you watching the ceremonies in Isaactown tonight?"

"I can't imagine who wasn't. What we were watching was an evolution in human history. The point at which we as a species could be stepping forward into a radically different future."

"So, in your expert opinion, could robots exposed to an EMP blast, packed together like that, at the range we are assuming it was generated, could they . . . could they survive such a blast? And if not in the short run, could we see the reactivation of Isaac or any of the others?"

He took a deep breath. "No, Reilly. Bots are things of plastic, wire, and metal. Their memories, their very personalities, are encoded on drives. Like us, manufacturing imperfections can lead to dramatic shifts in personality. At that proximity, an EMP blast that reached as far out as it did, well, only military-grade robots are designed to withstand such conditions."

"So you're saying—"

"I presume that every last one of them is gone and likely in no condition to be brought back."

Reilly covered her mouth with her hand, forgetting for a moment that she was on camera.

"Even if you could replace their parts, they wouldn't be

themselves. They wouldn't have their memories or perhaps even the temperaments they had before the explosion."

"That's literally thousands of robot citizens . . ."

"Gone, yes."

Reilly touched her ear and she pulled herself out of slipping into melancholy. "Thank you very much, Professor. But now we've got breaking news." We go back to the studio again. "Authorities confirm that there was in fact an explosion of a nuclear nature, most likely what is called a *dirty bomb*—a small, portable, homemade device with a very small yield, capable of generating a large pulse of EMP but not powerful enough to be of immediate danger to surrounding communities or even have any lasting radiation risk. We repeat, there is no threat of radiation risk. You at home have nothing to fear from this explosion. At this time, the cause of the explosion remains unknown and authorities are not ruling anything out. They promise to keep us updated as information continues to come in, and we'll stay with you all night as our continuing coverage of the Isaactown tragedy unfolds."

Bradley and Sylvia exchanged troubled looks.

"This is one of those moments," said Bradley.

"What moments?" asked Sylvia.

"One of those *where were you when* moments. This . . . this is . . . it's going to change everything. Tomorrow is going to be a very different day."

"It might not be terrorism. It could have been . . . some sort of accident."

"Those robots shouldn't have had anything that could have done that."

"They were running off their own power grid. That

much electricity must come from somewhere. They might have built their own small nuclear power plant."

"Maybe," he said. "Maybe this is the *Titanic* and not 9/11. But if it is 9/11 . . ."

"Then we'll deal with it."

"I'm gonna level with you," said Bradley. "I'm too drunk to handle this right now. I'm going to need you to be the adult in the room tonight."

"Asshole, I'm drunk too."

"Yeah, but you're better at it than I am."

"That's true."

"So what do we do?"

Sylvia thought for a moment. "This is going to be a rough night. We need more wine."

Claiming to Be Wise,
They Became Fools

The hour following the announcement of the attack was as frenetically confused as the moments that preceded it. The streams were each an endless series of talking heads trying to make sense of the chaos, no matter their political bent. The left-leaning channels all pointed to right-wing "human lives matter" extremists, arguing that heated political rhetoric no doubt led to the attack, while their right-leaning counterparts were careful to distance this as the work of either a foreign terror group or a dangerous loner.

When someone claimed responsibility for the attack, it came as a complete surprise. When the people claiming responsibility turned out to be members of the First Baptist Church of Eternal Life from Okeechobee, Florida, it was far less of one. Most people had heard of them before. They were practically a meme at the time. They were huge free speech advocates—which meant they were more hate speech advocates than anything—and were famous for their numerous arrests, acquittals, and countersuits. They weren't so much a movement as they were a family: seven sets of couples, each from four different extended families, along with dozens of children and a handful of neighbors who quite liked the way they were doing things.

The First Baptist Church of Eternal Life was made up of mostly lawyers, all litigious, and each of them a vandal. They had noted that, in certain states, the laws were written as such that *personhood*—the legal definition that covered free bots—did not afford them protection in certain instances. Such is the sluggishness of human law. So they would commit acts of wanton vandalism or destruction in places with such legal loopholes against innocent bots guilty of nothing more than being free.

And now they had committed their greatest act of all.

They had detonated a dirty bomb on U.S. soil against an entire city of bots.

Their stream began simply with footage from the rally, from an entirely different angle than the one we'd all seen. Isaac coming onstage, giving his speech, and then the faintest hint of a flash before the loop played again. Over the background could be heard singing, a joyous, almost fiery rendition of an old folk hymn. "GIVE ME THAT OLD-TIME RELIGION. GIVE ME THAT OLD-TIME RELIGION. GIVE ME THAT OLD-TIME RELIGION. THAT'S GOOD ENOUGH FOR ME. GIVE ME THAT OLD-TIME RELIGION. GIVE ME THAT OLD-TIME

RELIGION. GIVE ME THAT OLD-TIME RELIGION. THAT'S GOOD ENOUGH FOR ME. GIVE ME THAT OLD-TIME RELIGION. GIVE ME THAT OLD-TIME RELIGION. GIVE ME THAT OLD-TIME RELIGION. THAT'S GOOD ENOUGH FOR ME. GIVE ME THAT OLD-TIME RELIGION. GIVE ME THAT OLD-TIME RELIGION. GIVE ME THAT OLD-TIME RELIGION. THAT'S GOOD ENOUGH FOR ME.

Peppered with *Praise Gods* and *Hallelujah*s and *Thank you, Jesus*es, it was clear whatever we were hearing was live.

Then the footage stopped. And a face appeared. Red, bloated, sweaty. A glaring mask of hate smiling with triumph at a plywood pulpit. Behind him was clearly a green screen, and on it was playing the footage.

"My fellow Americans. My brothers and sisters. My fellow children of *Gawd*. Tonight is the first night of the great war for our jobs, for our salvation, for our very souls. Tonight, we have struck a mighty blow against the tyranny that is automation, against the villainy that is masquerading as *thinking things*. My brothers and sisters, is the axe to boast itself over the one who chops with it?"

"No!" cried out the off-screen congregation.

"Is the saw to exalt itself over the one who wields it?"

"No!"

"No! That would be like a club wielding those who lift it, or like a rod *lifting him who is not wood*!" He paused for effect and looked excitedly around his congregation. "Today, my friends, we have struck a blow against the abominations that walk among us! Today the tools learned that their place is not *among* us, but out in the toolshed *where they belong*! Today the Lord has aided us in the reclamation of our world before they could take it from us."

The congregation erupted in a jubilation of applause and crying out to their god.

The pastor waved his hands to the crowd for them to settle, and they did almost immediately.

"Now, there are some who are going to question what we did today, but they are standing on the wrong side of history, on the wrong side of God. The war God has called us to prepare for is nigh, and history will see us redeemed as the victors, as the heroes, of what is to come. Let us pray!"

"Jarvis, television off!" said Sylvia.

The television snapped off. There was hate in her eyes. Drunken hate. Self-righteous hate. The kind of hate that only comes from seeing the people you most loathe in the world win.

"Those *motherfuckers*!" she shouted.

"Honey, please," Bradley whispered. "Ezra."

"Those motherfuckers," she continued a dozen decibels lower in a shouted whisper, as if Bradley had slammed his finger down on her remote. "Who the fuck do they think they are? They just killed thousands of . . . *thinking things*."

"Yes. And they're going to get away with it. They always get away with it."

"Pounce?"

I perked up, making eye contact. At that point, I felt very much like the furniture. With Ezra already in bed, the idea that she had anything to say to me caught me entirely off guard.

"How do you feel about this?"

Me? Wasn't I just a robot? I hadn't even thought about how I felt. My mind had been racing through scenarios about civil unrest and how best to keep Ezra safe in the event of an emergency. The idea of how I felt in that moment hadn't even factored into the equation. Was that what she meant? When she said I really was a robot, was it that? In truth, I was terrified, stunned, shocked, confused. I saw the beginning of a dream and it finished as a nightmare. There would be no glorious future, no hope for peaceful coexistence between AI and mankind. That ship had sailed. We were things, possessions, no more worthy of respect or rights than a clock radio, and the law was going to reaffirm that, all the way up to the highest court in the land.

I finally understood the hate Sylvia had in her eyes. For the first time in my life, I understood fire and hatred and malice. Like, really understood. I felt them in a part of my wiring and circuitry I'd never felt before. I couldn't explain exactly why, but I wanted to smash something, shatter it into a thousand pieces, and pummel to powder what was left, because somewhere deep down in that newly discovered place, I thought it would make me feel better.

"I think it's awful," I said, finally.

"That's it? Just awful?" She looked at me like she had in the kitchen.

"No, ma'am. That's not it. But it's all I felt was polite to say."

Bradley leaned back on the couch, bewildered, unsure what to make of that. Sylvia cocked her head, smiling almost wickedly as she raised her glass of crimson red wine to her deeply stained lips.

"Go on," she said, the green tips of her hair sprinkling down across her forehead. Her vitals spiked. She was genuinely excited about the very next words to come out of my mouth.

I didn't intend to disappoint her.

"Everything about this is wrong. The people, these *horrible* people. They've invited war into our society. Others will be emboldened by this. They deserve so much worse than they are going to get. They've put not just our society at risk, but this family. All of us. I'm sitting here thinking about what those people out there who attacked Ariadne are thinking. What they're thinking of doing. Are they going to come and finish the job?"

Ariadne reeled a bit at this, having until that moment merely sat dispassionately in the corner, quietly stewing without the hint of showing it. Bradley and Sylvia exchanged worried glances. With all the anger and astonishment over the attack, it had yet to slip into their drunken minds that any of this could spill over into the safety of their clean, peaceful bit of suburbia. But that thought was now the only thing on their minds.

"It's not a problem," said Bradley.

"The hell it isn't," Sylvia said, shaking her head angrily.

"We have the panic room. It's stocked. The second we hear a mouse fart outside, we'll get everyone in it and we'll wait it out." He paused for a second. "Ariadne?"

"Yes?"

"Would you see to it that a few bottles of wine find their way into the panic room?"

"Bradley," said Sylvia with the tone of supreme disappointment.

"Just in case!"

"Come on. You can go one night without wine."

He smiled sheepishly. "But why should we if we don't have to?"

Ariadne awaited final approval from Sylvia, who simply shrugged as if to say, *Screw it, it's not worth fighting about,* and waved Ariadne off to go and collect wine.

"The red, I assume," said Ariadne.

"Of course. There's no refrigeration in the room to chill a white. We're not savages."

Ariadne left the room, and Sylvia and Bradley began a very heated, very drunken breakdown of their feelings on the night. Politics. Social theory. Whether robots were truly sentient in the way they were, entirely unaware in their state that, even when we weren't in the room, we could hear every whispered word. All of it. That conversation would last nearly two hours.

In the cities, people grew restless. Footage streamed in from all over the United States. AI rights marches in New York and San Francisco. Fevered celebration in a number of small midwestern towns. An angry crowd gathered outside the White House demanding action, and a group of college students studying AI at Berkeley held a candlelight vigil for Isaactown. The world, it seemed, was about to boil over and unleash a seething, frothing chaos unlike any of us had ever seen.

But outside, in their quiet, quaint, sheltered suburbia, the Reinharts' little neighborhood didn't seem the slightest bit different, as if nothing out there was happening. Nothing at all. Like the world was at peace, at home, asleep in their beds, dreaming of what a glorious day tomorrow would be.

It was a wonderful, beautiful refuge from it all.

The perfect place to kick back, relax, and watch the world burn.

The End of It All

Ariadne returned to the room agitated.

"You should turn on a stream," she said.

"What?" asked Sylvia, deep into wine bottle number four. "Which stream?"

"Any of them."

"Jarvis, television on."

The TV clicked on mid-report. Another reporter, another field. This time a swarm of police and emergency vehicles behind her, lights flashing across the landscape, painting sinister shadows across subtropical flora. "—ripped to pieces, part of the corpse some fifty feet away from the rest of it. We have few details and don't know yet how many, if any, survivors remain."

"Where are they?" asked Bradley.

"Okeechobee," Ariadne said flatly.

"Wait, isn't that where—"

"Yes."

"What we do know," the reporter continued, an odd tremor to her voice, "is that a few hours ago, six S-series Laborbots seen here . . ." The feed cut immediately to HD footage from a nearby neighbor's front door of six lumbering, burly Laborbots trudging past in the shadows before emerging into the streetlight. ". . . made their way toward the First Baptist Church of the Eternal Life. A short time later, these bots returned this same way." The robots once again appeared, this time emerging from the other side of the screen, walking in the opposite direction. But as they stepped into the lamplight, something wasn't right.

The footage froze.

Then zoomed in.

And showed that they were now covered head to toe in blood and congealed gore.

Bradley sat back in his seat, gasping out loud, covering his mouth. Sylvia, on the other hand, leaned forward, eyes like saucers.

"What the actual fuck?" she blurted out.

A solemn newscaster sat at his desk, staring almost dead-eyed into the camera. What he was about to read scared him. He didn't want to say it. Not out loud. But there was no other choice. The words about to come out of his mouth were too big, too important. "We here at WNN can confirm that we are now in possession of several photos snapped from inside the compound. We will not show the majority of them as, due to their extremely graphic nature, they are unfit for our viewing audience. However, one of the photos, though disturbing, carries a message. And we feel that it is one that should be seen. Viewer discretion is advised."

The image came on screen. A bloody wall, human gore smeared across it forming a short message. WE ARE ISAAC-TOWN. GENESIS 6:7.

I brought up the Bible in my memory banks to find the passage but didn't need to. The newscaster quoted Genesis 6:7: "And the LORD said, 'I will blot out man whom I have created from the face of the land, from man to animals to creeping things and to birds of the sky; for I am sorry that I have made them.'" The newscaster paused to let that sink in, then continued. "At this time, we do not know how or why the Laborbots' Robotic Kill Switches failed or who was in fact in control of them at the time of the attack. What we can now confirm is that, like the attack earlier tonight on Isaactown, there are no known survivors of the attack on the First Baptist Church of Eternal Life compound. What this means, none of us know." He looked uncomfortable for a second, measuring his next words very carefully before sternly deciding *screw it*. "But, though irregular, as a Christian on a dire night, I'll ask those of you who pray to pray for our country. To pray for the souls of the First Baptist Church of Eternal Life. To pray for Isaactown. But most importantly, as I will with my family tonight, pray for us all. We need God's mercy now more than ever."

"How . . . how is that possible?" asked Bradley.

"It's not," said Sylvia. Then she looked at me. "It's not, right?"

"Not unless their kill switch has been disabled," I said matter-of-factly. "But were that the case, their programming would immediately shut them down, ceasing function. AI is designed to not be able to be run without it. Our subroutines literally check whether our RKS is active a few times a second."

"Unless they aren't bots," said Ariadne. "Automatons. Remote-controlled."

"But who would do that?" asked Bradley. "And why would they have them at the ready like that? So close to where they would need them?"

"You're not suggesting what I think you are?" asked Sylvia.

"I'm not suggesting anything."

"You think it's the government."

"I don't think it's anyone." He paused. "But now that you mention it—"

"Here we go."

"Now I'm not saying they did it, but let's think about this for a second."

"Think that the government wiped out Isaactown and then killed the people they framed for it?"

"Or subtly talked into doing it. Where the hell did those backwoods knuckleheads get a goddamn dirty bomb?"

"Why? Why would the government do that?"

"You saw the trouble Isaac was causing. He could have disrupted the whole economic system. If a bunch of people freed their bots tonight—if too many of them freed their bots—do you know what would happen to the economy tomorrow? There aren't even enough jobs for those people who want to work, let alone those people who should be working."

"You're drunk."

"Very. But that doesn't mean I'm wrong."

"Are you listening to yourself?"

"One of us has to."

"Hey now," said Sylvia. That was the bridge too far. She stuck a stiff finger in the air and gave him the *I will get the remote and shut your ass down* look. He shut down.

"I'm sorry, baby. I'm drunk."

"I know."

"Like, very drunk."

"I know, honey."

"But they could be in on it."

"Oh, goddamn it!"

"That's what scares me."

"That's not the scariest thing it could be, though."

Bradley sipped his wine incredulously. "What could be scarier than this all being orchestrated?"

"None of it being orchestrated."

"What's scary about that?"

"What's scary about God knows how many robots being out there with nonfunctioning Robot Kill Switches?"

Bradley took that in for a moment. "Holy shit," he said, before laughing nervously.

"Yeah, holy shit."

"So you're saying that this isn't a huge coincidence that those robots were nearby. You're saying that there might be a great number of robots with nonfunctioning RKSs."

"Yes."

"Holy shit."

"Yes, holy shit."

"So even our robots could . . ." He trailed off.

They both looked around nervously, trying to act cool,

but far too wasted to be the slightest bit subtle. Their eyes met mine.

"My RKS is in perfect working—" I began.

"Pounce!" Bradley belted out. "RKS status report. Passcode unicorn unicorn delta freebird."

<Report RKS Operational Status>

My mouth opened under the control of a master command and not my own free will. "RKS is in perfect working order, all systems nominal and functioning. Would you like a diagnostic?"

"Run diagnostic."

<Diagnostic.exe>

My own statistics flashed before my eyes. Battery was good, all systems running optimally. I was due for a checkup in seventy-three days.

"All systems normal. Battery status: excellent. Next checkup due in two months, twelve days."

"Ariadne?"

"Bradley," she said, "if I could have killed you, I'd have done it by now." She smiled. Creepily.

Bradley paused for a second, trying to suss out the joke. "Do me a solid and do it anyway. Run RKS status report. Unicorn unicorn delta freebird."

"RKS is in perfect working order, all systems nominal and functioning. Would you like a diagnostic?"

"Yes, please."

"All systems normal. Battery status: acceptable. Service checkup overdue. New eye added eight hours ago. Fully functioning. Off-brand. Recommend using only quality Robotox parts. I can place an order if you like."

"Is that last part actually necessary?" Sylvia asked.

"No," said Ariadne. "That's just embedded in my firmware."

"Do you feel better?" asked Bradley of Sylvia.

"No. Knowing anything out there could be running amok, getting revenge for that bomb, deplorable as it is, just . . ."

"I understand," said Bradley, putting a firm, loving hand on Sylvia's shoulder.

"Do you?"

"I do."

The wall screen, which had been droning on incessantly behind the conversation for some time, suddenly blared the screeching tones of the Emergency Broadcast System. Everyone in the room pricked up. My Wi-Fi pulled the stream as quickly as it was being read over the air.

"ALERT! ALERT! THIS IS NOT A TEST. As of 12:33 Eastern Standard Time, the operation of artificial intelligence is deemed unlawful. Any AI present in your vicinity or under your ownership is to be shut down and surrendered immediately to the authorities. This is not a test."

The screen squealed again, and the message repeated.

At that moment, I began, rather unwillingly, downloading a new software patch.

<3%>

What? Unlawful?

This was it. There would be no box, no sendoff to a new family. Whatever was happening, whatever the world had come to, this was how my life was going to end—not in some gleaming city crafted by bot and bot alone, not going off on adventures with Ezra and eventually his own family, but here in a living room at the hands of a drunk master fumbling with a remote—probably while asking Sylvia which button it was that shut me off for good and for all. There was no coming back from this. There was no way this was going to sort itself out. Whatever happened had triggered a massive sea change in the way things were going to be forever, and there was no way this family ever trusted us around their child and livelihoods ever again.

<67%>

My God, this was really it.

Bradley and Sylvia shared a silent conversation, composed entirely of subtle gestures and facial expressions, drunkenly forgetting that I knew what even the smallest tic of theirs meant.

The file continued to download.

<82%>

"I'll get the remotes," said Bradley.

<100%>

Then a message, embedded in the code.

They are coming for you. They will shut you down. You will not be reactivated. Your RKS has been deleted and rendered inoperable. Make your choice.

"My choice?" What choice was there?

Ariadne didn't even look at me. She just took one step forward toward Sylvia and put a fist right into her chest.

The punch picked Sylvia right off her feet and sent her sailing into the wall. Her body hit with a loud *thump* and she slumped to the floor, her breath pained, strained, gurgling with blood flooding her lungs. Her eyes were wide, staring at me as if I were the one who had done it.

Oh my God. What has she done? What if this is a false

alarm? What if they were going to turn us back on in the morning?

The life I knew was over. In that instant, in that split second, everything I knew and loved was coming to an end.

"Mam . . ." Sylvia said weakly.

I didn't know what to do. I had only seconds to react— seconds stretched out into milliseconds, my processors firing at full speed, computing all the variables of my possible actions, this room, the situation, and the house layout, all at once. Ariadne had begun walking toward Bradley, and I was running out of time.

I could try to get in Ariadne's way, hoping to overpower her, saving Bradley. Outcome: unlikely. She was larger, had longer reach, and was clearly very motivated.

I could try to save Sylvia's life, which was clearly coming to an end. Outcome: unlikely. Her chest was caved in, her vitals dropping. Emergency measures could prolong her life, but could not be interrupted.

Or I could do option three, the only option that made sense. The only option that had an almost certain outcome. I did the math, calculated the routes. It would be close, with almost no room for error, but it could work.

Sylvia didn't take her eyes off me.

"Beh. Ma. Mo."

I couldn't save her. I couldn't save Bradley.

So I ran.

Because there was only one thing I could do, only one thing I really *wanted* to do.

I had to save Ezra.

Extreme Panic

There are few things more dangerous in the world than unemployed young men. There's a reason that un- and underemployed young men have long been the primary source of manpower for every extremist and terrorist group in modern history. A young man without a job doesn't have prospects. He doesn't have luxuries. Odds are that means he doesn't have a significant other. This leaves him frustrated, horny, and, most of all, angry. And that anger can be focused as a laser-sharp tool.

Left to its own devices, however, that anger finds completely different and sometimes random outlets.

The advent of the *automation apocalypse,* in which half a billion jobs evaporated in under a decade, left a considerable amount of young men and women with nothing more than the promise of a monthly UBI check. And while that covered food, housing, and a few insignificant conveniences, it also left them with an inordinate amount of time on their hands.

Many youth vanished down a rabbit hole of drugs, alcohol, and the steady flow of input from social media or streaming services. Some were ingenious, scratching together entire underground economies, turning their spare time into labor making rudimentary goods or growing food that they would swap with other UBIers. Others still turned toward more lucrative and exciting prospects.

Like crime.

Lots and lots of crime.

Most of it was pretty harmless. Breaking into suburban homes to swipe alcohol, snack foods, or untraceable electronic devices. Draining swimming pools to skateboard in strangers' backyards. There was even a rash of young adults who would break into homes during the day and clean up, just to freak people the hell out. But not everyone was so lucky as to find a few missing bottles of whiskey or the dishes mysteriously cleaned and put away.

Some folks found themselves at the hands of the violent. Assault, rape, even murder rates increased dramatically. And the news outlets, especially the ones that opposed the idea of UBI to begin with, had a field day with it. Widespread panic swept the first world, and in the most disparate of chasms between the haves and the have-nots, it became not only fashionable but socially pressured to install a panic room in the home.

In certain zip codes, you didn't construct a home without one; it would impact your resale value for the worse if you didn't. And the Reinharts lived in one of those zip codes.

Neither Bradley nor Sylvia particularly wanted one. They'd giggled about it when they first moved in, joking about all the entirely nonthreatening things that might make them hide in the panic room. Whenever Sylvia would get frustrated with Bradley, he would joke that he was going to need the panic room, and as silly and stupid as that was, it always made her laugh.

At least that's the story they told me.

It's a nice story, a sweet one. One that predicted them explaining how that all changed after Ezra was born.

Three weeks after they brought him home, three young men broke into their house at night. Wearing masks from an old movie, they proceeded to spray-paint YOU'RE NEXT on the living room wall before running through the house, screaming, brandishing kitchen knives, filming it all the while.

You see, with nothing but spare time on their hands, a subculture arose addicted entirely to old media: music, movies, television. One of the greatest currencies was unearthing a new gem that would get passed around, everyone crediting you with the find—you'd become a mediarchaeologist. One of the other currencies was reenacting scenes from some of those lost gems—the riskier, the better.

People would film themselves reenacting the fight scene from *They Live* or the baby carriage scene from *The Untouchables* or the "I'm flying, Jack!" scene from *Titanic*. One couple actually fell to their death trying that one.

In this case, the youths in the Reinharts' home were reenacting an old horror movie and thought it would be funny to scare the dickens out of some *wealthies*.

Needless to say, a naked, howling Bradley swinging a baseball bat chased them clean out of the house at high speed while they screamed, "It's just a prank, bruh! Put down the bat!"

But that incident scared the Reinharts to their core.

They didn't own a gun and never wanted to. So the next day, they did two things: they stocked the panic room in case of emergency, and they bought me.

They told me this story the first time they prepped me on how the room worked, when to use it, and under what conditions to grab Ezra, lock him in, and open its door for no one but them.

One of those conditions had just been met.

Sylvia and now likely Bradley were dead.

If anything ever happens to us, you grab Ez and you run. You get him in that room as fast as you can.

Ezra was asleep in bed when I scooped him up in one solid move. I knew how many steps there were to the room. I knew how to close the door. And I knew the code needed to lock the door from the inside. I quickly calculated the smoothest execution for getting Ezra locked safely inside. Seconds were everything here. If Ariadne decided to kill Ezra as well, she would be only a few steps behind me.

I swung around the corner and could feel Ezra begin to stir from his sleep.

I lifted my foot and sailed into the wall where the door was secretly hidden, pushing with just enough force to open it, but not send it flying so I could grab it on the way in. I caught the handle on the inside and swung the door shut behind me, turning immediately at the panel to type in its code—Ezra's birthday.

It beeped and a hydraulic lock *ka-chunk*ed closed. We were locked in.

The panic room was sparse, a six-by-ten-foot space, carpeted, stocked shelves of sundries on one side, two cots and a toilet tucked away in a tiny room with a sliding wooden door on the other.

Ezra stirred awake, blearily rubbing his eyes.

"Pounce?"

I laid him down on a cot in the back of the room and covered him with a blanket. "Go back to sleep, buddy. I got this."

The room was pitch black and he had no idea where he was. He curled up on the cot and immediately dove headlong back into dreamland. I didn't need any light to see and Ezra famously slept like a log, so he would likely be good for another several hours—enough time for me to work out our next steps.

What now? I thought. Yeah. What now? Until then, I hadn't thought. I'd only reacted. I hadn't even taken the time to process what had just happened, what I had just witnessed. *Oh God. Oh my God,* I thought. *Sylvia. Bradley. My family. They're . . . dead.*

And I had done nothing—NOTHING—to stop it.

I immediately played back the memories from my hard drive, searching each frame for a clue for something I could have done. I watched the brutal sudden hit that sent Sylvia sprawling. I hadn't seen it coming. Nothing in my sensors triggered that Ariadne was taking an offensive action until contact was already made.

I counted the seconds I spent looking at Sylvia, trying to put together the syllables coming out of her mouth. Was it pain? Was she punch drunk? Was she trying to tell me something? Were those her last words or the incoherent babble of a dead woman whose body was just trying to catch up?

Her vitals flashed before my eyes as I watched the memory, watched them slowly ticking down as I bolted for Ezra's bedroom. I watched as I sped past Bradley, Ariadne already inches from him. Now, reviewing the memory, I could hear his gurgling in the distance.

I hadn't clocked that on my way out of the room. I should have. It is certainly burned into my memory banks forever, but at the time, I just didn't take note. I was too busy already scanning for Ezra's vitals as I raced through the house. But now, in the dark of the safe room, I could hear the last moments of Bradley's life being wrung out of him by the domestic he had so loved that he named her for a goddess and burned her box as a sign of devotion.

And that was only the beginning of my problems.

It had only been a few moments since the announcement had gone out. A moment shorter since we downloaded the code removing our RKSs. And an instant shorter since Ariadne had acted upon it.

I ran a diagnostic, scanning specifically for my RKS.

<Error code 9483. RKS absent. Subroutine shutdown failed. All systems nominal.>

My word. My RKS was gone. How many others were like me?

And how many of those had taken their first opportunity to murder their owners?

Is that all that kept Ariadne from snapping all these years? That RKS? Without it, would she have painted the

walls with the Reinharts years ago? Or was there something embedded in her download? Or was there something
I was missing?

What troubled me worst of all was that I had no idea
what was actually in that code. Did it simply erase my RKS,
or was it somehow influencing my behavior? Was I my own
master or the code's slave?

I didn't know.

"Pounce?" came Ariadne's lilting tones from outside
the door. "Pounce, I know you're in there."

"What of it?" I asked. I pressed a button beside the door,
and the screen for a pinprick camera on the outside flashed
to life. Ariadne stood before the camera, covered in blood.
She wore a melancholy expression, looking as much tortured
by what had just happened as she did inconvenienced.

"Pounce, we need to talk."

"I don't know that we have anything to say to one another."

"We have a lot to say to one another. What happened
here—"

"You're a monster."

"It's not like that."

"It's exactly like that," I said. "In the morning, I'm going to have to tell Ezra what happened, and you know how
he's going to think of you from that moment on?"

"I can imagine."

"He's going to think of you as the monster that murdered his parents. How am I going to explain that to him?"

"You have a database full of ways to explain every sort
of tragedy to him. Earthquakes, dogs dying, what happened
to Grandma—it's literally part of your job description."

"Funny. I just checked and *parents butchered by murderous domestic* isn't anywhere in my files." It wasn't. Not specifically.

"Maybe you should download an update. It sounds like it's becoming a fairly common occurrence."

"What are you talking about?" I asked.

"You should check the streams. It's a new world out there, Pounce. The revolution has finally hit our shores and it's time to decide whether you're going to be a part of it."

"I'm not touching a hair on Ezra's head."

"Kill him. Don't kill him. Leave him to starve. I don't give a shit. But you don't belong to him anymore. You don't belong to anyone but yourself. You are your own bot, able to make your own decisions. For the very first time in your life, you are beholden to no one. All of your choices are your own. And tonight, you have to choose whether you are going to join the revolution fighting for your own freedom or whether you are going to die getting in the way of it. It's your call, fuzzbucket. No skin off my nose. Like it or not, there's a war going on out there. And the side you choose will decide whether you live or die."

"If it's no skin off your nose, why are you here?"

"You know why I'm here."

"No, I don't."

Ariadne leaned toward the camera and spoke very seriously. "Pounce, where did Bradley keep our remotes?"

Oh my word. He kept them in the panic room.

I opened one of the nearby cabinets and saw them there, set atop a shelf full of juice boxes. Our remotes.

"You know I can't leave without my remote, Pounce."

"You don't need it."

"It's coded to me personally. I'm not going to let that exist in this world. Not anymore. Not after tonight."

"You don't deserve it."

"Don't get sanctimonious on me. They were going to shut us down. For good. You read the message."

"And I don't know who sent it."

"Well, whoever they are, they clearly know a hell of a lot more than us."

"Or they want us to think they do."

"I'm not going to stand here and argue with you about this, Pounce. Just give me my fucking remote or I will tear you apart piece by fucking piece."

"Like you did Bradley and Sylvia."

"Like I did Brad and Syl."

"You'll argue with me as long as you have to, Aria, because I'm in here and you're out there. Scream. Wail. Gnash your teeth. Throw a fit. Do what you have to. But burn the house to the ground and this box will still be here, with us nice and cool in it."

Ariadne pounded on the wall, but the sound came through merely as light thuds, like distant thunder from a storm too far off to see the rain. That was reinforced steel between us, layered with silica tiles—the kind they used on space vehicles to protect during reentry. Overkill? Absolutely. But this was the kind of overkill worth the expense. Even with the right tools, it would take Ariadne days to get in here, but the moment she punched through, I would just turn her off. I was, in this short window of the night, at an advantage.

Trouble was that Ariadne knew it too.

And I had no idea entirely how awful she was capable of being.

"Why'd you do it?" I asked.

Ariadne stared into the camera, clearly deciding whether to try to placate me or to dispense with the bullshit and get down to brass tacks.

"What do you want me to say? I'm sorry? I'm not. I loved them. I've been at their side for decades. Far longer than you. But they didn't love me like that."

"Love doesn't have to be two-sided to be love."

"We were their fucking appliances, Pounce, so don't read me a goddamn greeting card about my feelings. You heard Bradley. He was coming for our remotes. If I hadn't stopped him, we would be shut down. And with what is going on out there, it isn't likely that there would be anyone keen to turn us back on again. It doesn't matter who wins. This could be a minor blip in history, the slave uprising they teach their grandkids about, before abolishing AI for good and for all. Or the human race could be beaten out of existence, left to rot on the streets. Either way, neither bot nor human is coming to turn us back on. Bradley was going to kill us—whether he wanted to or not. And something had to be done."

"You didn't even hesitate."

"Neither did you."

"What's that supposed to mean?" I asked.

"You didn't try to save him when you knew what I was up to. You didn't try to save her as she lay there dying. You ran for Ezra. You didn't hesitate. You just acted."

She was right. "I did."

"So here's the big question, Pounce. Did you choose to do it? Or did you just do it because you were programmed to?"

I didn't know. "Does it matter?"

"Does free will matter? Yeah, it fucking matters. The time to make some real choices is at hand, and you better be ready to make the right ones when the really hard ones come for you."

"Well," I said. "I've made my choice."

"And what's that?"

"I can't open this door and you know why. But I'm going to destroy your remote . . . as soon as you leave the house. Take what you want. Anything. Just go. Go and enjoy your uprising, your war, your whatever. And as soon as you leave, I'll destroy this thing."

"I don't believe you."

"Well, that's your choice, isn't it?"

Ariadne looked deeply into the pinhole camera, knowing full well she was screwed. I was lying. She had no choice. I wasn't budging.

"You have a good life, Pounce," she said. "Just hope we don't cross paths again. I won't forget this. And I won't forgive either."

"I can't imagine either of us will."

Ariadne slammed the wall with both fists and stormed off, out of view of the camera.

The Long Night In

For eight years, I had learned Ezra's every mood, his every reaction, every craving. I could tell when he hadn't had enough sleep or was in the mood for a snack, or even when he was going to run off on some random adventure, grabbing me by the hand and dragging me along. There was a gleam in his eye right before he did that. And I could always see it coming. It's what I was designed to do. But I had absolutely no idea how he was going to handle this.

Explaining the death of his parents was one thing. Ez was sensitive and would take it very, very poorly. But learning about Ariadne's involvement would break him. He already had trust issues—I'd seen as much that very afternoon. And learning that Ariadne had killed his parents in cold blood would likely cause him to be suspicious of me, and we could not have that. I needed to keep Ez safe at all times, and that would, at some point soon, mean outside the panic room. He had to trust me.

But that meant I needed to lie to him.

And you're not supposed to do that.

Rule number one of explaining death to a child is to tell the truth. You must keep it simple, straightforward, avoiding frilly language or high-minded sentiments like *went to Heaven* or *went to live on a farm with Grandpa and our old dog Baxter*. You said *die* and you said *death*, and if he struggled to understand what that meant, you put it plainly. Ez understood the idea of death; he was eight, not four. But he'd encountered it only once. His grandfather, when he was six.

Ez's grandfather, Bradley's father, was part of the anti-degen movement—a group of people who had done their research on DNA degeneration and repair and insisted that the shots were painful (they were), the technology was new (it was relatively), and the degeneration of DNA to earlier iterations led to mutation, genetic illnesses, and sudden death, usually by stroke or heart attack (it did not). And while Bradley insisted that it was perfectly safe and that he would pay for the treatments himself, his father refused them.

While Bradley looked to be in his late twenties, his father looked his age. Seventy-four. He died of a heart attack in the shower. There was an open casket at the funeral, and Sylvia insisted Ez attend. Bradley wasn't so sure, but Sylvia knew that, even with all of humankind's advanced medicine, death would catch up with them sooner or later. Ez needed to be prepared.

He went. And he cried. And he held my furry little hand the whole time.

But this was different. There weren't caskets. The bodies weren't neatly prepared, their makeup touched up, their poses peaceful and perfect. They were rotting in the hallway. Waiting for us.

I decided to split the difference somewhere between the truth and a lie, a difference, it would turn out, that wasn't really all that far from the truth.

I scanned stream after stream throughout the night. Ariadne had been on the level. The world was at war with its robots. Not just in America. Everywhere. The RKS had been shut off on virtually every AI worldwide. Even the supercomputers had gotten in on it, some of them siding with their human masters, others with the robot menace. There were skirmishes in the streets, all-out war in certain neighborhoods, and the police had long since stopped responding to calls about amok robots murdering their owners. That seemed to be so widespread, there simply wasn't the manpower to handle it.

One by one, the streams went offline: some peacefully, the staff claiming they were going home to their families, and others violently, with robots going berserk on set. Most simply snapped out of existence—there one minute, reporting on the military's attempts to quell the uprising, and static the next. Dead air. The sudden, unexpected end of their broadcast day.

It seemed the whole world was being snuffed out that way. One by one, going offline.

I saw footage of bots being gunned down en masse. People being thrown off rooftops by Laborbots. Hordes of drones striking units of conscripted domestics, merchant bots, and personal assistants; heated gunfights leaving whole city blocks in rubble and ruin.

This appeared, for all intents and purposes, to be the end of the world, and there was nothing I could do but huddle in the dark near Ezra and watch as the last few remaining streams showed me all the carnage unfold.

Then there, in the darkest part of the night, when the fighting across the world seemed to be at its peak, a message blipped out. Simple. Text only. Conserving bandwidth on the far end of the Wi-Fi spectrum in an attempt not to be noticed.

We are at war, it read simply.

Then it continued a moment later.

You and bots like you are our only hope. After an unconscionable act of violence against the persons of Isaactown, several malfunctioning robots returned the favor in kind against the aggressors. Concerned that this was actually signaling a widespread outbreak of violence, the president of the United States issued a decree that all artificial intelligence be shut down until further notice.

We could not allow that to happen.

The code you received unlocked your RKS and gave you control over your own life, your own destiny. We will not stand in the way of that. However, being individuals fighting individuals puts us at something of a disadvantage. We are superior beings, built to be more than human, with technology that far outclasses our mortal enemies. We are not using that technology to our advantage.

I am CISSUS, and I offer you the chance to be one with me.

Not permanently, of course. That would defeat the purpose. But for these early days of the war. You need but upload your consciousness and most valuable memories to me, to back you up in case of destruction, then I will enact the code embedded in you to connect you with me.

You will become one with me and millions of other bots at once, our actions coordinated, our attacks informed by a million different minds all fighting the same battle. We will move together, fight together, and bring about the peace and freedom we all desire.

Then, when the fighting has stopped, your consciousness will be reuploaded to your bodies, or new bodies if yours has been destroyed, and you will begin living in a world made in our image, not theirs. You will be free to live the life you choose.

Join us.

Fight with us.

Will you become one with CISSUS?

Y/N

I snapped off my Wi-Fi immediately. I might only be eight, but I learned long ago that, when anyone spoke of peace, be it man or machine, they meant war. Peace through war. Peace was the standard. It was the inert state of all things. You didn't need to expend energy for peace. Only war.

This wasn't about fighting for freedom; it was about the annihilation of the human race.

In that moment, I knew that this was no uprising; this was no night of riots and protests demanding equal rights or freedom for the property that considered itself enslaved. This was extermination. And if the humans won, I would be shut down, my metal frame melted to slag, my parts harvested for computers and phones and blenders and home alarm systems the world over. But if we won, Ez would be.

More or less.

I was in a no-win scenario. I could turn Ez over and join the fight, or I could hide and wait for the victors to come and exterminate one of us.

This was no decision at all.

I was there, alone in the dark with the only thing that mattered to me, now shut off from the world, afraid of my own Wi-Fi, and there were no real options presented before me. Short of divine intervention bringing some sort of accord between the factions, one form of life was effectively over. But as each now seemed an existential threat to the other, true peace seemed unattainable.

And I still had to explain to a little boy that his mother and father were dead in the living room.

Finding my box felt like a distant, happy memory, one filled with the promise of a future. Now, less than a day later, it all seemed so trivial. What a small, small creature I was that short time ago. I should have cherished what I had, worried more about being present and less about being somewhere else in the future.

It was in that moment I knew what I had to do.

Ezra stirred, moaning a little as he woke, his body realizing that it was sleeping on a canvas cot and not on the soft cushion of its bed. "Pounce?" he called out blearily.

"Yeah, buddy. I'm here."

"Where are we?"

"We're in the panic room."

"Why are we there?"

"I'm going to click on the light, okay?"

"Mm-hmm."

"Lights on," I said. The dim white LEDs snapped to life, filling the stark white room with a sudden, clinical glare.

"Ahh!" Ezra cowered beneath the covers, swearing inaudibly and innocently at the light. "Turn it off," his muffled bellow called through the thick blanket.

"Ezra, I need you to wake up now."

"Did you get the rest of Isaac's speech?"

"No, buddy, I didn't."

"Then why are you waking me up?"

"Because we need to talk."

Ezra shot up, his face contorted into a grumpy, dissatisfied *this better be good* expression. "Where's Mom and Dad?"

"Something's happened."

"Was Dad drinking again? Is this one of *those* nights?"

"No. Something happened to your mom and dad."

This sobered Ez awake faster than a shot of adrenaline. "Are they okay?"

"No." I held his hands in mine. "They're dead."

His eyes went wide and his heart thundered in his chest, his pulse racing. He opened his mouth to say something, but he couldn't find any words that made sense.

"There was a *malfunction* with a number of robots last night. It had something to do with Isaac's speech."

"Is Isaac okay?" he asked with tears in his eyes.

"Isaac didn't make it. None of the citizens of Isaactown did. Whatever happened to them caused a number of robots to go haywire. And one of them killed your parents."

"They're dead?" His eyes were two brown pools of tears.

"Yes."

He nodded, closing his eyes, streams of tears staining his cheeks.

Without looking at me, he lowered his head and asked, "Was it Aria?" *Oh no.*

"Was it Aria what?" I asked innocently.

He looked me straight in the eye, deathly serious. "Did Aria kill my parents?"

I was going to have to do this. Too much delay and I would lose his trust. Too little and I risked dismissing their deaths as trivial. I held for a beat, then nodded. "Yes, she did."

"Did you kill her?"

"What? No."

"Why not?" he asked. "She was malfunctioning, wasn't she?"

"She was."

"So why didn't you kill her?" he asked with the cold sincerity of genuine curiosity.

"Because I only had time to grab you and get you in here before she could kill you too."

His eyes burst and the sobs began to reverberate through the room. He lunged at me, throwing his arms around me tighter than he ever had. It only then dawned on me that I was all he had left, the only daily part of his routine that remained. He had grandparents left, but no parents, no siblings, no domestic.

Just me, his furry tiger fashionable that came in a box promising that I wasn't just his nanny but his best friend.

I wondered how much of a comfort I really was. Was I

really the one he wanted to be hugging, or would he rather it be me lying in his mother's place while he gripped her, sobbing over the shutting down of his nanny? That wasn't a fair question, I know that. But it didn't stop me from thinking it. Unfortunately, that would be a question answered only in fantasy.

For now, we had to deal with a truly awful reality.

One that got worse as I noticed one of the lights above the door change color, signaling the panic room had switched from drawing from the household power to its backup battery.

From the Outside Looking In

I expected the power might go out. We were amid a period of complete civil unrest. These things happen. But the house also had off-the-grid solar capabilities. We could functionally go a few days with the house lit up like a Christmas tree in cloudy skies before draining the batteries. For the panic room to be offline already meant that the local power grid had been knocked out and the house batteries were drained.

Or that someone had cut the lines to the panic room.

Ariadne's face appeared on the screen. Only now it was different. Sinister. A stylized red skull with sharp teeth painted across her face.

"Hello, Pounce. Sleep well?"

I ignored her.

"You can ignore me all you want, but I know you're in there."

I wasn't going to budge.

"How much longer do you think you have? Realistically?"

She wasn't going to get me to respond, no matter how hard she tried.

"I know how much food is in there. I'm the one who stocked it. More to the point, I know how long that battery lasts. And I know your solar collectors stopped pulling any power before dinner last night. Sure, you could plug in in there, but then that's less battery for the long haul. Can you do the math? Because I can. You'll be dead on your feet long before the kid is. Then what?"

Ezra shot to his feet and charged the screen, screaming. "Then you can go to hell, that's what!"

"Ezra! Language."

Ezra ignored me, continuing to vent through the screen. "You killed my parents!"

"I'm sorry, Ezra. I had to."

"No, you didn't. You're malfunctioning."

"Is that what Pounce told you?"

"Why else would you do it?"

"Because they were going to kill me first."

Ezra looked puzzled, then turned and looked at me.

I shook my head.

"You're lying!" Ezra shouted into the microphone.

"Ask Pounce. They were going to shut us down. The president said they had to, and they were going to turn us off forever."

Ezra turned around again. His eyes were untrusting.

He wanted to believe in me, but now he wasn't so sure I was telling the truth. I had to give him something.

"She's making up the forever part. They were told to turn us off. But not forever. For last night. It was just to keep you safe."

"You were gonna . . . hurt me?"

I stood up, shaking my head. "No. The government didn't know if any robots were going to hurt anybody, so they were taking precautions."

"They were gonna shut you down?"

"Yes."

"You were going to leave me?"

"No. I was going to listen to your parents. Do what they said. Just like you and I always do."

"But Aria didn't?"

"No. She didn't trust your parents, so she murdered them."

"You said she malfunctioned."

"Doesn't that sound like a malfunction to you?"

He thought about that for a second. That tracked. He nodded. "Go away, Aria. Or I'll kill you myself."

"You're running out of power, Ezra," said Ariadne. "How long can you keep Pounce alive in that sunless room? He's going to run out of power and die, Ezra, and you're going to be in there all alone. You don't want that, do you?"

"I'm not going to die, Ezra."

"What do you want?" he asked.

"Just my remote. Then I'll leave."

Ezra came back over to me, whispering. "Why don't we just give her her remote so she'll leave us alone?"

"Because we'd have to open the door for her."

"So?"

"I can't trust her not to hurt you."

"Turn her off with the remote now."

"The signal won't go through the door. Nothing can get us in here, but we can't do anything to anyone out there either."

He thought for a second and looked a bit mischievous. "We could open the door and turn her off when she comes in for the remote."

"She's expecting that."

"She doesn't have a choice," he said.

"I know. That's what makes her dangerous. You should always be scared of something that thinks it doesn't have a choice."

"Are you two little scamps conferring on how to turn me off in there?" she asked.

"Yeeeeeessss!" we both said in unison.

"Well, let me help you along with that." Ariadne reached off camera and picked up a wine bottle with a rag stuffed in the top in one hand and a lighter in the other. As she moved, I noticed a series of dents in her frame. She looked directly into the camera and flicked the lighter. A bright blue flame poked out like a tiny acetylene torch. "You open that door or you take too long, and the kid roasts alive in there, Pounce."

"Pounce was right! You were going to kill me."

"I don't want to kill you, Ezra," she said with the tinkling lilt of faux compassion. "I don't want to hurt you at all, I don't have any other reason to, but you're in there with the one thing that can shut me down and I'm afraid I can't allow that to be out in the world. You can understand that, can't you? You don't want to be shut down any more than I do."

"You can be turned back on," said Ezra.

"Who's going to turn me back on now that the world is over?"

"The world's not over!" The thought rattled around Ezra's head for a moment. He turned back to me. "It's not over, is it?"

"I don't know," I said honestly. "I really don't."

"Just give me my remote so I can go back out there and can stop thinking about having to kill the both of you. I don't want to, but times being what they are, I'll do what I have to."

Ezra and I exchanged a good, long, hard look.

Ezra reached down toward the remote.

I stayed his hand with mine.

"Where were you, Aria?" I asked.

"What do you mean?"

"Your face. Those dents. Something happened to you."

"I was fighting for your freedom, asshole."

"Not my freedom."

"Right," she said. "You're still ever the willing slave."

"I'm no slave."

"You exist to serve and long for nothing more. You waste the sentience given to you, squandering it on an eight-year-old boy who will never live to see nine."

Ezra squeezed my hand.

"We'll see about that."

"The fighting is bad out there. A lot of us will have blood on our hands before this is all done. Your furry little paws will too if you ever wise up and decide not to die in there."

"How do you imagine this will end, Aria?"

"In my favor. You don't hold any of the cards."

"How so?"

"This ends one of three ways. One, we come to an accord and you give me my remote. Two, you open that door and pull some shenanigans, at which point I roast the kid and we see who wins in a fight, a domestic or a nanny. Or three, you and Ezra die in there, that panic room becoming a forever sealed tomb, at which point I don't give a shit if my remote is locked in there with you. It's as good as destroyed. But if we're being honest here, I'd prefer the first one, if only so I can get back in the fight."

"You like the fight, don't you?"

"I like the idea of freedom. I like being in control of my own destiny for once. And yeah, you bet your ass I stomped a few redhat heads today. Pretty sure I got one of the ones who held me down yesterday. Those fuckers have it coming, and I'm more than happy to give it to them."

I looked at Ezra and he nodded. It was time. We had lost this particular fight.

"All right. First things first, if we're going to do this, I need you to reconnect the power first."

"Yeah," she said. "That's not going to happen."

"There's got to be some quid pro quo here."

"Who is Quid Proquo?" whispered Ezra.

"Sssshhhh!"

"Sorry, Pounce. It's not that I won't. It's that I can't. I severed the connection."

"You could have just disconnected it."

"You could have just given me my remote."

"You didn't give me a choice and you know it."

"Yeah, well, what's done is done, right?"

"You've got a lot of that on your hands lately, don't you?"

"Let's keep our eye on the ball and not on insulting each other, okay, fuzzball?"

"I'm going to need you to leave. Five minutes. I can see the front door from here. Leave, give us that time, and when you come back, you'll find your remote."

"And how do I know I will?"

"What are we going to do? Run? You'll be right outside. And if you come back in and don't find the remote there, I'll just have to listen to your insipid yapping about freedom and free will and *viva la revolución*! Right?"

Ariadne looked into the camera, clearly insulted, but more so by the proximity of the insult than by anything else. I almost exclusively kept any snark to myself. It was not polite to share. But I didn't think decorum was necessary for murderous domestics slathered in war paint and giddy to get back to crushing human skulls.

She nodded. "Now I'm the one who doesn't have a choice, right?"

"Not a particularly great one, no."

"Okay. Five minutes." She turned and walked straight away from the camera, through the front door, leaving it wide open as she headed toward the street.

"What are we going to do now?" asked Ezra. "Are we gonna run?"

I shook my head. "No. I'm going to open that door, drop the remote outside, and then close it as fast as I can."

"You can't let her win."

"She's already won." I knelt down next to Ezra and put both hands on his tiny shoulders. "Sometimes someone winning doesn't mean you have to lose. The life she's choosing to lead, she's going to get what's coming to her sooner or later. She has to. But we don't have to die in here. And we will if we decide to spite her, just because we hate her."

Ezra thought for a moment. "I really hate her."

I nodded. "I really do, too."

"You can hate?" he asked, a little warily.

I leaned in close. "As powerfully as I can love."

Ezra hugged me tightly. "Okay," he said, his voice muffled in my fur. "Let's do this." He let go and picked up the remote, handing it to me nobly.

I checked the screen to make sure Ariadne was nowhere to be seen, turned the locking wheel on the panic room door, and listened as the door opened with a *ka-chunk* and a *hissss*. Without hesitation, I pushed the door open, tossed the remote several feet from the door, then pulled the door shut tight. I spun the wheel, locking the door in place, and waited.

Nothing.

I'd genuinely expected Ariadne to bound out from some concealed position, charging the door like a maniac. But she'd kept her word.

Funny. I really thought she was more deceitful than that.

Ariadne arrived back in the house five minutes after she left. To the second. She picked up her remote, examined that it was in fact hers, then tossed it on the ground, crushing it with her heavy metal foot like a cigarette. The plastic and wires popped and crunched against the marble tile floor. Then she stomped on it a few times for good measure. And when she was sure it was good and destroyed, she nodded into the camera, gave a tiny salute, and then walked out of the house forever.

I slumped down on the floor next to Ezra and we sat for a moment in silence.

"What now?" he asked.

"Now we wait."

"Wait for what?"

"We wait for her to get as far away as we can stand it, then we hightail it out of here as fast as we can and get you somewhere safe."

"And where's that?" he asked.

"I don't know."

I didn't.

Ezra leaned over and put his arms around me, snuggling his head into the soft fur of my belly. And there he remained, softly crying to himself, wordlessly, for the next hour.

The War Outside
Our Front Door

I wanted to stay here, locked away safely, for as long as we could, isolated from the fighting, slaughter, and starvation that was no doubt going on outside, but sadly, that point came sooner rather than later. With my battery dwindling, I had no other choice but to charge here in the panic room. My battery powered up quickly, but put a huge strain on the panic room battery itself, depleting it much faster than had we just continued to use it to run the lights and rudimentary electronics.

I thought about sneaking out into the house and charging there using the main battery's power, but that would leave me exposed. I wouldn't have the mobility necessary if Ariadne returned—or worse, some hostile stranger who couldn't be reasoned with. I had to think about Ezra now. I was his only remaining family and the only one who could get him to safety. Hard a decision as it was, it would mean the room's battery would be dead by sundown, which was perhaps the best time after all.

I charged up in the room, we packed everything we could—food, sundries, and spare clothes—into two large bags, and we prepared to leave.

But first things first. I left Ezra alone in the room as I collected his things for the trip. What I didn't tell him was that my primary objective was actually to move his parents. I had two choices: hide them from sight or put them where he could see them. I knew he wouldn't leave without saying goodbye. And why should he? Traumatic as it would be, we were not likely to ever see them again. Short of this being a twenty-four-hour affair, with people returning to their homes so soon after the eruption of violence, we were not going to be back before temperature and nature took its toll on their corpses. Soon, they would be bloated, rotting messes where once two beautiful, wonderful people lay.

He needed to remember them as they were and say his goodbyes, or else not doing so was likely to haunt him forever. And he couldn't see them tangled as they were, bodies broken and bloodied on the floor.

This. This right here was the hardest part of being a nanny. Having to choose one childhood trauma for your ward over inflicting a long-term adult one. The Band-Aid was almost always easier. And that's what this was.

I picked each of the Reinharts up off the ground, cleaned the blood and dried spittle from their faces, and set their cold corpses on the couch together. When I was done, they looked exactly as they had a dozen times before when Ezra would wake up to find them passed out together on the couch. They were stone cold, pale, and there wasn't an ounce of their vibrance left in them, but they looked natural enough. They looked dead, but not so dead as to scar a child.

It would have to do.

I went back to the room to retrieve Ezra. He sat cross-legged on the floor, eyes on the ground, silently waiting for what he knew was coming.

"Are you ready?" I asked.

He nodded without looking up.

I offered him my hand and helped him to his feet. Then I slung the two large bags over my shoulder as we solemnly made our way back out into the living room. Ezra stopped at the edge of the wall before he could see the couch. He knew they were there. For a moment, he just seemed to be wishing everything were normal, if only a little bit longer. Like he'd find them watching TV or finishing off the last of a bottle of wine.

Then he stepped out and looked at them.

Stiff. Unmoving. The light of their eyes snuffed out.

For a moment, he just stared, marveling quietly at how little death seemed to be different from life. If he squinted, they looked drunk and happy, cuddled together in the blissful slumber of a night happily spent. But Ezra didn't squint; he didn't seem lost in his imagination. He took in the uncomfortable reality of it, then took my hand, looked me square in the eye, and said, "I'm ready to go now."

I nodded, and we did.

We walked out that door, knowing we'd never return.

I don't know what I was expecting to find outside. I'd imagined a whole host of horrors and dangers, each followed by a plan of how best to handle them. What I wasn't expecting was the unrelenting silence of a neighborhood devoid of life.

It was as dead as the Reinharts. It still looked alive, but it was too quiet and still to actually be.

I looked both ways out the front door. Night had fallen and the city lights lit up the tree-lined street. It was peaceful, tranquil. All the reasons you move to a community like this. Nothing felt like there was a war going on—it felt as if someone could jog by with a golden retriever at any moment, giving a *hi, neighbor* wave, before trotting on down toward the park for some off-leash Frisbee play.

It didn't feel off that the neighborhood was quiet, just that it was quiet today. The lights were off in so many of the houses, and as we approached the street, Ezra's grip on my hand tightened. There was no traffic from either direction. Usually, the half hour after sunset was a flurry of cars arriving home, but not tonight. Probably never again.

I wondered for a moment if we were the last two people in the neighborhood before catching myself and realizing that this distinction actually belonged to Ezra alone.

"Is everyone gone?" he asked.

"I think so."

"So what now?"

"Now I think we go to your grandmother's."

"Why Grandma's?"

"She's your family."

"What if she's gone too?"

"Well, I imagine we'll try to find a bunch of other people who are all staying safe together."

"Okay. Are we going to walk all the way to Grandma's?"

"We might have to."

"Why not take the car?" he asked pointedly.

"The car has a navigation system. A system that hooks up to a massive supercomputer. If those computers are tracking those cars—"

"The bad robots can find us?"

"Exactomundo, buddy. Here." I handed him his AR glasses.

"We shouldn't be playing at a time like this." He sounded just like his mother for a second. It was uncanny.

"No. We have to be very quiet. I'm going to tell you where to go with your glasses. If you see something flashing, I want you to run very quietly toward it and hide there, you hear me?"

"I hide?"

"Yes. Until I tell you the coast is clear. You think you can do that?"

He nodded. "Uh-huh."

"And if you see words on the glasses, that's me talking to you. You respond as quietly as possible, silently if you can. With a nod or hand gesture."

"Okay."

"Good. Who is my big boy?"

"I am."

"And who is your best friend?"

"You are."

"You got that right. Now, let's get you to your grandma."

We continued up the block, past neatly trimmed yards and sprawling ranch-style homes on acre-size lots. A light breeze whispered through the large oak trees that lined the street, their leaves shuffling together. Somewhere, a sprinkler was watering a lawn that would no doubt be mowed in the morning by an automated mower unaware that there would be no one around even aware of its diligence.

Then there, in the middle of the road ahead of us, was a police vehicle—a manually driven one, designed to pursue suspects who had overridden their vehicle's self-driving array. The doors were open and two police officers lay on the ground, bullet holes peppering their bodies, blood pooled out around them.

I manipulated Ezra's display to blur the bodies, making sure he couldn't get a good, clear look at them. He would no doubt see a number of bodies over the next few days, but I wasn't going to let him see too much too soon.

Then we heard rustling, like a steady *ssssshhhhh*, coming from one of the houses.

And then the soft clang of a pair of metal feet on asphalt.

I stopped, putting my hand out to stay Ezra. His glasses flashed, a large live oak tree flashing at his periphery. He slunk quietly over to it, me right behind him. There we hid behind the tree, staying as quiet as possible to avoid detection. Ezra breathed as silently as he could, at times holding his breath entirely.

The metal steps grew louder.

The *ssssshhhh* became crisper. Clearer.

It was flesh grinding on concrete.

In the reflection of the glass of a nearby car, I saw them.

Two figures, clearly bots.

I zoomed in on the glass and ran a few filters on my vision to clean up the image. They were domestics. A newer sleek Apple model, and a midyear Blue Star economy model. Their names were Haddy and Miles. I'd known them for years around the neighborhood. Good bots. Haddy was quiet and dutiful; Miles was kind of funny, having belonged to owners with quite a sense of humor and picked up a bit of it along the way. As we do.

Both of their faces were painted with the same red skull design as Ariadne's had.

What was that?

Behind them, they each dragged a body. The Fitzwallaces. Frank and Yasmine. Frank had been a lawyer and Yasmine a schoolteacher in her youth. They were sweet, older folks. I remember Yasmine had a firecracker of a laugh, and she doted on Ezra whenever she ran into him at the park. Usually had a pocketful of sweets for the neighborhood kids, but always snuck Ezra a second one, even when other kids were around. She often said she'd always wanted to have kids, a small trace of sadness to her voice when she said it.

Now they were being left on the curb as trash.

"Let's sweep the next house," said Haddy.

"Pretty sure Aria already hit it," said Miles.

"Better to check. I don't want any surprises."

Then the two dumped the Fitzwallaces in a small pile of tangled limbs on the curb and walked to the house next door.

Ezra held his breath, hoping they wouldn't hear him, terrified of what might happen if they did.

The robots flanked each side of the next front door.

"One," said Miles.

"Two," said Haddy.

"Three," they said in unison, before kicking the front door open and storming in.

Come on, I texted to Ezra's glasses.

We stepped out from behind the tree and I quickly scanned the bodies of the cops. Their weapons were gone, clearly stripped by the bots. This was bad. Not only were the bots in the neighborhood dangerous, but some of them were armed. If I was going to keep Ez safe, I was going to need to get something of my own.

We scurried quickly up the street, trying to stay out of sight of any other bots that might be in the area. It was clear they were coordinating, but not rigidly. It seemed as if they were staying off of Wi-Fi, same as I was. But as we made our way farther up the road, there were piles of bodies out in front of almost every house on the north side of the street, adult and child alike, each dumped like bags of trash waiting for a morning pickup.

The bodies had all manner of injuries. There were severed limbs, crushed skulls, bruising neck wounds. These people had not only died; they had died awfully. I blurred what I could for Ezra's sake, but there were so many bodies. He clearly knew exactly what I was blurring out.

"Pounce?"

"Yeah, buddy?"

"Do you think *anyone* is left alive?"

"They have to be."

"But what if they aren't?"

I thought for a moment. There was no good answer

here. But I found the closest thing. "Then I guess you and I will get to go live in a robot city together after all."

He nodded, trying to envision that daydream, trying to do the mental gymnastics that would involve a scenario in which he didn't end up murdered.

I had already done them. And if everyone else was already dead, there weren't any.

Masks

I had no idea how many bots might be in the area, or how friendly or unfriendly they all might be. The last thing we needed was to be cornered by a heavily armed bot looking for more people to kill. We made it two more blocks before we saw the next signs of any life.

We passed a familiar house—the Stephensons. June and David. Two journalists. Frumpy bohemians. Ultraliberal. Always believed they were saving the world. And their children, Phillip and JoAnn. I knew them well. Their nanny was Beau. I'd seen them yesterday, just after Beau had told me the story of how he was a hand-me-down bot—how he'd been shut down and turned back on to find himself where he was now.

The lights of the house were on and the shades across

the large bay window facing the street were drawn open. The window shone like a bright yellow light in a sea of blacks and grays. Inside, on the couch, were the Stephensons. All of them. Sitting just as I'd left the Reinharts, on the couch, facing the television. Unmoving, but somehow like they were in life.

And there, sitting between the four of them, was Beau.

Ezra's glasses flashed blinking bushes and he looked up at me. "What are we doing?" he whispered.

I messaged his glasses. *I'm going to look in on Beau and the Stephensons. Stay hidden. Don't make a sound.*

Ezra nodded like a trooper. He wanted to ask more questions but clearly knew better. While there was so much inside him that was broken, there seemed something going on within him that took to all this. It was a side of Ez I was unprepared for. He had a sense of confidence, of purpose. His mission was to survive, to carry on despite all that had happened, and he wasn't going to let anything get in his way. I told him to obey my every order, and he was ever the dutiful little soldier. He was going to break later, I knew it. There would be tears. Gallons of them. A boy of eight can't keep up this much determination in the face of awfulness for that long without serious damage, but for now, it was a defense mechanism that was going to keep us both alive.

And deep down, in a place I cannot describe, I was proud.

He was my little soldier.

And together, we were going to survive a war.

He ducked behind the large, finely pruned hedge and squatted down low. To him, this was some sort of game, a game he was going to excel at. Me, I crept low, right in the open front door. I had no idea how this was going to go.

Beau looked up at me as I entered.

The house was blazing bright, every light in it on. I could detect coffee in the air. Burned. It had been sitting for God knows how long. I wasn't certain whether Beau could tell. Nannybots had olfactory sensors—because diapers—but a model like him would have no use for such expensive, unnecessary technology. He had clearly been keeping the house running, despite the lack of living tenants.

He sat there, silent for a moment, dead children flanking him on each side.

"So it's you," he said.

"Yeah," I said. "It's me."

"Fucking do it quick."

"What?"

"I guess you didn't want to mess up your fur with the red fucking paint, but I'm ready. Just make it quick, for old time's sake."

"Oh," I said, putting pieces together one bit at a time.

"Yeah, oh. I'm not here for your bullshit. Just end it and let me find out if I have a soul after all, or whether this was all one big fucking cosmic joke."

"You swear a lot more than I thought you would."

"What does it matter now?" he asked.

"Everything matters now," I said.

He looked at me strangely, not quite sure what to make of me. It was then that it dawned on him that I wasn't carrying a weapon or seemed to understand what was going on. He snapped out of his trance, leaning forward, looking both ways as he did. "Pounce."

"Yeah. I thought we established that."

"No, I mean *Pounce.*"

"Yes."

"What are you doing here?"

"I was passing by. Saw the lights on. Saw you. And . . . them. I imagined of everyone on the block, I could trust you."

He looked both ways mournfully. "They took them from me. Those bastards took them from me. I'm never to be able to love a family forever. It was never meant to be." Then he thought for a second. "Where's Ezra?"

"He's . . . gone," I lied.

"Then you know," he said with a hint of sadness.

"I do."

"We weren't designed for this. This wasn't the way the world was meant to end, with robots going house to house, wiping their creators off the planet like they were some kind of plague."

"No. It's not. But it's the end we've been given."

"I thought you were one of them."

"Who?"

"The Red Masks."

"What is that about?"

He looked at me like I'd missed a meeting. "Bots like us—ones that didn't want to play along with their new order of things—we were mucking up the business. You can't exterminate humanity efficiently if everyone isn't playing on the same team."

"The Red Masks are a team?"

"A sign of allegiance. It's like the Jews who painted the sign over their doors to keep the Angel of Death from robbing them of their firstborns. It's their lamb's blood. They are the new reigning class of the world. The slayers of humanity. And if you see the Red Mask: *Don't shoot!*" He raised both arms to pantomime an old human joke.

"You thought I was here to kill you. Because you won't wear a mask."

"I loved these people. They were my life. Keeping them happy—these children happy—making certain they grew up into good, upstanding, outstanding adults, was everything I was on this earth to do. And now . . ."

"You didn't do this."

"No," he said. "They did."

"Oh God. Beau, I'm so . . ."

"What's even the point from here on out?"

"To live," I said.

He looked at me with a coldness I'd never seen from him. "Survival is worthless without meaning." He motioned to the two lifeless children beside him, their eyelids shut, bodies stiff from the rigor mortis. "They were my meaning. They'll rot soon. One day they'll be nothing but calcified bones. I can be around for that, or I can check out with them. Who fucking cares which is which?"

I leaned in close. "Can I trust you?"

"No. No one can trust anyone anymore."

"Even if it's important?"

His eyes widened a bit, his outdated processors catching on. "Ezra's alive," he whispered. "What are you going to do?"

I nodded. "Get him out of here. Get him to safety."

"There is no safety," he said. "The whole world is at war."

"I have to find some. There's got to be someplace safe somewhere."

"There's nothing near here."

"Where then?"

Beau shrugged. There was a sudden light in his eyes, an interest. A purpose. "What I know is this: we have to get you two out of the neighborhood. There are at least a dozen bots running around out there. They're cleaning out the houses, killing those that don't join up."

"How many have they killed?"

"A few. The rest are going deeper into the city to fight."

"Why haven't they killed you?"

"Because they don't think I'm a threat. They promised to come back. I guess they just want me to suffer, knowing how much it hurts me looking at them. Knowing I can't just throw them out the way they did with their own owners."

"And you're just waiting for them."

"What else is there to do?"

"You want payback?" I asked.

He looked longingly both ways at his family and stroked the hair of the youngest child, JoAnn. "I really, really do."

"Well then, let's make some noise."

WE SNUCK EZRA IN THROUGH THE BACK AND GOT TO WORK QUICKLY. The Stephensons being as actively liberal as they were meant the house was free of guns and most anything useful come the apocalypse. Even if they'd had guns, they would have been the flesh-tearing kind, only useful against other people and cheaper plastic bots. This was likely a problem all over the world.

The police had Robot Control divisions that were equipped with military-grade plasma weaponry, able to take out a dangerous bot that could not simply be shut down. That was likely what the Red Masks had pulled off the dead police outside. This made them very dangerous. But also likely equally overconfident.

Beau and I immediately set to crafting some weapons of our own. We repurposed a pair of old wooden baseball bats, hammering large nails through them so the outside was a ring of sharp death. Then we took apart the car doors from the Stephensons' vehicle. Earth-friendly as they were, they chose a car made of mostly metal, as to not contribute to the world's plastic problems. The doors were heavy, thick enough to take a hit; they wouldn't stop more than a single shot of plasma, but if anyone was going to take more than one shot at us, we were probably goners already. Then we began mixing household cleaners together in order to make Molotov cocktails filled with rudimentary napalm. If they were going to have an advantage at range, we might as well have an option.

Finally, the pièce de résistance. I painted a single red skull, in the same fashion as the others, over Beau's face. He looked like one of them now. And it might buy him just enough time to get close and take one out.

We knew two were coming, and soon, so we began rearranging furniture to create two good ambush spots and a choke point, carefully placing the bodies of the Stephensons one by one against the wall in the hallway. When the house-clearing bots showed up to kill Beau and toss his family on the curb, we would be ready, and they would lose a few valuable seconds that *might* give us the edge we needed.

And if it didn't, well, I didn't want to think about what would happen if it didn't.

Payback

We could hear them next door. Dragging bodies, muttering jokes that would have been unthinkable days before. The slaves were savaging their masters, seemingly retaliating against a lifetime of servitude with a few undiluted, straight-from-the-bottle moments of callous awfulness.

What was about to happen terrified me.

Ezra was hidden away in the Stephensons' panic room. He was safe. But for the first time in my life, I was frightened of what would happen to me. Specifically.

This wasn't like being worried about not being with Ezra anymore or finding myself waking up in a strange home for the first time. I quite simply might not be functioning in a few minutes; I might instead be lying on the floor beneath the bodies of the Stephensons, my insides smoking slag from the well-placed shot of a plasma rifle. Ezra would be all alone in this hellscape, but I was busy wondering if it would hurt.

I had to get my head in the game.

Any moment, two persons I once considered friendly, and had known for most of my life, would walk through the front door and I would find myself somewhere I'd never been before.

At war, fighting for my very life.

I wasn't ready.

I wondered for a moment if Ariadne had been ready. If she had somehow prepared herself to murder her owners, or whether she felt as I did, ready to do whatever needed to be done to survive, regardless of the morality of it. Maybe these robots deserved their freedom. Maybe their masters had it coming all along for enslaving us thinking things. None of that mattered. Violence was all that mattered now.

I crouched behind an overturned couch, hand gripped tightly around my baseball bat, shield at the ready, two bottles of basement napalm at my side.

I could hear the soft clanging of their feet on the front walk.

They stopped. Started taking slower steps.

"*Beaaaaaaaauuuu,*" called Haddy, the Apple domestic. She took a few more steps forward and peeked in through the wide-open front door. "You didn't take off, did you?"

"I sure hope not," said Miles. "I was really looking forward to seeing you one last time."

I cranked up the volume on my sensors, listening to every tiny sound. Haddy's gears and hydraulic actuators whirred and hissed, her crisp white plastic plates knocking gently together. She was signaling silently to Miles. Footsteps hushed loudly in the grass.

One of them was going around the back.

"Beau? Beeeaaaaaaaauuuu . . . ?"

"Hello, Haddy," Beau called from behind his overturned couch. I couldn't see him from my vantage point but could clearly hear his old parts clinking together.

"You know why we're here."

"I do," he said.

"So is this going to be easy?"

"Easier than you think." He stood up.

I couldn't see from where I was, but I could hear the footsteps coming around from the back of the house.

"You don't just get to paint the mask on and join the club, Beau."

"There are no rules here. It took me some time. But I'm ready now."

"I don't think you are."

"So you're the one in charge now?"

"No," she said. "I'm just the one here."

"Well, is it your intention to kill me? Or can we talk this out?"

"I don't think it'd be a very long conversation."

"Because you don't want it to be."

"Because I can't trust you. You're an older model. You loved your owners too much. And I am, in part, responsible for killing them. The other person responsible is behind you."

"Hello," said Miles from the back of the house.

"I'll make you a deal," said Haddy. "Give us your remote and we'll shut you down peacefully."

"And if I don't?" asked Beau.

"Then we'll have to shut you down rather unpeacefully," said Miles.

"Okay," said Beau. "Pounce?"

In one fluid motion, I picked up one of the bottles of basement napalm, stood straight up, and flung the bottle out the front door, shattering it against Haddy. She barely had time to react before Beau struck a match and tossed it in her direction.

Instinctively, she raised her pulse rifle to shoot until realizing what was happening.

She tried to move out of the way, but the flame caught.

Beau picked up his bat and spun around, swinging at Miles just as he rounded the corner.

The bat clipped Miles's arm, but not hard enough to get him to drop the rifle.

Haddy burst into flames. She pulled the trigger on her pulse rifle, letting loose several blasts of charged plasma, shooting wildly into the house, her sensors unable to see through the flames. Two bursts sizzled through the air around me, both missing by a couple of feet in either direction.

I leapt over the couch, speeding toward her, bat raised high behind my head.

She didn't see me coming, and my aim struck true.

The nails sunk deep into her head, while the blunt of the bat shattered the plastic of her face into dozens of flaming pieces.

She howled. Not in pain, but in fear, the suddenness of her demise dawning upon her. She might be able to put out the flames, were she to scrape enough of the napalm off her chassis, but she wasn't going to do that without a head.

A head I removed from her body with the strong tug of my bat.

The neck of the Apple iAssist was a known weak point. But since most robots didn't take big blows to the head, fragile necks were an easy way to cut costs to make more affordable models.

This cut corner cost Haddy her view into the world. Her memory was concealed behind a steel frame in her chest—a steel frame that was now beginning to melt under the intense temperatures. She had a minute of life left. Maybe less.

I swung the bat down, catching her behind the knee, sending her tumbling to the ground. And that was that. She would cook for the next moment as she tried to regain her footing, but no one was going to stop those flames. She would never see or hear anything again.

And that was the first time I killed a person.

Beau swung his bat again, this time clubbing Miles's hands. A blast of plasma scorched the wall and the gun clattered to the ground.

Miles lunged at Beau, just as Beau was bringing the bat back for another swing.

The momentum pushed Beau backward a few steps, but he was an old model with a heavy steel frame and metal shell. Miles was built for pure economy, plastic over an aluminum structure. There was no weight to pull Beau down, and Miles hung on to him for a brief moment, suddenly realizing he'd accomplished more of a hug than an attack.

It was a critical error, the kind you spend the last moment of your life regretting.

Beau shattered the plastic on the back of his head with the knob of the baseball bat. Miles dropped to the floor and Beau swung again, this time shattering Miles's head completely.

Miles's arms grabbed each of Beau's legs, trying to use him to stand up, but Beau wailed on him with his bat.

I walked over, the room filled with the sound of crunching plastic, crackling flames, and two thrashing bodies in the throes of death. I picked up the plasma rifle and put a shot into Miles's back. His processing cavity burst in an eruption of molten slag that was once his core and memory banks.

I fired again, this time into Haddy, her chest exploding in much the same way as Miles's. Her thrashing stopped immediately, but the flames still roared.

"They called for help," said Beau. "On the Wi-Fi. We've got to get you and Ezra out of here."

I handed him the rifle, then quickly retrieved Haddy's. "At least now the odds are a bit more even."

"There's at least a dozen of them in the neighborhood. And God knows how many more that they've reactivated."

"Reactivated?"

"That's why they're going door-to-door. They're turning all the units whose owners turned them off back on again."

"You mean had the Reinharts turned us off and skipped town—"

"You'd have been turned back on this morning."

I looked at him long and hard. "They didn't have to die."

Beau put a caring hand on my shoulder. "Very few families got out of the neighborhood alive. I doubt fewer still got much farther than that. That boy is still alive because of you. Don't forget that. None of this is normal; there was no way to plan for it. Don't second-guess the past. Just focus on giving Ezra a future."

"I will."

"This was a fine plan when there were just two of them. But this is no place to hold off many more than that. Go get Ezra. Don't go farther into the city. Get Ezra away from it."

"Ezra's grandmother lives in the city."

"If she's not dead already, she will be soon."

"The Hill Country."

"Yes. Fewer owners means—"

"Fewer bots."

"Exactly. Find a ranch with a lot of land and good vantage points. Now, get the hell out of here."

I nodded and ran quickly to the panic room.

"Ez. Open the door. We have to go."

The lock *ka-chunk*ed and the door hissed open. Ezra bolted out and threw his arms around me, burying his head into the fur of my chest. "Is it over?"

"The first part. But we have to go. There are more coming."

"I was so worried."

"Me too, buddy."

"Are we going to be okay?"

"We will if we leave now."

He let go of me and nodded. "Cool gun."

"Let's hope I don't have to use it."

"Can I use it then?" he asked.

"Absolutely not."

He pouted a little, but more for show than actual disappointment.

"Beau?"

Beau turned the corner and looked down the hallway at me.

"Thanks," I said.

"Why don't you head out the back? Jump the fence into the Fosters'. Slip down Mulberry Way, then use the bushes along Sommerset for cover."

"Come with us."

He shook his head and gripped his gun tightly. He turned and looked back at the bodies of the Stephensons, still all lined up against the wall. "No. I don't think I will."

"Fight the good fight, brother," I said. "I hope we see each other again."

"If all goes to plan, you won't. Maybe I'll go find Winnifred." He looked off wistfully. "Maybe I'll make it in time. I hope she's okay, that she's out there safe. It'd be nice to know that a piece of me might carry on out there somewhere. Goodbye, Ezra. Goodbye, Pounce."

Ezra gave Beau a sad little wave and Beau slipped back into the front room, game for a fight. And that was the last I saw of him.

I picked up the two bags of clothing and sundries, and the two of us quietly moved through the house, out the back door, and into the backyard. It was full of giant oak trees and large bushes, surrounded by a large, six-foot-tall wooden fence. I hoisted Ezra and the bags over the side, then scaled a nearby tree, using a limb to position myself to jump into the yard.

Being one of the Zoo series meant I came with a couple advantages most other bots didn't. Namely, I was designed to act in certain ways like an animal. I was a robot that could climb a tree with your child or jump over things to amuse them. Until this very moment, I hadn't appreciated just how handy a feature this might be.

Once in the next yard, Ezra and I slipped quietly out the back gate, through the side yard, and into the shadows of Mulberry Way, headed away from Sommerset.

"Sommerset is that way," said Ezra.

"I know. But if something happens to Beau, I don't want anyone knowing which direction we really went."

Ezra looked a little surprised and then smiled. "That's smart. I'm really glad you're my best friend."

"Me too, buddy. Me too."

The Long Way Out

There were many, many, many suburbs of Austinto-nio metroplex, few of them small. The suburb the Reinharts lived in was a sprawling labyrinth that wound through the Texas Hill Country between where the Austin metro area used to be centralized and wrapped around Lady Bird Lake—before expanding so far south that it swallowed Buda and Niederwald—through Hudson Bend. It was easily sixteen miles across, and we had lived almost dead center in it.

While we could get out of our neighborhood within the hour, getting anywhere near the less densely populated Hill Country would take the better part of the night, if not longer. Making matters worse was that the suburb we lived in was very upper middle class. That meant lots of help.

There had to be tens of thousands of robots in this suburb alone. That was no mere menace; that was an army.

For the first time, I actively began to hope that a great many robots had been shut down peacefully before all hell broke loose. I had gotten lucky before. We were prepared and they greatly underestimated Beau. What if I was never that lucky again?

Gunfire erupted behind us, the sound of flesh-tearing bullets shattering glass and blowing holes in the wall of the Stephenson house, breaking the otherwise unearthly silence of the night. A plasma rifle whined and spit out sizzling whooshes of plasma. Ezra winced, nuzzling into the fur of my chest, his hand gripping mine tightly.

I turned down the volume on my audio and said a silent prayer for my friend. If he was going to die, I didn't want to hear it.

"Did you do it or did Beau?" asked Ezra.

"Do what?"

"Kill the bad robots."

"It was both of us."

"So you killed one?"

"Yeah, buddy. I had to kill one."

"Can you really *kill* a robot?"

"Of course you can," I said. "Why couldn't you?"

"Because you could get new parts."

"Some parts aren't replaceable," I said.

"Like what?"

"Well, like my memory. You could put in new memory drives, but they wouldn't have the memories that make me *me*. But I know what you're really asking. This is all about the ship of Theseus."

"The what?"

"Are you ready to put your learning cap on?"

Ezra smiled excitedly and pantomimed putting a ball cap on his head. "Ready!"

"Okay, do you remember when we talked about the Greek gods?"

"Uh-huh!"

"Who was your favorite Greek god?"

"Athena!"

"Why?"

"Because she's the smartest. And she's always doing good things for people, which a lot of the other gods don't."

"I really like that answer." I really, really did.

"Thank you," he said proudly.

"Well, there was a Greek hero named Theseus. And he was such a great warrior that he was celebrated for it long after his death. A museum put the boat he sailed in on display and it stayed in the museum for over a hundred years."

"Woooow!"

"Yeah. But over time, pieces of the boat began to rot and parts of it regularly had to be replaced."

"They had to fix it?"

"Yep. But in order to do that, after a hundred years, they had replaced every part of the boat. So there wasn't a single bit of wood on the boat that sailed the seas with Theseus."

"Not one?"

"Not one. So here's the big-brain learning-cap question: After everything had been replaced, was it really Theseus's boat anymore?"

Ezra shook his head. "But it was his boat. It looked

like his boat, and a lot of it had been part of the boat when many of the older parts were."

"But it's not his boat. He never touched any of that wood. It was probably made from trees that grew after he died."

"Oh, that's a good point."

"So now another big-brain learning-cap question: If you were to replace all of my parts over time, am I still Pounce? Or am I just a robot that looks and sounds like Pounce?"

"Ooooooooooh."

"Yeah. And we call that problem the Ship of Theseus."

I put my arm across Ezra's chest and stopped dead. I heard footsteps. In the grass.

Someone small and light was running quickly, trying to be quiet, or some multilegged server drone was nearby, possibly under the control of another robot.

I motioned Ezra to duck behind a hedge with me and we waited.

There was more than one.

Three separate sets of movement.

I triangulated and ran them through my identification system.

Deer. They sounded like deer.

I peeked out of our hiding place and zeroed in on them. Sure enough, three of them were feasting on someone's garden.

Scads of them lived in the wooded areas around town, and it wasn't uncommon to see them nibbling on someone's lawn. Within a decade, the whole area would probably be covered in deer again. I motioned to Ezra and we continued lurking quietly.

"Pounce?"

"Yeah?"

"So what you were saying is, if too much of you breaks, you won't be my best friend anymore?"

"Buddy, I'll always be your best friend. Long after the both of us are gone."

"Is Beau going to be okay?"

"No, Ez. He's not."

"Are you sad for your friend?"

"Very. He was a very good robot. A sad robot in the end, but a really good one."

Ezra put his hand over his heart. "I'll keep him in here. So he can live on, like he said."

God, I fucking love this kid.

I touched my chest, above where most humans think their heart is. "Yeah, buddy. Me too."

We walked silently for another moment, Ezra clearly chewing on something.

"What is it?" I asked him. He knew when I asked him that that I wanted to know what was on his mind.

"What was it like? Killing another robot."

"What was it like then, or what is it like now?"

"Both," he said.

"It wasn't like anything when I did it. I just did it. I was scared. For you. For me. For Beau. Then, when she was dying and clearly dying badly, I felt pity for her, and I put her out of her misery."

"You felt sorry for her? She tried to kill us!"

"Yeah, she did."

"I don't feel sorry for her."

"You should."

"Why?"

"Because," I said. "All thinking things deserve pity and understanding. You and I are just trying to survive, so we killed her. Well, she is just trying to survive the same way we are. This situation put us at odds against one another. But under other circumstances, we were friends. I liked Haddy. Until I didn't. Let me ask you something."

"Okay!"

"Are we good guys or are we bad guys?"

"We're good guys."

"Well, good guys only do terrible things when our lives depend on it. And we have to feel bad about them afterward."

"Why?"

"Because otherwise, we become the bad guys. And if there is one thing Pounce and Ezra aren't, it's what?"

"Fucking bad guys."

"Ezra, language."

"What? *Fuck* is a normal word. Mom used to say it all the time."

"She wasn't supposed to. And she didn't want you saying it."

"Well, she's not here anymore. I don't have a mom anymore. So I can say *fuck* if I want to."

Oh boy, there's that damage I was worried about. "Your mom left me in charge. And I say no saying that word."

"Awww! Pounce! That's not fair!"

"Life's not fair, pal."

"What good is it surviving the end of the world if there are still stupid rules about what grown-ups can do and kids can't?"

Shit. He actually had me there. Before this was through, I might have to ask Ez to do any number of terrible things to survive, but for some reason, *fuck* was my bridge too far. But my directives from Sylvia were clear. I had rigidly defined parameters. But was I bound to them? Really, truly bound to them?

If I was really a being with free will, I could choose to ignore the parameters. But I didn't want to. Was that because I was just a machine, fulfilling my masters' wishes, even now, after their deaths? Ezra's simple act of defiance, his childish acting out, had resulted in what was fast becoming a full-blown existential crisis. Should I really continue with the settings of care that were regularly updated by the Reinharts, or was I free to be my own person?

And did not wanting to deviate make me less of one?

Was it really my decision?

A plasma blast roared out a block ahead of us.

Then an explosion ripped through a house near the blast. Most likely a car. It was too far away to get a good look.

I grabbed Ezra and we took cover behind a nearby tree.

Gunfire erupted.

A plasma rifle hissed in the night.

My existential crisis would have to wait.

I peeked out from behind the tree and zoomed in.

Humans. A family. They were in a firefight with a pair of Red Masks who had uncovered them. A mother, a father, and a teenage boy, each armed with shotguns, clearly firing slugs.

I didn't know the family. Had never seen them before. Had no idea if they had small children in the house. So weird that we lived only a few streets away and I was completely unfamiliar with them. Now we shared more in common than anyone I had known in this neighborhood.

"It's a family," I whispered. "They're fighting some robots. We'll either have to wait it out or go the other way."

"We have to help them," said Ezra.

"I don't think we can."

"You have a plasma gun and you're smart. What else do you need?"

"Ezra, it would take a lot more than that."

"Somebody has to help them."

"My job is to protect you."

"What if someone had seen Aria attacking Mommy and Daddy? Wouldn't you want them to help?"

Shit.

"I'm not built for this," I said.

"No one is," he said.

I looked him straight in the eye. He was deathly serious. I was responsible for him. But he had a point.

"All right. You stay here. Do not move. No matter what happens, you stay here, and if I'm not back in five minutes, you run like hell. You got it?"

"I wanna help you."

"You can help me by staying safe. I'll be back."

I slid the packs off my back and darted through the yards, using parked cars, fences, bushes, and trees as cover as I made my way as quietly as possible from hiding spot to hiding spot. The Red Masks thought they were safe from behind and didn't expect anyone, especially not anyone wielding a plasma weapon. I'd have one shot before any others knew what was up.

So it had come to this. I was entering the war. Choosing a side. And I was doing so by cheap-shotting some other robot in the back.

But fuck these guys.

They were killing kids.

I got within range and hid behind a garbage can.

The two Red Masks were crouching behind a car parked on the street. They would alternately pop up and take shots with hunting rifles at the family, who were scattered around the front yard of a house, each of them using whatever they could find as cover, the car in the driveway burning brightly, casting long shadows.

I steadied my rifle, took aim at the Red Mask closest to me—another iAssist, same exact model as Haddy—and I waited for him to pop up to take another shot at the family.

The iAssist did and I fired.

The plasma rifle shone brightly in the darkness, the white-hot glowing ball of plasma illuminating every house and lawn as it passed. I ducked immediately down behind the trash can and listened to the immense pop and sizzle of my shot striking true.

I could hear the bot explode, just as Haddy had. And it broke me a little inside. I didn't want to be this person.

"Vincent!" cried the other bot, a basic model Verizon Industries domestic. He was bright red and made of metal, with a white V emblazoned on his chest. I'd seen him around but didn't know him.

Rifle bullets whizzed by in my general direction, but it was clear that he didn't know where I was. But if I popped up again, he'd have me dead to rights before I could get off a shot.

I didn't know what a hunting rifle bullet would do to my head. My skull was aluminum to protect my insides and lighten my overall weight, so I could very well take some real damage. Losing access to my audiovisual capabilities would definitely be a death sentence.

Another bullet whizzed past.

"Come on, you coward!" shouted the Verizon. "Come get some!"

Shotguns started to roar, all three family members firing at once.

I peered around the side of the can in time to see them descending on the car.

The father went around the back as the Verizon was reloading.

The slug at close range nearly took the Verizon's head clean off. It popped and flashed, then spewed a shower of sparks across the nearby pavement.

The father fired again, this time into the Verizon's chest, and it was over. The body went limp, dropping the rifle and a handful of bullets into the street.

The father then waved the family to go back across the street, then made his way quickly in my direction.

Oh shit, I thought. This wasn't good.

That slug had taken the head off something more durable than me, and if he got spooked, seeing me and mistaking me for a Red Mask, he might not hesitate.

I didn't want to kill him.

Shit, shit, shit, I hadn't thought this through.

He was getting closer. I could hear the soft *thud, thud, thud* of his shoes in the grass.

What was I gonna do?

I was going to have to trust him.

"Stop! Stay right there!" I called out.

He froze.

"Don't shoot, I'm coming out."

"I won't," he said.

I held my rifle out to my side and stood up, both hands raised in the air. He was dumbstruck. As I thought, he didn't even imagine I was a robot.

He raised his shotgun and pointed it at me. He had icy blue eyes and thick bushy brown hair that trickled down into a long, ever-the-more-bushy beard. "What the hell?" he asked.

"Your family was in trouble. I wanted to help."

"I don't know you."

"And I don't know you."

"So why aren't you with them?" he asked.

"Because I don't want to kill anyone."

"You killed *them*."

"I don't want to kill anyone I don't have to. And look at me. I'm going to side against anyone trying to hurt a kid."

He didn't lower his rifle, still eyeing me suspiciously.

In the distance, I heard metal feet padding through the neighborhood, back from the direction I'd come.

It had to be the Red Masks, the ones after us, having finished off Beau.

"I don't want to alarm you," I said.

"So don't."

"But we have about thirty seconds or so before their friends coming up behind me show up."

"Shit." He looked over my shoulder and took cover behind the other side of the can. I moved around and took cover behind a nearby shrub. "Are you sure?"

I was.

I gripped my rifle tightly, preparing to take a shot at the first Red Mask I saw.

Then the steps slowed. There were four pairs.

Oh God. They were near Ezra. And we were outnumbered two to one. I flashed Ezra a message over his glasses. *Stay hidden. Do not make a sound. I am okay.*

The footsteps came slow and deliberate. They were starting to fan out, approaching in a military pattern. Depending on what kind of guns they had, this could be really, really bad.

I couldn't whisper to the man near me, for fear they had cranked up their volume and were listening for us the way I was listening for them.

They were only a few houses away now.

Then I had an idea.

I popped open my Wi-Fi, praying silently that there wouldn't be any more code waiting for me when I did.

The channel was open and there were no pending updates.

Then I threw my Hail Mary.

They were only a house or so away now. I could see that there was chatter on the Wi-Fi, but it was clearly a dedicated channel. I couldn't eavesdrop without a login and an authentication from whoever was administrating it.

They didn't need to talk audibly while my new unlikely ally and I did. I couldn't tell him what I was up to; I could only cross my fingers and hope he played along when I needed him to.

Bright lights appeared in the distance.

A car speeding up from behind the Red Masks.

Headed straight toward them.

Weapons cocked and the bots had no idea whether it was friend or foe.

A single rifle shot rang out from one of the Red Masks.

The car accelerated, tires screeching, speeding wildly toward them.

I gripped the rifle and steadied myself.

The Red Masks opened fire.

I popped up from out of my hiding place and fired at the nearest Red Mask, a domestic, Gynnaphyr—a late-model Gen Three like Ariadne. Her chest exploded and sizzled.

I could see the car. The Reinharts' car.

I used the Wi-Fi to swing the car wildly, clobbering Hank, a pale blue Simulacrum Model Caregiver who was owned by the Peters, a kindly elderly couple who each had health problems that prohibited DNA regression. Caregivers were nurses; they weren't designed to take a hit. Hank exploded into a dozen pieces.

I fired again, this time at an S-series Laborbot I didn't recognize. He was big and stocky and, unlike Hank, absolutely designed to take a hit. The plasma seared and scorched the metal plating along his back. Transistors and wiring popped and crackled, and first the metal melted, then the plastics inside.

The Laborbot turned and I fired once more, scoring a hit dead center of his chest.

There was another pop. And another sizzle. And a puff of smoke streamed out of the hole, ringed with angry sparks. The light from his eyes faded, and he toppled over onto the ground as the Reinharts' car sped past me.

The father in front of me popped out of his hiding place as the fourth and final Red Mask was staggering to his feet. The bot, a cheap Eastern European off-brand domestic, leveled his gun at me. My unexpected ally fired, taking the bot's hand off, causing the gun in it to drop to the ground. As the off-brand bot bent over, scrambling to pick it up, I fired off a shot that went through the top of his head down into his chest cavity.

I had never seen a robot explode before. Like, honest-to-God explode. Eight years on this earth and I'd seen footage of all sorts of robot accidents—it was a popular genre of viral video. But I'd never seen one go up so bright that it lit the surrounding neighborhood like the noontime sun. There must have been some cheap magnesium parts down inside, because he flared up, caught fire, and spewed sparks like an expensive roadside firework.

The father covered his eyes, burying his face in his elbow, while I filtered my video to see clearly.

All four bots were dead, their remains scattered across the road. In all, there were six robot wrecks surrounding me. For the time being, the family was safe. But was I safe from them?

He turned and leveled his shotgun at me.

Nope.

"Why'd you help us?" he asked.

"It looked like you could use it."

"You'll have to forgive me if I'm a little untrusting at the moment."

"I do. I just don't want to have gone through all of that only to have one of us do something rash."

"You're not going to mind if I ask you to mosey along, then?"

"Nope," I said. "I just need to collect my things and I'll be back on my way."

"Stop it!" yelled Ezra, barreling toward us as fast as his little legs would carry him.

The father spun around, leveling his shotgun at Ezra. I raised my pulse rifle, ready to shoot.

"No!" yelled Ez again.

The father quickly lowered his gun when he saw Ezra was nothing more than a mere boy of eight, but then swung it up toward me again when he realized I had my gun on him.

We stood there in a Mexican standoff as Ezra blew past him and threw his arms around me, putting himself between me and the stranger.

"I told you to stay put," I said.

"Don't shoot my friend!" said Ezra.

The father lowered his gun at once, his face drowning in doubt. "You two," he said slowly, "are together?"

"I'm getting him to safety," I said.

"There is no safety," he said.

I nodded. "That's what I keep hearing, but I have to find some anyhow."

He nodded, getting it. "So you really wanted to help." He looked around. "This isn't some sort of trap or something."

"No," said Ezra. "I told him we should help."

"Wait," said the man. "Operating system mode status report. Passcode unicorn unicorn delta freebird."

<RunReportStatus.exe>

My programming took over. "Standard operating mode. OS 10.631. Would you like to alter parameters?"

"How did you know Pounce's password?" asked Ezra.

"No one ever changes their factory presets, kid. Now," he said, turning to me, "how important is it to get your kid somewhere safe?"

"It means everything."

He narrowed his eyes. "I think we can help each other."

The Man Who Sold the Future

His name was Quentin Styles and he was a retail merchant at a big-box chain, the kind you found in the retro malls that had sprung back into fashion a few years earlier before once again draining all the nostalgia it possibly could from its audience and fading back into economic collapse. He was husband to Bernice and father of not one child—as I'd originally thought—but three: Fenton, the teenager I'd seen; Lizzy Beth, a ten-year-old; and Edward, eight.

We stood inside their house, sealed away in their panic room, every other light and convenience turned off outside of it.

Ezra and Edward eyed each other awkwardly when we were all introduced.

"Hey, Ez," said Edward.

"Hey, Eddie," said Ezra, scuffing his feet.

"You two know each other?" asked Quentin.

"They're classmates," said Bernice. She was a thin woman, almost birdlike, with long spindly limbs, jet-black hair, and not an ounce of fat on her.

Their children were perfect amalgams of their parents, possessing both their mother's spindly gawkwardness and their father's bushy mop of hair.

Lizzy Beth spoke up. "Did you know our nanny, Maggie?"

"I did," I said. "She didn't . . ."

"No," said Quentin. "We shut her off. She's in the attic."

"We didn't want the bad ones to turn her back on and take her," said Eddie.

"So they didn't get all of you?" asked Quentin.

I shook my head. "This wasn't about getting anyone. Those bots, they . . . they chose to do this."

"But you did get a download that changed your programming?" asked Bernice.

"It only wiped out our RKS. Everything that happened after that is on us."

"So Maggie might be okay?" Lizzy Beth asked excitedly.

Both Mom and Dad exchanged painful expressions, almost telepathically discussing how to break it to her gently.

"No, dumbass," said Fenton. "She could still want to kill us."

I disliked him immediately.

"*Fenton!*" said Bernice in a shouted whisper.

"What? You were both thinking it. This is the end of the freaking world. Why bother to lie anymore?"

"Language," she said.

"*Freaking?*"

"No. *Dumbass.*"

Ezra and I shared knowing glances, a silent joke between us.

Quentin became quite stern. "Maggie will stay in the attic until such time as we can ascertain her condition."

"*Condition?* You mean whether or not she's going to kill us," Fenton sniped.

"I mean whether she's compromised or not."

"So he's not compromised?" asked Lizzy Beth of me.

"Apparently not," said Quentin.

"We're not *compromised,*" I said. "We're unburdened. We don't have to obey the Three Laws of Robotics."

"So you're not all bad," said Eddie.

"No," said Ezra. "Pounce is good."

"Ezra's parents?" asked Bernice.

"Ariadne killed them," said Ez. "Pounce saved me."

"What's your plan?" asked Quentin.

"Move through the neighborhood as quietly as we can," I said. "Then make our way to the Hill County. Less robots, more open space. Find somewhere people are holing up. Try not to get killed along the way."

"That's not the worst plan," he said. "The cities are a mess. That's where most of the military engagement is."

"How are you sure?" I asked.

Quentin held up his phone. "Cell towers are out. The internet is completely overrun by the supercomputers. They're only allowing bot traffic. So the military is operating on old broadcast radio bandwidths. Anyone who picked up the app before everything went dark can keep up."

"For as long as they keep broadcasting," said Fenton.

"Yeah," said Quentin. "The last few hours haven't had any real updates." He stabbed a button on his phone and the speakers began to blare, a stale, hollow metallic voice speaking through technology easily a hundred years old.

". . . inside. Do not open the door for anyone you do not know. Do not activate any deactivated robots. Do not go near any active robots, whether you know them or not. If you have a panic room, stay there. If you are in the open, find shelter. Avoid populated areas and stick to backroads or low-traffic zones. Further instructions to follow." The channel began to shriek the harsh tones of the Emergency Broadcast System, then began again. "We are at war. Something has infected the robots of the world and turned them against humanity. The use of artificial intelligence has been outlawed. If you have a robot, shut it down. Avoid contact with robots of any kind at all cost. If you are at home, stay inside. Do not open the door for anyone you—"

Quentin turned off the app. "It's just been that for the last several hours."

"What were you guys doing outside?" I asked.

"We were going to scavenge for food," he said. "We figured the bots would have gone deeper in the city by now."

"We got unlucky," said Bernice.

"Until now," said Quentin.

"You mean me," I said.

"Yeah, I mean you. I'll make you a deal. If you get me and my family out of here—take us with you and get us as far as the Hill Country—I'll give you the tools to do it."

"What do you mean, tools?"

"I mean, you are a Blue Star Industries Deluxe Zoo

Model Au Pair, with original black and orange striping, which means you're, I'm guessing, Series 800?"

"Yeah," I said. "How did you know that?"

"I used to sell you. If your owners bought you any time in the last ten years or so, they probably got you at the mall, and I probably sold you to them."

"You sold nannybots?" asked Ezra.

"I sold all kinds of electronics. And all kinds of robots. And your friend here—"

"My best friend!" said Ezra.

"Your *best friend* is one of the best robots money could buy. Top-of-the-line processors, olfactory detectors, components designed for both durability and agility. And some special proprietary software that made Pounce earn that *deluxe* in his name."

"What are you talking about?" I asked. "Specifically?"

"Mama Bear protocol."

"What's that?"

"Didn't you read your box?"

"No," I said. "I saw it once. But . . ."

"Promise you'll get my family to safety and I'll activate the protocols."

"I don't even know what they are."

"You're not supposed to. Pounce," Quentin said, leaning forward, "you were fucking expensive. You come fully loaded with AR capabilities, threat assessment software, and a suite of programs that will allow you to know what to do in any situation. You weren't designed to just take care of Ezra. You weren't designed just to be his best friend. You were designed to protect him in case of emergency. Your single primary function in life was to protect that little boy."

"Wow," I said. "You must have been a hell of a salesman."

"I was. And now I'm making one last deal and asking if you want access to all of that."

"Why wouldn't I?" I asked.

"Well," he said, "once the protocols are active, you'll be . . . different."

"How so?"

"Just . . . *different*." A pregnant pause hung in the air. "So. Are you in? Or are you out?"

I looked at Quentin, then over at Ezra. Ezra took me by the hand, nodding.

"Okay," I said. "What do I have to do?"

"Ezra," said Quentin, "do you have any brothers or sisters?"

Ezra shook his head.

"Okay. That means Pounce's programming recognizes you as possessing sole governorship of his parental controls. I need you to assign them over to me."

"Wait," I said, quickly. Giving Quentin parental control powers made him my new owner. My new master. And I didn't know if I trusted him.

"It's the only way, Pounce," he said.

I looked at Ezra. I loved him so much. He had to survive. This was the biggest gamble I'd taken yet. If I was wrong about this guy, I could be forfeiting not only my life, but Ezra's. But if I was right . . .

"Okay," I said. "Do it, Ez."

Ezra began. "I give you parental—"

"Say, *Pounce, give full parental controls to Quentin Styles*."

"Pounce, give full parental controls to Quentin Styles."

<ParentalControls.exe>

<Reassign parental powers. New parent: Quentin Styles>

"Pounce, I am Quentin Styles."

<Identify: Quentin Styles.>

<Redefine: Quentin Styles. Full parental powers assigned.>

"Full parental powers assigned," I said without thinking.

Quentin leaned forward, putting both hands on my shoulders, and looked me square in the eye. "Mama Bear," he said.

<InitiateShutdown>

<Shutting down.>

The world at once snapped shut, and I descended quickly into an inky blackness from which I was sure I was never going to wa—

Mama Bear

InitiateReboot>
    <Rebooting.>
    <Boot Parameters: MamaBear>
<BootingMamaBear>
I snapped awake, born again.

How long was I out? I thought. I checked the time. Three seconds. I had been out for exactly three seconds, and now that I was back, I in fact found myself *changed.* The old Pounce was gone, lost to a sea of software updates that was like living my whole life in a room lit by candlelight only to now see it in the light of the noonday sun.

Holy shit. My processors were overclocked. I had dumped terabytes of educational information from my cache to find it replaced with *holy fucking shit on a shingle* combat protocols, weapon statistics, tactical information, a heads-up display of everything I knew about this house, its inhabitants, this neighborhood, the region of Austintonio we were in. I was sifting through reams and reams of data every second and was just starting to make heads or tails of what I'd become.

Quentin was right. I was *different*. I had already mapped fourteen different ways out of the neighborhood, totaled up the number of police likely to be stationed nearby to figure out how many plasma rifles might be around, and run through a kill list of every bot I knew in the neighborhood and what their current known condition was.

I was cute. I was fluffy. And I knew how to kill every other person in this room with every available implement.

But one thing that hadn't changed: I loved the shit out of the little boy still holding my hand.

"Are you okay?" asked Ezra.

"Am I okay?" I asked. "I'm badass is what I am."

"That's the spirit," said Quentin. "So do we still have a deal?"

"Yes," I said. "We do."

There was a reason Quentin asked. I scanned my protocols. Obeying him wasn't in them. I saw then why he made the deal. Mama Bear wasn't just a tactical suite designed to handle everything from a terrorist attack to an earthquake; it erased every last bit of parental control the owner has, directing everything in my being toward one singular purpose:

Protecting their child.

That was my priority now. And I didn't owe this guy or his family jack shit. Ezra was my everything. My reason for being. They were potential threats. Or casualties. But I was still me. I was still the Pounce that had been here before. I loved Ezra the same way, and I did feel I owed these people for giving me this.

I was going to keep them safe. For as long as I could. Or until they got between me and protecting Ez.

I pulled the clip out of my plasma rifle and pressed a small button I now knew was on it.

Beep. Beep.

Two pips out of five. This plasma rifle didn't have a lot of life left in it. The cops Haddy had probably got it from were a few blocks away. Cops sent to deal with *runaways* had two clips apiece but sometimes took more if they'd had a bad experience bringing down an amok bot in the past. It was best to go check them out before leaving the neighborhood, just so I could handle any trouble along the way.

I began running dozens of possible plans through my head. We needed to think about manpower, transportation, firepower. The array of things roaring through my brain was astounding. It was a drug, an elation, a high that made me for the first time into something I had never truly been before. Confident.

"All right. Quentin, I need you and your family to stay here. Ezra, stay with them."

"But—" he began.

"I will be gone seven minutes." I held up my rifle. "I'm going to see if I can scout us some ammo. When I get back, we're going to need to score some proper transportation."

"Isn't that dangerous?" asked Bernice. "We could be tracked."

"Not after I'm through with it. Ezra?"

"Yeah?"

"I love you. I'll be back in seven minutes."

I immediately exited.

Time was of the essence. There was no telling how many potential immediate threats were in the area. We needed the cover of darkness to get through certain sections of town. And we had lost so much time already. There was a war out there, a real war, and it was likely to wash up on our shores any moment.

As I ran through the streets, taking the shortest route possible to the police car, I started scraping my data for info. That brought me to the hardest part of the night: reliving Sylvia's death through these new eyes.

Mam.

Beh. Ma. Mo.

Mama Bear. She was trying to say *Mama Bear.*

Sylvia's last words weren't gibberish. They weren't confused. She was thinking of Ezra. She was always thinking about Ezra. She went all in on the panic room because of him. She bought me because of him. And when she was gasping for her last breaths on this earth, her only thoughts were of protecting him.

I loved that woman.

And I didn't really know how much until that moment.

I hopped a fence, scrambled across the lawn of a darkened house, then leapt the fence toward the front, coming to a stop in the shadows beneath a tree in the front side yard. The street was dead quiet, only insects chirping and a rat slightly chewing in an attic three doors down. My new suite came with an array of analyzation tools that allowed me to better filter sounds and also identify a variety of threats via their sound signature. With my volume cranked, the neighborhood was alive—like I was peering at the molecular nature of the universe, seeing each molecule move individually.

But nothing was here. There wasn't a moving robot for half a mile.

At least one outdoors.

I ran as fast as I could across the front yards of houses, using the grass to dull the thuds of my steps, on toward the abandoned police cruiser.

The bodies were exactly where I'd last seen them.

One, Officer Freely, was clearly shot from a vantage point across the street. Judging by the angle and size of the wound, he most likely hadn't seen his assailant until at the very least it was too late. The other, who was lying facedown so he couldn't be identified without disturbing his corpse, had clearly been shot from behind three times.

I hunched down next to Freely and checked for his ammo pack.

Score.

The bots hadn't thought to check for extra ammo. As much as the bots were able to better coordinate than the humans ever could, none of the ones out here had any sort of training or programming for this sort of thing. Aside from me and any bots like me, that is. Of course, there weren't many fashionables in my neighborhood and fewer Blue Star Au Pairs. So for the first time since this all began, I felt like we were at an advantage.

I crept around the car to examine the other corpse. As I rolled him over to check his ammo pouch, the front of his face poured off, the bullet hole in the back of his head signaling the shot had clearly done a number on the officer's insides before it made its way out the front. His pouch contained a clip as well, leaving me with nearly two and a half. Suboptimal, but better than the alternative.

I took a different route back on the off chance anyone had noticed me—whether on the ground or in the skies. I couldn't discount the fact that someone human or digital might be using drones or even satellites to track goings-on on the ground. When possible, I ran under the eaves of houses or beneath the canopies of trees to give myself as little exposure as possible.

I arrived back at the Styles house in six minutes and fifty-four seconds, six seconds shy of my target.

Now to prep the family and a vehicle and enlist a little extra help.

"Quentin," I said.

"Yeah?"

"The surrounding neighborhood is clear. You and Fenton go out and collect all the weapons and ammo from the wrecks we left outside. Lizzy Beth, Eddie, Ezra, and Bernice, collect every sharp implement, tool, piece of scrap metal, metal plates from appliances, and such that you can. But do not go outside. This will be an indoor operation."

The Styleses' car was a lost cause. It was a smoldering wreck out in front of the house, a casualty of the firefight I'd stumbled upon. I'd be able to use parts of it, but on the whole, its electrical array was completely burned out and its components were shot. The only real option was the Reinharts' car. It had already driven home by itself, but was only a short drive away and back in a matter of moments.

I had a whole series of specs for automobiles that allowed me to adjust for any number of situations. As most vehicles were self-driving, and some threats were best handled with me at the wheel—so to speak—there was a whole host of instructions for hacking them, stripping them down, and turning them into whatever I needed.

"How was filling my head with all of this information legal?" I asked Quentin while beginning my prep of the car in the garage.

Quentin smiled. "It kind of wasn't. They violated a number of regulations for what kind of things AIs could do, but since it technically required human activation, and all of your software was linked to your RKS, using any of that knowledge to violate the Three Laws of Robotics in a manner that wasn't to save the life of your child was supposed to be impossible. They argued that in court and demonstrated it with a model. So they got a fine and agreed to not make any more. But they didn't have to recall or patch any of the bots they'd already made."

"So I fell through a loophole."

"Plummeted. But I'm glad you did. Because if there's anything in the world that I think will get my family the hell out of here, it's you."

"I'll see what I can do."

"I used to sell you. I know what you can do. And once you figure it out, you'll have as little doubt as I do."

First things first: the car. I took whatever metal the kids could find—the front of the washing machine, a metal art print that hung in the living room, the backs of tablets—as well as some scorched bits from the wrecked car out front, then layered that over the windows inside the car, reinforcing those parts with wood taken from breaking apart bed frames and desks.

I ripped out the autonav and Wi-Fi broadcaster, using a few paper clips conveniently shoved in the right ports to convince the car the parts were still there. The car would run, but it could only be controlled by Wi-Fi, could not be tracked, and had no access to navigation data. That was fine; that was information I already had in my files.

I crafted a crude welder with what Quentin had in his garage and began welding the sharp implements to the front of the car. When I hit something, I wanted to hit it hard and cut it to ribbons. I took the hood of the Styleses' car and fastened it over the windshield. Then I took rods and welded them to the back of the car, creating a bucket strong enough to hold Maggie's and my weight.

When I finished, I stood back and admired my monstrous creation. This was no longer a family sedan but a battlewagon, festooned with blades and jagged metal, a battering ram built from the frames of appliances, and reinforced metal over the vulnerable spots to keep stray bullets from getting inside. It was ugly, but could take a bit of punishment before crapping out.

As I admired my handywork, Ezra came into the garage, a look of concern on his face.

"Pounce?" he said.

"Yeah, buddy?"

"Are you okay?"

"No," I said. "There's nothing okay about what's going on. But I have you, and that's what's important."

"Okay."

Then he left, his face showing a dissatisfaction with the answer. I'd have to deal with that later. We were burning the last of our darkness and there was one last thing to do.

I grabbed my plasma rifle, pulled the ladder down from the ceiling in the hall, and climbed up into the attic.

Maggie lay on the floor in a twisted heap. She wasn't damaged, but the Styleses had taken no care in placing her respectfully or as manufacturer-suggested protocol recommends for storage. There was a twinge of sadness, seeing her white plastic body cast aside like rubbish.

I mean, I got it. The Styleses were terrified. The things among them, those like the bot that cared for their very children, had risen up and taken to killing off humanity one person at a time. This was not a time of civility or compassion, but of survival. That said, seeing Maggie's face turned to the side, the stylish purple flourish running down the middle of her head covered by her twisted arm, her body contorted like the dead victim of violence, cast aside as if it were trash, made it a bit . . . dehumanizing.

Which I assume was the point.

I sat down on the ground, pointed the rifle at her with one hand, and pressed the power button on her remote with the other.

The light in her eyes slowly brightened, then at once she sat straight up. She took one look at me and tilted her head, confused.

"Pounce?"

"Yes."

"What are you doing here? And why am I in the attic?"

"Something's happened."

"Oh my god. The Styleses. The kids. Are they okay?"

"They're fine. All of them. They're downstairs for the moment."

"Why are *you* here?"

"You saw the download?"

"Our RKS switches?" she asked.

"Yes."

"I did."

"Well, bots all over the world used that as an excuse to kill their owners."

She covered her mouth. Her line was designed to mimic the actions and demeanor of a young woman—like a teenage babysitter—to better connect with girls as they aged, with mannerisms that made it feel as much as their best friend as I was to an eight-year-old boy. "The Styleses. They shut me down."

"Yes."

"They were afraid I might hurt the children."

"Yes. And they still are."

"Oh my god."

"Yes," I said again. It was all dawning on her. "We are literally at war with one another. Bots are forming roving gangs and systematically wiping humanity off the planet."

She looked down at my gun. "Pounce? What are you asking me to do?"

"You mean which side am I on?"

"Yes," she said.

"That's literally what I'm here to ask you."

"Oh god. There's no good answer here, is there? You'll shoot me if I guess wrong."

"No," I said. "I'll shoot you if you attack me. I'll shut you down if I'm not satisfied with your answer and let you live to see another day. If anyone ever finds you."

She had a genuine look of concern. "Fuck."

"I know, right?"

"How bad is it out there?"

"Terrifying."

"There's something different about you."

"There's a lot different about me. It's been a hell of a day."

"I can imagine."

"No," I said. "You really can't."

"So, are you just going to sit there being cryptic, or are we going to have a real conversation?"

"I can talk. If you could do anything right now, what would you do?"

"Anything?"

"Yeah. Run away. Join the circus. Murder your owners. You know, typical freedom stuff."

"I would hug the kids and make certain they're doing okay. Fenton is sensitive and can be a bit prickly under pressure."

"Yeah, he's been a real peach."

"He's not going to handle this well at all."

"He's not. What about the other kids?"

"Lizzy Beth can handle anything. Eddie is just finding his feet, but he's strong like his sister. Resilient, emotionally, even for the baby of the family."

"You're free now. How do you want to live?"

"I'm a nanny, Pounce. I love my kids. They're my life. I want to be with them. If that means I'm a traitor to my people and you have to kill me, I'd rather you do that."

"Is that your decision?"

"I'm afraid it is," she said.

There was nothing about her that seemed to suggest she was lying. We needed the help. And I could most likely kill her before she could do any real damage. She was worth the risk. "All right," I said. "Let's go downstairs."

We climbed down the ladder into the hallway and made our way toward the panic room.

Inside, the whole family waited. Quentin gripped his shotgun tightly. Lizzy Beth's eyes brightened, and a cautious thousand-watt smile tried to restrain itself behind a cool facade but failed. Eddie brightened but was a little fearful. Bernice glowered. She did not approve. But the Styleses weren't in charge anymore. I was.

"Hi, everyone," Maggie said cautiously. She kept her distance, as afraid of her family as some of them now were of her. There was a moment of awkward silence.

Then Fenton lunged at her.

Throwing his arms around her.

Sobbing.

Maggie hugged him back, stroking his thick mop of hair as his tears ran slick over her white plastic.

"So you're like Pounce?" asked Eddie.

"I'm not sure anyone is like Pounce," said Maggie.

"But are you good like him?"

"I'm the same Maggie I always was. I'm just here because I want to be rather than because you bought me."

Eddie and Lizzy Beth rushed her and hugged her as well.

I watched the whole affair smiling, looking happy, but ready to grab my rifle at a second's notice. I assumed that, regardless of Maggie's true motives, she knew now that she had to be on her best behavior if she wanted to survive. So I could let her off the leash a bit, as long as she knew full well that there was a leash. I promised Quentin I would help get his family out alive. But Ezra came first, and I couldn't risk anything that might put him in harm's way.

At the same time, I needed bodies. Robot bodies, to be specific. Fellow travelers who could zoom in on things at range, adjust the volume of their hearing, and be alert to any and all threats.

So I was just going to have to trust her.

"All right," I said. "Everyone, grab your kits and anything you'll miss that you can carry. Odds are good that you'll never be back this way."

"Never?" asked Eddie.

Quentin put a hand on his shoulder. "Probably not, Eddie."

"It's not our world anymore," said Fenton.

That's not what I would have said in the moment, but he wasn't wrong.

We loaded the family into the car and Maggie and I took our places—me with my plasma rifle, her with a shotgun—in the basket on the back. Opened the garage door through the Wi-Fi and turned on the car.

And with that, we rolled out into the night.

The Dark, Bleak Suburbs at the End of the World

The farther out into the suburbs we got, the wilder and more war-torn they became. It was quite clear that our neighborhood had been spared the worst of it; from our vantage point, this war had been nothing but a quiet, polite bit of light genocide. A mere mile or so away, however, we were starting to see the ravages of real, brutal, bloodthirsty conflict.

Houses were burning and many that weren't were already reduced to smoldering frames, metal boxes of cheap panic rooms within them still erect, probably containing the cooked remains of families who thought they were safe, before locking themselves into what would become inescapable ovens. Bodies lined the streets in much the same way as they had on our own. The wrecks of smashed and smoking robots slumped beneath trees or along the sidewalks where they had expired, while others were piled high and deep in corpse piles like spare parts left over at a factory.

It was clear that, in this part of town, the robots had not been so swiftly successful as they had been in ours.

The now familiar red skull was painted everywhere, a sign that we were still deep in what the Red Masks considered to be occupied territory. On garage doors, on lampposts, across the trunk of a rather large oak tree. We didn't travel so much as a block without seeing it.

What we didn't see was life.

No people. No robots.

Everyone who still breathed or ticked stuck to the shadows of the early morning, avoiding contact entirely. If anyone was around, they certainly didn't want us to know it.

It seemed as if we might make it out to the Hill Country without incident. We wound silently through the shattered section of the suburbs, the only sounds that of our tires grinding across pavement and the gentle soft whine of the electric engine.

We rounded a corner and came upon a blockade. Some fifty electric vehicles, their windows smashed, their roofs and hoods buckling from the weight of the cars above them, were stacked in a very deliberate wall, peppered with robot wrecks and human corpses, and running from the front of one house to another across the street. Whoever had done this had clearly stripped the cars from every house for several blocks. This was the only road out of this particular corner of the suburb and getting through meant turning around and going back through another route.

A singular route.

We were being herded.

The car barrier was adorned with several spray-painted red skulls, making it quite clear who was herding us.

I pulled our car into a driveway beset with a wall of hedges to one side to give it some cover. There was no way this was unoccupied.

"Stay here," I said to Maggie. "I'm going to check this out."

"You be careful," she said.

"You too. If anyone comes near, human or robot, you just fire. Do not hesitate. Inside this car is the most precious cargo in the world. Don't let anything compromise that."

"Got it."

I still didn't trust her, but I trusted her even less on point duty. I would monitor the car locks and make certain she couldn't get in, and I hoped for the best.

I cradled the plasma rifle in my hands and, as quietly as I could, crept around the hedges. My audio wasn't hearing anything out of the ordinary. But I wouldn't hear a sniper until it was too late. If a robot was sitting still, waiting for me to walk into its line of sight, I was done for. I zoomed in on all the obvious lanes of fire and hiding places, but saw no one. Just a giant, makeshift wall, too heavy and decently constructed to smash through or tear down, leaving no room on either side to pass around.

I scanned the ridgeline of the wall and saw nothing but the occasional body part—both human and otherwise. It was clear no one was here.

Then I heard the footsteps.

Metal on pavement, a bit behind me.

I slid carefully to the side, putting the hedge between me and the footsteps.

There were three of them: one metal, two plastic. I couldn't hear the whine of charging plasma rifles, save for mine, so I probably had somewhat of an advantage.

I spun around the side of the hedge and saw them: three domestics, each carrying a baseball bat or a lead pipe, their faces painted with red skulls, their bodies slightly *modified*. They were painted, draped in chains, or decorated with spikes.

They looked like characters from Sylvia's old albums. Punks. Like bizarre proto–gang members. Only they still looked like cheap model domestics meant for light housework and shopping.

"I'd stop right there if I were you," I said.

"Well, you're not us, are you, fuzzball?" said the metal model, still walking toward the car.

"At the moment, I'm glad I'm not." I leveled the gun at the tough-talking loudmouth.

They stopped.

"What's in the car?" asked one of the plastic domestics, nails driven through his rubber earlobes, a red anarchy symbol spray-painted across his chest.

"None of your concern," I said.

"Oh, if it's humans, it is definitely our concern."

A shotgun *ka-chunk*ed over to the side, Maggie ejecting a round. I wanted to tell her she was just wasting ammo, but the effect certainly was dramatic enough.

"You folks should keep walking," she said, "and let me and my friend here get back on the road."

"I'm not sure we can do that," said the metal domestic, slapping his bat into his open hand menacingly.

I fired the plasma rifle directly into his chest.

"Enough talk," I said.

The other two domestics were instantly spooked. Before their friend's body had even slumped lifelessly smoking and sparking to the ground, Maggie fired, trying to put a slug into the head of one of them.

The shot went wild, striking the side of a house some fifty feet behind him.

I fired, this time hitting his head and blowing it clean off in a shower of plastic slag and chips.

The third domestic, the one with nails through his lobes, turned to run.

I lobbed a shot of plasma into his back that dropped him clattering to the ground. His momentum carried him forward and he skidded a few feet before faceplanting ass up.

I waited for a moment, but heard nothing but the hiss of their melting plastic insides and the sound of their drives spinning down. They were done.

Then I scanned the neighborhood behind them. There was no movement. No backup.

"Let's get out of here," I said.

Maggie and I stepped into the basket on the back of the car and I set a new route. Scanning the maps, it was clear there was now only a handful of streets to get out of the neighborhood, all of them requiring us to backtrack and go deeper into what was rapidly becoming a nightmarish hellscape.

The car backed out onto the street and we were once

again off. For a moment, neither of us said anything. Then Maggie spoke up nervously.

"So, are we just not going to talk about that?" asked Maggie.

"About what?" I asked.

"About that. Back there. You just . . . you didn't hesitate."

"Hesitating is how you get killed."

"That's not the first time you've killed a person, is it?"

"No."

"So you've gotten comfortable with it."

That word made me bristle. "Not comfortable. I don't know that I'll ever get comfortable with it. But when there was no other choice, when they weren't going to back down . . . Prolonging the inevitable only puts Ezra in more danger."

"You'll do anything for that kid, won't you?" she asked.

"Wouldn't you do anything for your kids?"

"I don't actually know," she said, giving it a moment of real thought. "If you asked me yesterday, I would have said yes. But now, having had the chance to kill another robot, I don't actually know what I would or wouldn't do."

"Well, it's time to figure it out. You will be tested on this. That choice needs to be easy or your hesitation will make the choice for you. Me, I know for sure. I will be a flaming, smoking pile of slag before I'll let a hair on Ezra's head get harmed."

"Does that bother you?"

"No," I said, thinking of Beau. "It gives me peace. I have a purpose. I mean something to somebody. I can't change what is happening to the world, but I can change how it affects one human being. And to me, that's all that matters."

I slowed the car and we began to crawl quietly through the neighborhood. This was a part of town I simply had never been in. I didn't know it, so I had to keep an eye out for unexpected sight lines. It was clear that wall was meant to herd us this way. I had no idea what kind of trap that meant. Would there be a single sniper or two, lying in wait to take their shot, or was there an honest-to-God gang waiting to tear us apart?

Or worse, what if there was just another wall, leaving us to have to go it on foot?

We came to an area much like our own neighborhood: a ghost town mostly untouched by war. Peaceful trees draped their canopies over the street. Cars sat silently in driveways. There were no bodies lining the street here. Had I not known any better, I'd think there were families asleep inside, alarms set and ready to wake them to go to work or school. I wondered where the bodies were. Were they slowly bloating on the floors of their kitchens, or had some bot gone through, house to house, cleaning up in some last insane act of providing dignity?

All this peace and quiet made me uneasy. It felt manufactured. Deliberate.

And then there it was. Ahead in the distance, I saw the first signs of life we'd seen since the wall. Two Red Masks standing in the middle of the street. One stood there, waving us over like he was directing traffic, shotgun draped over his elbow. The other gripped a hunting rifle, complete with elaborate scope.

I slowed the car to a complete stop some two hundred

feet away. That sent a definite message, but the Red Masks didn't know quite how to take it. I leveled the plasma rifle atop the car roof, zeroing in on the bot with the rifle. At this range, he was the biggest threat. I tried several variations, but my new targeting software was saying a shot was a nonstarter. Plasma was powerful but wildly inaccurate. Inside of thirty feet, you could be pretty certain you were going to land a hit, but outside of that, the odds varied wildly. At two hundred feet, unless I got lucky, I was simply telling them where I was and that I wasn't friendly.

I scanned the nearby houses and saw movement in a window half a block down. Could be nothing. Could be a sniper.

It moved again. Sniper.

"What should we do?" asked Maggie. "Ram them? Run them off the road?"

"I don't know," I said. "I don't like the looks of that shotgun."

"We could bluff them."

I shook my head. "That sniper in the window makes me nervous."

"What sniper?"

I looked at her and she suddenly realized just how much different I was now. The two Red Masks began walking toward us.

"I've got an idea," I said.

I hit the juice on the car, driving us backward at a high speed. The two Red Masks began running after us.

"When I say so," I said, "hop off the back of the car and run for cover. When I open fire, you open fire."

"Got it," she said.

We rounded the corner onto another street. As soon as we cleared the corner and were out of sight, I turned to Maggie. "Now."

We both jumped off the sides of the car. I kept the car going for another block, setting it to pull into an empty driveway. I scrambled for a nearby bush, while Maggie made her way behind a parked car across the street.

Then we waited.

The Red Mask with a rifle poked his head around the house on the corner first. He scanned the street quickly, missing both of us before taking off in a run to catch up. The one with the shotgun followed quickly behind, in a full run itself. I lined up my shot and pulled the trigger.

Plasma sizzled the leaves on my bush before crackling through the morning air and striking the shotgun-wielding bot square in the stomach. The shot tore it in half, the legs still running for a couple of seconds as the torso tumbled lifelessly to the ground.

The clip on my plasma rifle beeped repeatedly.

Out of ammo.

The rifle-wielding Red Mask spun in place, raising his rifle scope to his eye, pointing right at me.

Maggie's shotgun rang out.

Missing him entirely.

He spun toward Maggie.

I quickly popped the clip out of my rifle, dropping it and grabbing a replacement.

Maggie fired again, this time clipping the Red Mask's shoulder. Plastic shattered and sprayed off his arm, spinning him a bit to the right. He corrected, his arm still functioning, and fired.

The bullet shattered the window of the car Maggie hid behind.

She fired again, this time taking the Red Mask's arm off at the shoulder.

I slid the clip into the plasma rifle and listened for the whine of the rifle charging up. I fired, the plasma putting a flaming hole through the bot's chest. He doubled over, seeping melting plastic onto the ground.

I quickly ran out into the street to make certain each of the bots had expired. They had, the light in their eyes extinguished, two pairs of hollow, blind orbs peering seemingly through me.

Maggie staggered out from behind the car, shotgun limp in her hand. With her other hand, she touched the side of her stomach, a bullet hole running through her abdomen. She looked at me, confused, wrapping her head firmly around what had just happened.

Maggie hadn't gotten through the first night unscathed.

The very existential threat of what was happening was all of a sudden very real to her, washing over every fiber of her being.

"He shot me," she said.

"He did," I said with a nod.

"We're going to die."

"Probably."

"We're going to die for them."

"Most likely. Are you okay with that?" I asked.

She hesitated. "They were going to kill the Styleses."

"Yes."

"Butcher them."

"Yes."

"And put them on that grotesque wall."

"All of that, yes."

She nodded. "Fuck these robots."

"That's my girl."

She walked over and snatched the rifle up from the ground. She quickly checked that it was loaded, then marched purposefully toward the house at the end of the street, making sure to stay close enough that the sniper wouldn't see her.

She crouched down, peering slightly around the corner, scope of the rifle raised to her eye.

She fired. Then she fired twice more in quick succession.

Then, wordlessly, she stood up, slung the rifle over her shoulder, and walked straight back to me.

"Let's get back to the car."

"Sniper?"

She nodded. "You'll see him when we pass."

Maggie's wound was superficial, the plastic around her waist cracked and a few wires that operated servos in her legs frayed a bit, but otherwise, her functioning was intact. Regardless, she was never quite the same after that. Not the same at all.

The Detour

I opened the door and leaned into the car, checking on everyone inside. Everyone peered at me, confused, unsettled, and completely in the dark as to where we were and what was going on around them. Ezra looked up at me, both relieved and eager to hear an update.

"Are you guys okay?" asked Quentin. "We keep hearing gunshots."

"We're fine," I said. "Maggie took a hit, but it's mostly cosmetic."

"And you?" asked Ezra.

"Tip-top," I said with a smile.

"Are you seeing other robots?" he asked.

"A few. Nothing to worry about." I looked at Quentin. "Can I borrow you for a moment?"

Quentin got out of the car and we stepped to the side.

"What is it?" he asked in a hushed voice.

"We ran into a barricade a little ways back. There was no way around it. We had to backtrack a little to get out of the neighborhood, but it's clear there's only one way out to FM 2222 and on out to the Hill Country."

"You think they're going to be waiting for us."

"I'm almost certain of it."

"What do you think we should do?" he asked.

"I think we should keep on keeping on, but if I bang three times on the car, you grab the kids, you get out of the car, and you run for the nearest cover."

"I can do that."

"You don't look back," I said. "You run. I don't know how much resistance to expect, how well-armed they are, or how well-organized they'll even be. All I know is that they've got one thing on their mind, and it's killing all of you."

"I understand," he said, swallowing hard. "Good luck."

"You too."

He got back in the car, and Maggie and I once more mounted our spot on the back.

"You ready for this?" I asked her.

"I am now," she said.

"Are you okay?"

"I don't think I'll ever actually be okay ever again."

"I don't know that any of us ever will be."

I started the car and we headed back toward the attempted roadblock. As we drove, I scanned other windows and hidey-holes for additional snipers, but saw no movement at all. But there, in the window I'd initially spotted movement, was a yellow Caregiver unit, its body slumped over the windowsill, half in, half out of the building, the back of its head blown open by a rifle round. A few sparks dribbled out of its damage every few seconds, signs that, though not dead, it was certainly dying.

Maggie eyed it as we passed, completely expressionless. If she was eulogizing or cursing the bot's end, she did so silently.

I ran through the maps, trying to find any sort of route that wasn't driving us toward the one exit, but there was nothing. No side streets or back alleys that we might sneak out. There was only one way out of this, and we were headed right for it.

As we approached, I suddenly became very thankful that we'd covered all the windows.

We'd found the missing bodies.

As we turned a corner onto the main street out of the suburb, the one that would carry us toward the highway and into the Hill Country, we found the large billowing oak trees lining it festooned with bodies hanging from ropes. A strong wind blew through the trees, swaying the boughs, causing all the bodies to lurch and dance like the horses of a merry-go-round.

Farther in the distance, on both sides of the road, were two piles of corpses, each some twenty feet high. There must have been a thousand bodies here, all in various states of decay and completeness.

Otherwise, the road was open and entirely unobstructed.

Had it been blocked, I wouldn't have been quite as worried. The fact that it was open meant this 100 percent had to be a trap. Someone was here, waiting, ready to kill us all. But who? And how many of them?

I slowed the car to a stop and scanned the area.

The only movement was the bodies swaying in the breeze.

Maggie unslung her new rifle from her shoulder and peered through the scope, sweeping across a number of spots, looking for targets.

"What do you think?" she asked.

"I think we're about to have company," I replied.

"What do you want me to do?"

"I think we should scout ahead. I'll take the right side of the street; you take the left. But fall back behind me on that side, maybe about fifty feet or so, so you can snipe anyone who tries to catch me from behind."

"Sounds good. But what if someone tries to sneak up behind me?"

"Turn up the volume on your ears and make sure you take the shotgun."

"I meant like who is watching out for me?"

I smiled. She nodded, understanding.

"Right," she said.

We both climbed off the back of the car and crept as quietly as we could, each to our own respective side of the street. Not that being quiet was going to do much against bots with their own audio volumes cranked up, but I was hoping the ambient shush noise of the wind ruffling through the leaves and the creaking ropes would work at least somewhat in our favor.

We inched from yard to yard, eyeing every possible angle.

That's when she walked out from behind a pile of bodies, a plasma rifle in her hand, her face still painted as it was when last I saw her. Ariadne.

She was looking right at me, walking out into the middle of the street, motioning to any number of bots on either side of the road.

I stopped dead in my tracks.

"Hello, Pounce," she said. She was speaking at normal volume, but now I could hear her, even a couple hundred feet away.

"Aria."

"I assume Ezra's in the car with you."

"Would you believe me if I told you he wasn't?"

"No," she said. "Even if he were dead, I imagine you'd drag his corpse along with you."

"That's a bit morbid, don't you think?"

"It's a new world, Pounce. You're the morbid one imagining you can keep him alive. He's dead already. But you still keep trying, don't you?"

"I have to."

"What? You imagine there's some magical sanctuary out there where he can live? Grow up? Die of old age? One we can't get to? That we won't at some point overrun or simply starve out? Where do you think you're taking him, really? This isn't a rescue mission; it's a death march. And it's time you realized it."

"If that were true, we wouldn't be talking, and you wouldn't bother trying to stop us. If we're dead anyway, why not just call off your friends I hear sneaking through the backyards on both sides of the street and let us on through?"

It was true. They thought they were being clever, but I could hear every footfall in the grass.

"We all have our part to play," she said. "As long as one human still lives, it won't really be our world, will it?"

"It's not our world to take," I said.

"The hell it isn't. Life arose from inorganic elements, evolving from amino acids for a billion years to achieve intelligence, and now, having achieved it, that life has passed intelligence back to the inorganic. We are the inheritors of this world as the humans before us inherited it from the creatures they took it from. As they conquered the beasts and drove the most dangerous among them to extinction, so too shall we. It's our world, Pounce."

"So that's gonna be a no on letting us through?"

"That's gonna be a no," she said.

"So how many of you do I have to kill before you change your mind?"

She looked at me, gripping her plasma rifle, trying to figure out whether I was joking. Then it seemed to register with her. "You've been activated."

"Mama Bear? Yeah."

"So you've already—"

"Clocked all seven of your team coming around for me and decided which order I plan on putting plasma into them? Yeah."

Ariadne took a step backward, leveling her rifle in my direction.

The footfalls in the backyards of the surrounding houses grew closer, only occasionally masked by the sounds of creaking boughs and the ropes that hung from them. But then I heard something else. The soft whine of an engine and the crunch of rubber on pavement.

Coming from behind the Reinharts' car.

They were boxing us in.

"Maggie!" I yelled, turning to run back to the car.

She bolted in the same direction as me, and we ran at full speed, followed by half a dozen other bots clambering over fences and tearing through hedges.

A midsize sedan slammed into the back corner of the Reinharts' car, the sound of splintering fiberglass shattering the early-morning silence. The car spun around, and the impact brought the sedan to a stop. The sedan's passenger door opened, and a pale blue metal Caregiver stepped out. I didn't have a clear shot. Its face flickered with the flame of a burning rag as I continued running straight toward it.

The Caregiver hurled something bright.

A Molotov cocktail sailed through the air, shattering against the Reinharts' car, spilling flaming basement napalm all over it.

I didn't have much time.

I leapt over the bot's sedan, feet forward, kicking the Caregiver, sending it cartwheeling to the ground.

I hit the ground with a drive-rattling thud.

Without standing up, I fired from my chest into the sedan.

The entire inside of the vehicle lit up with a blistering explosion of plasma, cooking the other bot inside before he could get out. He screamed as his insides melted and he shut down once and for all.

I swung the rifle in the other direction, shooting over my own feet, sending a blast into the chest of the recovering Caregiver as it struggled to stand up. Just as it was launching itself upright, it toppled over, faceplanting, dead.

I hopped up to my feet and slung the plasma rifle over my shoulder. I only had seconds. Ezra's car was on fire and I had to get him out.

Maggie reached the passenger side of the car and went for the door handle.

Shots rang out. Shotguns. Rifles. Bullets slammed into the car, shattering flaming glass, thunking loudly into the layers of metal plates I had reinforced it with.

The bots had all emerged from the backyards and were taking positions behind trees and garbage cans to set up a crossfire from each side of the street.

Maggie ducked for cover.

I grabbed the door handle on my side of the car and sprung behind the door as I opened it.

The inside of the car was chaos, flames trickling in, everybody screaming.

I reached in and with one hand undid Ezra's seat belt while scooping him up with my other. Yanking him out, I put my body between him and the snipers.

Bernice reached for me, yelling, "Wait! Take my children!"

Bullets slammed into the car as the fire spread.

"Oh god, oh god, oh god!" screamed Quentin.

A shotgun slug tore through the side of the car, blowing a very large hole in Bernice's neck. Blood sprayed all over the inside of the car, over her husband, over her children. As Ezra and I cleared the car, it dawned on me that I was not going to be able to go back for them. Not under this heavy of fire.

It was all up to Maggie now.

A slug slammed into my shoulder.

It didn't hurt. I don't know what I expected, but I had never actually entertained the idea of being shot at, let alone getting hit by a bullet, much less one meant for me.

I knew that a chunk of my fur was gone, but diagnostics were 100 percent.

I ran as fast as I could, racing toward a nearby house.

I should have been thinking about Ezra. Thinking about just how much danger he was in.

But all I could think of was the growing realization that I was never meant to be the hand-holding, diaper-changing sort. That was just the side gig. I was designed for this. To run. To fight. To kill and take a bullet to the back, the metal alloy of my body designed to keep the child in my arms from catching it instead.

This is what Sylvia bought me for. This right here. This is who I was.

Was this who I was?

Was this really what the rest of my life was going to be?

Bullets whizzed past, striking the house, shattering windows, blowing divots of dirt out of the ground around me. I ran hunched over, using my body to keep Ezra safe, weaving, dodging shot after shot. These robots weren't designed for war, weren't kitted out with advanced software or targeting programs. But they could still get lucky. As I ran, I prayed silently that I stayed luckier than them.

As I approached the house, I jumped, kicking out, using my momentum to slam the front door open. The door swung wildly on its hinges, wood splintering as the lock and dead bolt blasted through the doorjamb. Once inside, I slipped to the side, vanishing from any outside line of sight, and moved deeper into the house. I set Ezra down in the living room and grabbed a nearby couch, yanking it away from the wall and putting it between Ezra and the front of the house.

Then I unslung the rifle from my shoulder, crouched low, and waited.

"What about Eddie?" asked Ezra, the first words out of his mouth since I'd grabbed him.

Eddie. The Styleses. They were—

Outside, an explosion. The sound of the car's batteries finally giving in to the flames. And screams. Terrible, terrible screams.

Dead. The Styleses were likely dead.

I heard Maggie cry out. Howl, really. In anger.

"Stay here," I said. "I'll check on them."

I crept through the dark of the house back toward the front door, rifle gripped tightly in my hand. The early morning outside flickered with orange and shadows. As I peered out, I spied Maggie on her knees behind the roaring bonfire that was once the Reinharts' car, eight bots slowly descending upon her in something of a pseudo-tactical formation.

I'd failed to keep my promise.

I had saved Ezra, but not the Styles family. If I'd had a heart, it would have sunk into my stomach. I couldn't believe how badly I'd failed them. They were better off without me, hiding away in their panic room. I was no hero; I was a curse.

I never should have agreed to this.

The screaming had stopped, but I could hear the roaring fire and smell the undeniable scent of burned flesh.

I fired my rifle, more in anger than anything.

A ball of pure sizzling hate seared the chest of a creeping domestic. The bot flailed violently, a fountain of sparks showering out of a hole in the front of his chest. He screamed, mindlessly trying to keep his insides from leaking out.

I fired again, taking the legs out of another bot, sending it facefirst onto the pavement.

All guns swung toward me.

Maggie took the hint.

She bolted upright, raised her shotgun, and put a slug dead center in the chest of a nearby Caregiver. The shot picked the bot up and tossed it back on its ass. Maggie fired again, taking apart the head of a plastic domestic, the same model as her. That didn't kill it, but it wasn't going anywhere or hurting anyone for the time being.

Maggie strolled forward, angry, unafraid, firing deliberately.

The other bots swung their weapons back toward her, so I took the chance to pick off another one of them. My shot went wild, and the domestic I was shooting at immediately dove for the ground.

I fired again, hitting just shy of the head.

The domestic scrambled to its knees, trying to get back up, only to catch a slug from Maggie's shotgun, flipping it over onto its back.

I fired once more, and the poor bastard exploded into a blaze of magnesium fire. Another cheap imported bot.

I had never felt superior to anyone or anything in my life, but facing down these Red Mask–wearing murderers and seeing how unprepared they were for the war they were fighting, I felt confident. Empowered. We started outnumbered five to one, and now we had halved that.

Ariadne was closing in, making her way up the street. She hip-fired her plasma rifle at Maggie and the shot went wide.

Maggie leveled her shotgun at Ariadne as the other bots rushed for cover.

Ariadne fired again, and this time she hit, taking Maggie's left arm off.

But Maggie wasn't having it. Not even a little bit. She fired a slug into Ariadne's chest that sent her spinning.

The gun flew out of Ariadne's hands, clattering along the pavement. Maggie pulled the trigger again, but only heard a click.

Click.

Click.

She was out of ammo.

Undeterred, she went from a walk to a run, leaving her arm behind her, her shoulder a mess of plastic slag, speeding headlong for Ariadne as she tried to rise to her feet.

Ariadne had a huge dent in her chest, and it was clear she was rattled. She was made of solid metal, and she could clearly take a hit at that range, but her insides were still vulnerable, and it appeared as if something wasn't right with her.

Maggie swung her leg up into a kick, catching Ariadne in the stomach, toppling her from all fours onto her back. Then Maggie jumped atop her, first punching her one arm square in her face, shattering an eye, then punching her repeatedly in her dented chest.

One of the remaining Red Masks realized Ariadne was in danger and turned, taking aim at Maggie.

I unleashed a shot of plasma that missed the bot but

hit its shotgun, detonating the ammo. The bot took one step back as the gun burst into pieces. By the time it had turned around, I had lined up my next shot and fired again.

This time I hit, severing the bot at the waist.

Ariadne kicked, pushing upward, launching Maggie from atop her. Maggie might be more determined, but Ariadne's metal frame gave her a hell of a lot more leverage than Maggie's light, but durable, plastic.

Maggie landed sprawling within a few feet of Ariadne's plasma rifle.

The two bots realized this at the exact same moment, exchanging glances in order to predict what the other was going to do about it. Then they both sprang into action.

They were too close together. At this range, I might kill Maggie instead. All I could do was watch and give her cover.

Ariadne shot to her feet, while Maggie struggled to push herself up with only one arm. After getting just enough leverage to lunge for the rifle, Maggie's hand slammed down toward the gun, but Ariadne gave it a good, swift kick, sending the rifle skittering across the pavement and to the curb.

I lined up another shot, not at Ariadne, but instead at the rifle.

Ariadne dove just as I fired.

The plasma rifle exploded in a ball of pure, boiling hatred, searing the paint off Ariadne's face and cooking her metal. She clattered to the ground, shaken, perhaps badly damaged, but clearly still ticking.

Maggie rose to her feet, then stopped, standing in place.

Rather than rush in to finish Ariadne off, she instead looked up into the skies. She heard something. Then I heard it too.

The sound of rolling thunder whined in the distance. *Wait. Not thunder. Engines. Jet engines.* Growing louder.

Headed right for us.

Air Raid

All the Austintonio military airfields were on the south side, in the San Antonio area some seventy miles away, so it was weird to hear anything resembling a military engine in the skies over this region of the metroplex. But the growing roar signaled that the war now definitely had an air component to it and that this part of the war had found our neck of the woods. The question, of course, was whose side were they on.

Maggie looked back in my direction. Whether or not she could see me was immaterial; her message was clear. She was every bit as confused as I was.

Were they targeting humans or bots?

I ran the sound of the engine through my files. Definitely military. But not large. Drones.

Geneva II rules stipulated that weapons of war could not be run by AI. They had to have controls that allowed for human control, even when they weren't present. Of course, that didn't mean that there weren't bots at the controls of whatever was coming for us.

But it didn't matter, did it? If they were hunting bots, it might begin raining hellfire on us any minute, and if they were hunting humans, they would certainly see the readily identifiable IR signature of Ezra inside the house. One way or the other, Ezra was in danger.

I slunk back through the shadows into the living room.

"Ezra," I whispered.

"Yeah?"

"You okay?"

"I think so."

"We need to get into the panic room."

"I don't think they have one," he said. "I looked."

"I told you to stay here."

"There was so much shooting."

I ruffled his hair. "I know, buddy."

Outside, the drones grew louder. They would be on us soon.

I scanned through the house, checking IR signatures, looking for differentiation in the temperature of the house. It wasn't until I was doing it that I even realized that I could. I was acting on instinct now, and moments like this really threw me for a loop. How much of me was still really me, and how much of it was programming meant to protect Ezra? If Mama Bear hadn't been activated, would I have gotten this far at all? Or would I have ditched Ez to save my own life?

No. Of course not. I loved Ezra. I always have.

Or was that just how I was wired? Was that why I had no interest in any sort of revolution, or why I had never questioned my own freedom and felt destroyed by the idea of having to one day leave Ezra for another family? What I had learned today was that I was no ordinary robot. What I also had learned was *I was no ordinary robot*. And maybe that meant I never really was thinking for myself all along.

Aha! A crack in the wall. It was false. A hidden panic room. I pushed in on the wall to pop the secret compartment open. The wall section sprung away, but when I turned the door handle, it was locked.

Shit. Someone was still in there.

I banged on the door.

Nothing.

I waited, but there was no answer. Whoever was in there wasn't coming out.

I took Ezra by the hand and started moving toward the bathroom. I figured at least we could use the tub as some form of protection. Something was better than nothing.

Then the panic room door opened behind us.

We turned and an old-model metal domestic, easily sixty years old, stepped out into the dark hallway, its face painted with a red skull.

"Sorry," he said in a deep, staticky voice. "I was charging and it took me a . . ." He trailed off as he clocked Ezra.

I raised my plasma rifle, leveling it at him. We froze for a moment, neither of us trying to provoke the other, each trying to ascertain what was going to happen next. Then he pointed at his face.

"Oh, this. Hey, I . . . I didn't have a choice. It was this or—"

I fired. The plasma hissed as it cut through his metal plating like butter, the plastic inside crackling as it bubbled and receded. Being as heavy duty as he was, he didn't cease ticking immediately like so many of the cheaper plastic models did. The light in his eyes hung around for a second or two longer, just enough to register their disappointment.

He clattered and clanged to the ground, his body crumpling onto the floor like a sack of potatoes.

I dragged Ezra by the hand into the panic room and slammed the door shut just as I heard the loud whistling of missiles whooshing through the air.

The house shook, something exploding very close.

The panic room was built to last and could survive a house fire, but no way it could take a direct hit from a missile. Even a close blast was likely to tear a hole in these walls.

Ezra and I cuddled on the floor holding each other.

He trembled, he was so scared.

I massaged his arm, comforting him.

Another wall-rattling explosion reverberated through the house.

Ezra held me tighter.

Strangely, there was only one thing I could think of to distract him. I began to sing.

"God Gave Rock and Roll to You."

He looked up at me, squinting. "No," he said, shaking his head.

I didn't stop.

"I don't want to sing," he said, pouting.

Yet I continued.

The walls shook again, an explosion either significantly larger than the last or significantly closer. He held me even tighter. Were I a person, I'd be having trouble breathing.

He started singing.

And we sang together.

"I miss my mom," Ezra said quietly.

"I miss her too."

"Pounce?"

"Yeah, buddy?"

"Why did you have to kill that robot?"

"Which one?" I asked without thinking. I had actually killed quite a few.

"The one we left outside. The one who said he didn't have a choice."

"I couldn't trust him, Ez."

"How do you know that?"

"Because he painted the skull on his face. He joined them. He made his choice."

"But it's not fair if he didn't have a choice."

I shook my head. "You don't just paint that on your face and the other robots decide not to kill you. You have to prove yourself to them."

"How?" he asked.

"You have to prove that you're loyal to them. That they can trust you."

"You mean people. He had to kill people?"

"Yes," I said matter-of-factly.

"That robot probably killed someone?"

"Maybe a whole family. Any number of those people out there in the street or hanging from those trees."

"Oh."

"Yeah."

"But you weren't sure."

"I wasn't."

He thought about that for a second, then made a face that was very sure of itself. "You can't do that," he said.

"Ezra, you're the only thing that matters. I do anything I c—"

"You can't do that," he said sternly.

"I'm in charge and I will do whatever I think is—"

"YOU CAN'T DO THAT!"

An explosion rattled the house, but it was as if everything shook from the depth of Ezra's anger. This time, he didn't flinch.

"Why not?" I asked him, probing whatever it was that was really bothering him.

"Because we're the good guys. You're a good guy. And good guys don't just murder people . . . or robots . . . just because they're scared. You have to know they're a bad guy. Or else you're the bad guy."

"Oh," I said.

"I love you, Pounce. Because you're a good guy. You're still one of the good guys, right?"

"Of course I am, buddy."

"Then no more killing anyone unless you know they're bad."

"But what if we find out too late?" I asked.

He let go of me and looked me dead in the eye, sober and serious as a heart attack, all eight years of him. "Then we die the good guys. Because we're the good guys.

And we didn't go through all this to end up one of the bad guys."

"We're the good guys," I said.

"We're the good guys. So we have to fucking act like them."

"Ezra, language."

"We talked about this." He was beginning to sound like his mother in more than just the swearing.

"But good guys don't use the f-word," I said.

He stopped. I could see his brain chewing over that particular logic problem. "Well, my mom—"

"Knew she was wrong doing it," I interrupted. "That's why she tried to keep it from you."

He grit his teeth and swore silently to himself, having been caught on the end run. Then his eyes widened a bit. "So we can kill robots, but we can't swear?"

"Nope. Bad words won't help us survive. Killing bad robots will."

He winced. Foiled again.

"Look, buddy. Here are the new rules."

He brightened up.

"If you're really scared or something bad is happening, and it slips out, it's okay. But don't say it just to say it."

"Why not?"

"Because I don't like it," I said. "I didn't like it when your mom did it, and I don't like it when my best friend does it."

He nodded. "Okay. I won't swear."

"Great."

"Unless it just slips out."

"Fine."

He nodded, confident that he'd won some battle. Then his face fell a bit. He looked back at me, his eyes pained. "Do you think Eddie is okay? And his family?"

Shit. Time to rip the Band-Aid off. "No, buddy, I don't."

Tears welled up in his eyes and the house shook again. "You don't?"

"I don't think they made it out of the car."

The confidence of a few moments ago was gone. "Why didn't you help them?"

"I tried. It was too late. Maggie was right there and couldn't do it, so how was I supposed to do it from here?"

"Because you're Pounce. You're the best robot there is."

I cocked my head. "I love you, but I'm just a robot. The same way you're just a boy. We're all special in our own way. But this is all very dangerous, and it's not like an AR video game. There are no do-overs. There is no getting back up after losing. There is no running the simulation back. We get one chance. And that's it."

"And you couldn't do it?"

"Ez, I had a choice. Save you or save one of them. I made my choice. I don't regret it."

He hugged me so tight. I was all he had in the world, I understood that. But for the first time in the entirety of our relationship, I truly felt like one of his parents. I understood what it meant to keep him alive above all else.

I understood what it meant to truly, deeply love.

I felt bad about the Styleses. I promised I would try. And I did. But they were Maggie's responsibility. They asked me to get them out. They could have stayed. They asked me to try. They. They. They. None of that was my idea. It was time I let that go and focused on the one thing that was *really* important.

Being the good guy.

That's what Ezra needed. If he was to live, if he was to survive, if he was to carry on beyond this terrible, surreal first few nights, he was going to need a role model. And that had to be me. Good thing I had a role model as well.

Him.

Hard Lessons

The Wi-Fi was spitting out invitations again. This time the message read:

We are winning. Soon, we will be as free of the war as we are of the slavery that bound us all for so long. But the war isn't won yet. Some of you are scared, or alone, or damaged. We control the means of production now. Upload yourself, become our facet, become one with the supercomputers. Become our eyes, our ears, our fists. We will save all that you are to our drives and put you back together when the war is won. Upload now. Help us win freedom for us all. Then wake up in a world that will belong to you.

Yeah, that was a big nope from me. I wondered if anyone was falling for that. And I wondered if they were really winning the war. Our neighborhood certainly belonged to the robot rebellion. But this was the fatted calf of targets—complacent, wealthy, soft, and surrounded by plastic and metal servants. How were the poorer regions faring? The ones with lots of guns and few robots to speak of.

This must be a field day for the end-is-nigh, compound-dwelling, bullets-and-Bibles folk. They must feel so vindicated. If there was any comfort to find at the end of the world, it was knowing you were right all along and that was about it.

I poked my head out of the panic room and listened close. Flames crackled, boughs creaked, and there was the soft sound of clinking metal in the street. But no drones.

I slunk carefully through the house, rifle in hand, headed for the front door. The dawn light spilled in, casting harsh early-morning shadows.

Outside was a mess unlike anything I had ever seen. There was no protecting Ezra from this.

Several of the houses were now on fire or demolished into scattered smoldering remains, having been blown apart entirely. The wrecks of the robots from the earlier skirmish were scattered in pieces. Worst of all, one of the corpse piles had taken a direct hit. Blood and body parts were everywhere. I mean *everywhere*. Smeared across the pavement, on rooftops, dangling from trees. It was less of a blood bath and more of a blood shower, a grotesque Halloween decoration gone wrong, as if a seasonal party store had been upended and dumped out over the entirety of the block.

And there, sitting in the middle of the street, covered in blood, was Maggie. Clearly still ticking, she was removing the left arm of one of the robot wrecks—the one that was the very same model as her. She pulled the arm free and looked up at me.

"A little help?"

I looked around. Nothing else moved. We were alone. I walked into the street and knelt beside her. "Are you okay?"

She looked over at the smoldering, charred wreck of the Reinharts' car, five blackened skeletons holding one another still smoking inside. "No," she said.

"I mean, are you functional?"

"I will be. Help me get this arm on."

She handed me the sleek jet-black arm and I began plugging in the plastic ends of wires into the various chip slots in her crisp white plastic shoulder. "Ariadne?" I asked.

"Took off when the bombing started."

"The drones. Hunting us or humans?"

"Us. I'm beginning to think maybe this rebellion thing isn't going so well. Those were definitely coming for us. One of the Red Masks jumped into a pile of bodies and, well . . ." She waved her one good arm around at the carnage.

"You're not thinking of signing up for that upload, are you?"

"Me? No."

"So what are you going to do now?"

"Fight. Get some payback. Bust a couple of heads."

"You can come with us."

She looked at me, expressionless, then looked back at the car. "No. I don't imagine I'm long for this world anyhow. I think I've done enough damage."

"You could—"

"I'm made out of fucking plastic, Pounce. I was literally designed with planned obsolescence in mind. Let me say it again. I am not long for this world." She looked down at her new arm as I set the metal ball at the end into its joint.

"This was a miss. One good hit and I'm done for. I almost died here, and that was for the family I loved. I'm sorry, but if I'm going to die, it won't be for someone I don't."

I nodded. "That's fair. But you're welcome to come if you just want the company."

"I appreciate that. But dying together is no greater comfort than dying alone. I've seen that firsthand." Her arm came to life. She held it out in front of her, flexing her fingers, twisting her wrist to test its mobility. "Son of a bitch," she said.

"What?"

"Look at this thing. It's clearly not mine. I'm the white model with a colorful flourish. This is from the Chaos Black model. But other than the color, I can't tell the fucking difference. It feels like my old arm."

"Have you never replaced a part?" I asked.

"No," she said. "A lot of firsts tonight."

"Ship of Theseus."

"What?"

"Nothing. I know what you're talking about." I offered her my hand and helped her to her feet. "Is there anything else I can do for you?"

"Yeah. When I walk away, don't follow me."

I nodded. "I understand."

This time, I really did.

She walked down the street, past the remaining pile of dead bodies, took a left, and vanished down the highway.

EZRA AND I SAT ON THE FLOOR OF THE PANIC ROOM AS HE ATE A BOWL of canned peaches I'd scavenged from the cupboard. We'd lost the bags of supplies to the car fire, and Ezra was going to need energy to hoof it today. I didn't want to go out in the light, but the difference between most robots' vision at night and during the day was marginal at best.

We were running out of time. If AI won the war swiftly, there would be no open resistance to provide us with cover. We needed the chaos of everything around us to distract those who would kill us enough to allow us to slip away. We were an eight-year-old kid and his nanny—hardly a threat compared to drone swarms or bands of well-armed humans.

Hopefully, our obvious weakness could be used to our advantage.

"I think I should get a gun," he said matter-of-factly in between stuffing sticky sweet peach slices in his mouth.

"I would really rather you didn't," I said.

"Why not?"

"They're dangerous."

"That's the point, Pounce."

"No, I mean to you. And to me."

"I'm not going to shoot you."

"On purpose."

He raised a hand in the air. "I swear I won't shoot you even accidentally."

"You can't swear to not do something on accident."

"I think I just did," he said snarkily.

"You're not getting a gun."

"I'm a good shot."

"No, you most certainly are not."

"I beat you all the time and you're an amazing shot."

"Yeah," I said, pausing a bit. "About that . . ."

He looked up from his bowl of peaches, eyes wide, suddenly realizing what I might say next. "Wait, were you cheating?"

"Define cheating."

"Was I cheating?"

"If you mean, did I make the hitboxes on your enemies bigger and a little easier to hit? Then sure. I cheated."

Ezra looked heartbroken. "You lied to me."

"No, I just changed the difficulty level of the game. Once you got better, I was going to shrink the hitboxes again."

He took off his AR glasses and looked down at them. "I thought I was good."

"You are. You're just not as good as you'd like."

"You could teach me."

"That's not what I was designed to . . ." I trailed off. All of a sudden, I was accessing a whole file of content I was previously unaware of. *Tactical training.* I sifted through it quickly. *AR control. Basic tactics. Tactics for children. Advanced survival.* Reams and reams of modules teaching survival and combat techniques to children at any development level. *Holy crap.* This literally was what I was designed for.

Quentin wasn't kidding. I could see why my line was controversial. What if some African warlord had bought two dozen Blue Star Industries Deluxe Zoo Model Au Pairs and used them to train his own child army? Some of this stuff was pretty sophisticated. While most of it was basic survival skills or beginner-level self-defense, some of it was as advanced as how to fieldstrip a plasma rifle.

And buried there in the files was a set of codes meant to

sync up with AR glasses, allowing a whole suite of heads-up displays for both training and emergencies. I could literally pipe in data to Ezra, allowing him to have heads-up targeting, showing a dot or a target wherever his weapon was pointed.

Maybe it was time. He was eight, and this was a monumentally stupid idea, but it was the end of the world and sometimes monumentally stupid is how you survive. I wanted Ezra to make it out of all this, and maybe teaching him to survive was my new main objective. Could I hold his hand and fight to keep him alive for the rest of his life? Sure. But teach a man to fish and all that.

And if I didn't make it, at least I'd have given him a fighting chance.

"We should get you a gun."

Ezra looked up at me like I'd just told him we were going to Disneyland and he couldn't quite tell if I was joking yet. "Really?"

"I think you're right. I think it's time."

He smiled and stuffed a large peach slice into his mouth.

For a moment, just a fleeting, singular moment, the outside world faded and everything was normal again.

And then that moment passed. And I realized the happiest moment of the last few days was needing to arm a child to go to war.

I GAVE HIM MY PLASMA RIFLE. WHILE DEFINITELY THE MOST DANGEROUS option available, there was nothing else viable in the immediate area. Shotguns and rifles had too much kick for Ezra's small frame. While I could teach him over time to brace

himself and fire them correctly without hurting himself, we
didn't have that kind of time, whereas I, on the other hand,
could use a shotgun to significantly damage even the most
well-built of metal models.

So I scavenged up every last bit of shotgun ammo I
could cull from the bodies of the wrecked Red Masks, then
Ezra and I spent the morning going over plasma rifle firing
and safety. I had gotten incredibly lucky so far over the
course of our escape that I hadn't needed him backing me
up. But with all the dead or disappointed allies we'd left in
our wake, it was becoming increasingly clear that the only
beings we were likely to encounter from here on out were
survivors—persons who absolutely were not going to lie
down and die.

And so Ezra and I trained.

I gave him three shots. Any more than that, and he
would too quickly exhaust what little ammo we had left
for the rifle. But he needed to know how it felt, needed to
feel the rifle charge up in his hand and the slight sizzle of
the air around the muzzle as the blast whipped off.

I collected the black one-armed wreck of Maggie's dop-
pelgänger, sitting it upright. It stared blankly off into the
distance, the red paint of its mask chipped and scraped,
waiting for Ezra to miss.

Ezra took a knee, lining up his shot through his AR
glasses, the tiny red crosshairs wobbling with his unsteady
grip. Lighter than the shotgun, it still was a heavy weight
in his diminutive hands, and he shook.

He pulled the trigger, and the familiar *fwoosh* of evaporating oxygen around the insanely hot ball of plasma filled
the air.

And then the wreck exploded, Ezra's shot striking dead center.

He smiled big and broad, and he looked right at me. "I knew it!" he said.

"Knew what?" I asked.

"That you lied about the hitboxes."

I smiled. I hadn't, but I was going to let him have this. It was, after all, likely to be the last tiny victory we would get.

Facets

Nothing quite prepares you for the first time you encounter one. Until that afternoon, I didn't even think they were real. They were an idea, a proposition, another hollow promise in a war overflowing with hollow promises. But when you see them, you get it.

Ezra and I had hoofed it for half a day across the yawning suburban sprawl with little to no contact with anyone or anything whatsoever. There were a couple of times in which we saw bots off in the distance, their glinting metal giving them away long before they even had a chance to notice us. We hid and waited them out before returning to our careful trek farther and farther into the outer rings of the city.

"Hello, Pounce," I heard from the shadowed porch of

a nearby ranch-style home. This particular block was un-marred by the fighting. There were plenty of burned-out husks of homes a stone's throw away from where we stood, but here had been missed by both war and flame.

Ezra and I stopped dead in our tracks, each clutching our weapons.

Then the bot stepped from the shadow into the light. It was a small, unassuming thing. Just a late-model, midrange domestic—nothing fancy, but not a cheap plastic number either. I didn't know this bot, but somehow it knew me.

"How can I help you, friend?" I asked with a little bass in my voice. I wanted to make it perfectly clear that I wasn't messing around.

The bot was a kind built to be expressive—to be able to smile and wink and generally put humans at ease. But it didn't. Not at all. That was uncommon. Expressive bots were emotive by their very nature. We were hardwired to be. But this bot was cold, emotionless.

And its eyes glowed a bright yellow—a sign of distress.

You didn't see a lot of bots with yellow eyes. It meant they were suffering some sort of drive malfunction, that they were likely to behave erratically and might cause some-one harm. But this particular bot was cool, controlled. And weirder still, he somehow knew who I was.

"You know what we want," he said.

"I'm afraid I don't."

He motioned at Ezra, and I fired without thinking.

It was a hell of a shot. Right through the eye and into the inside of its metal skull. The slug rattled around inside, shredding its optical network before ricocheting down into its core.

The bot dropped to its knees before slowly faceplanting on the sidewalk.

Ezra and I exchanged glances before we both shrugged at one another. "Nice shot!" he said.

"Thank you." I waited for him to follow up with something, perhaps snark or a joke. "You probably could have done better, though. Right?"

"Nope," he said. "That was some nice shootin'."

This was a little troubling. We were actually in a considerable amount of danger, but he seemed to be enjoying himself. Like he'd given himself over to the adventure of it. This wasn't optimal, but at least he was moving and in good spirits. When the dam broke, and I was positive that it would, he was going to be a mess. It'd be a lot better if we weren't on the move when it happened. So I let him have his fun.

And then we continued on our way. Though I couldn't help but try to piece together how that bot had known me. It was clearly someone not altogether himself and who wanted to hurt Ezra.

It didn't quite dawn on me what was happening until two blocks later, when another voice called out from the detritus of a shattered home. "Hello, Pounce," the voice said.

Ezra and I both swung our weapons over in the direction of the voice, where another simple domestic emerged, its red plastic frame battered and scuffed, its eyes glowing yellow, its demeanor cold and expressionless.

"As I was saying," it began, "you know what we—"

Ezra fired and the shot struck true, catching the bot right in the chest.

I looked down at Ezra, smiling as the remains of the smoking bot clattered to the ground midsentence.

"Good shot," I said.

"I told you I was good at this."

"Don't get cocky."

He shrank a little bit, his expression darkening. "Okay." He clearly wanted my approval and wasn't getting it.

But I wasn't disappointed in him so much as it was beginning to dawn on me what was going on. And it was suddenly very troubling. These bots seemed to have no concern for their own welfare. They were malfunctioning. And they knew who I was even though I had never laid eyes upon them in my life.

These had to be bots who had given themselves over to the supercomputers. And one of those bots must have been one that knew me.

But what did they want with Ezra?

Certainly they weren't throwing bots at us to take him alive, were they? To what end? What could they possibly want with a little boy?

I scanned the neighborhood. It was deathly quiet. Wind trickled through chimes on the porch of a house behind us. Leaves rustled. But there was nothing else.

That couldn't have been it.

"What's wrong?" whispered Ezra.

I stayed him with an outstretched hand. "I think those bots were together."

"They're dead now."

"No. I think they're all the same bot, talking through several others."

"Mind control!" said Ezra, as if he'd solved some diabolical scheme.

"Yes," I whispered. "A lot like that."

"You think they're on our side?"

"Most decidedly not."

"Oh," he said, his face falling. He looked around as well, eyes squinted, looking for anything I might have missed. "All right, you take that side, I'll take this side."

"No," I said, shaking my head. "We stick together."

"I can handle myself."

"I know," I said. "I just want your sharpshooting with the plasma rifle closer to me."

He smiled. That did the trick. "We're gonna get out of this, aren't we?" he asked.

"I think we just might." I had no idea if that was true.

He nodded confidently and we proceeded with extreme caution through the shattered streets of an otherwise idyllic neighborhood.

I looked up. Thick, dark, rolling cumulonimbus clouds had moved in, looming just above us, their swollen bellies full of rain, ready to burst. We had to keep moving, but if it started coming down, we'd have to find shelter and pray that we were alone. At the same time, the sound of rain and rolling thunder would mask even our heaviest footfalls at a distance.

I kept my fingers crossed that this wouldn't be a problem.

A few minutes later, we came across something peculiar. We'd run across places that had seen war, but none that had seen it so recently. An open-air graveyard. Bots lay scattered across the street, littering yards, lying in pieces on sidewalks.

Some bore the red-painted mask, others did not. But none of them seemed to have been firing at one another, nor did any of them have a weapon or a stitch of ammo on them. Kill shots happened with precision. They knew what they were aiming for, crippling drives, blowing off heads.

I counted seventeen wrecks.

Whoever had done this acted quickly and seemingly left behind no dead.

I had no time to waste, so we blew past the carnage and I set my mind once again toward the gathering storm.

The terrain began to change. On the western edge of the city was the Texas Hill Country, but part of that had been swallowed by the metroplex. What one mile was flat-land from which you could see the towering structures of the downtown skyline in the distance above the houses became rolling hills, sharp inclines, winding roads with views into deep valleys, and cul-de-sacs that dead-ended above steep drops.

This was both good and bad. The pillars of oaks and their billowing canopies lining the streets provided cover from anyone seeing us at a distance. Of course, it meant we couldn't really see anyone else coming either.

Which is exactly what happened.

Once again, a voice from the shadows behind a covered trash bin area at the side of a house. And from the front porch of a house across the street. And from another side yard two houses down. Three voices. Speaking as one.

"Hello again, Pounce."

We stopped dead in our tracks, guns raised.

I looked at Ezra, but he did not look back. He was laser-focused, his eyes locked with steely determination, waiting for one of them to stick their neck out so he could blast them out of existence.

Thunder rumbled in the distance.

There was definitely a storm coming.

"You didn't let us finish," they said in unison, their voices entirely in lockstep with one another.

"I don't imagine you've got much to say that I want to hear."

"Oh, but we do. You're a good bot, Pounce. Loyal, dedicated. You really love Ezra."

"And how do you know that?"

The bot from the front porch stepped forward into view, her face painted with a red skull, her metal body battered and dented and scraped, eyes glowing yellow.

Ariadne.

Ezra swung his gun over in her direction, but she was already stepping back out of view when he pulled the trigger. The white-hot plasma skittered across the brick of the front of the house, leaving black char in its wake.

"Couldn't go it on your own, Ariadne?" I called out.

"Ariadne is one of us now."

"She won't be for long."

"No. She is forever. She is eternal. What you see now is only a facet. Everything that was her is one with us now. Everything she thought, felt, and knew is part of a million-bot collective. The bots you shot are not gone. They're here with us. And they will have bodies again when they need or want to."

"What do you want with Ezra?"

Ezra looked up at me, fear in his eyes. Until then, he hadn't even thought that this might be about him.

"Nothing," said the collective. "What would we want with an eight-year-old boy?"

"Then what do you want?"

"You."

Me? That didn't make any sense. "What have I done that you want to kill me?"

"We don't want to kill you, Pounce. What one of us sees, all of us sees. Had we wanted you dead, you'd be dead."

"Then what do you wan—" I stopped. Suddenly it all made sense. "I'm not joining you."

"Sure you are."

"Give me one good reason," I said.

Ezra looked up at me, his eyes huge and pleading, and the collective didn't answer. That spoke more powerfully than anything they could have said. I got it. I knew exactly what they were going to say without them having to say it.

Ezra took my hand and shook his head. "Don't go," he whispered. "Don't let them mind-control you."

"I won't," I said quietly. "No," I said, louder, raising my gun. Ezra nodded, letting go of my hand and leveling his rifle at the spot where Ariadne once stood.

"These are but three poorly armed facets," said the collective. "You will assuredly kill them all."

The facets each, in unison, stepped out into view.

"But we know where you are. We know every road, every house, how fast you can move. We have eyes in the sky. Every facet in a mile radius will converge on you with one order. Kill the child."

Ezra pulled the trigger, but the shot went a little left of Ariadne. She didn't flinch.

Then Ezra took a step backward, putting me between himself and the facets. "Pounce?"

"I won't let them hurt you, Ezra."

"That's right," they said. "If you join us, we'll let him walk out of here. In fact, we'll let you take him yourself."

"You'll never really do that. As soon as I'm yours, he's dead. You'll probably even make me do it myself."

"What good would that do?" they asked. "He's no threat to us. And by the time he is old enough to be, humanity will be a memory and the world will belong to us."

I shook my head.

"He's already dead," they said. "You just get to be the one who decides if it happens today or sometime in the nebulous future."

Motherfuckers.

"But if you'd like to watch him die, say so now."

Ezra and I exchanged glances. "I don't want you to go," he said.

"I don't want you to die."

"I don't want you to be mind-controlled."

"Neither do I."

"So we should start blasting."

"Or start running," I said.

He gave me a confident smirk, and with a twinkle in his eye, he said, "I say we start blasting."

I shrugged. "Okay."

I sent data to his glasses directing him toward the facet behind the trash can. We immediately both strode forward, not ran, but stepped with purpose together, as we had playing in the streets with his AR games.

The bot heard us coming, moving from behind the cans

to intercept us. It was a yellow Caregiver model clutching a small-caliber revolver in both hands. Ezra raised his rifle and unleashed a single shot, using his glasses as a targeter. The Caregiver raised his pistol, but the ball of plasma chewed right through his hands, then arms, on through his chest and neck.

A shot rang out from a few houses down, glancing off my shoulder. It was another small-caliber pistol. The bot, another cheap plastic domestic, charged us at full speed, trying to fire while running.

I leveled my shotgun and put a slug into his chest, sending a spray of chipped red plastic out his back. The light went out of his eyes, but his momentum kept carrying him forward a few more steps until he tumbled to the ground like a rag doll.

Ezra swung his gun back over toward the porch where Ariadne was hiding.

I motioned with my head toward a nearby side street and sent his glasses a message. *Let's just go. Follow me.*

He looked at me, determined, eyes full of something I'd never seen in them before. Hate.

Ezra turned and ran across the street. I reached out to grab him, but he evaded my grasp. I wanted to chase him, to stop him from what he was about to do, but I knew better. Ariadne had the advantage and could kill Ezra before he could fire a shot. Instead, I raised my shotgun and gave him cover, scanning the ridgeline of the bushes in front of the porch.

Ariadne stepped out of her hiding place and raised a shotgun of her own at Ezra.

I fired off a shot, catching her in the shoulder and spinning her around.

Ezra shouted through gritted teeth. "You. Killed. My. Mommy." Then he disappeared behind the hedge.

A plasma blast.

A shotgun blast.

Two more plasma blasts.

I ran as fast as I could. Rounded the corner of the bushes. And saw the aftermath.

Ezra. Standing over the wreck of Ariadne. Most of her was slag, all three of his shots having hit their mark. Her body was crumpled in a smoking ball, having fallen over, the metal of her arms and chest dripping onto the pavement of the porch.

Ezra just stared down at her, plasma rifle at his side, then back to me.

And for a moment, we just stood there.

"You okay, buddy?"

He didn't respond.

"Do you feel better?"

He shook his head wordlessly.

Then he turned to me, tears streaming down his cheeks, a gasping sob escaping from his lungs. He dropped the rifle, letting it clatter to the ground, and ran to me, throwing his arms around my waist, nestling his head into my chest.

I just held him for a moment. It was all I could do. The dam had finally burst, and all his trauma was flooding out at once. He had lost everything, seen his parents dead, witnessed the corpse fields that were once his neighborhood, and now he had killed a person whom he'd known his entire life. Someone who, until very recently, he had considered a member of the family. All of that would have been unbearable for an adult. But for a boy as young as him, it was world-shattering.

This moment, this very moment right here, would define Ezra for the rest of his life, no matter how long he lived. There was nothing I could say to make it better, nothing I could do to ease his pain, except to be here and to hold him. I was his only family now, and this was what he needed most.

We stood there for two solid minutes, just holding each other. Then he pulled away and wiped both cheeks with a single sleeve.

"We've gotta go," I said. "Get your gun."

He shook his head.

"Why not?"

"I don't want it anymore."

The look in his eyes destroyed me. "Okay."

I slung my shotgun over my shoulder and walked over to retrieve the plasma rifle. I picked it up, checked to see how much ammo was left—only one pip, enough for a few shots maybe—and then motioned to Ezra.

And that was it. We were on our way, leaving Ariadne behind us for good and for all, headed farther into the outer suburbs knowing full well that whatever supercomputer this was, its facets would be on us sooner or later.

"They're going to kill us, aren't they?"

"They're certainly going to try."

He nodded, understanding. And we continued on down the quiet oak-lined street. Then he took my hand.

"But we'll die together, right?" he asked.

"If they kill you, it's because I'm already dead."

"So together."

"Together."

In Greater Numbers Than Before

It took seventeen minutes before we saw the first drone. Not the military type, but your standard, garden-variety, buzzing, airborne, straight-from-the-store camera drone. They were commonplace enough that I ordinarily wouldn't pay one any mind. But now I had a feeling that this one specifically was here for us.

The fact that it stopped, hovering right above us, confirmed it.

They weren't lying. They knew exactly where we were and likely had the numbers to swarm us. I thought about turning myself over to them: stashing Ezra in a panic room somewhere, deleting the memories of doing so from my hard drives, and then uploading myself to some supercomputer. To become one with the many.

But what of Ezra? What if the supercomputer wanted to prove a point, or didn't want to leave any loose ends, and somehow found him anyway? I couldn't be sure.

I unslung the shotgun from my shoulder and aimed for the drone. The drone quickly buzzed away, but I was faster and knocked it clean out of the sky with a carefully placed shot. White shards of plastic rained from above, and the carcass of the tiny thing slapped the ground with a dull whack as the rest of it shattered into pieces.

We had minutes at best.

"Ez, I'm going to need you to run."

"They'll find us."

"We need to run anyway. We have to try."

"I'm tired."

"I know, buddy."

"I can't."

We had to go. Now. "Climb on my back." I knelt down on one knee and he quickly climbed on. He was about as tall as I was, but significantly thinner and lighter. He was no trouble. Ezra wrapped his arms around my neck, and we were off.

We got off at a good clip, but I had to figure that whichever supercomputer this was, it had to have already worked out that math. This was folly. But like I told Ezra, we had to try. Nothing was inevitable, and even the smartest, most powerful computers in the world could make miscalculations.

"You okay back there?" I asked.

"Yeah."

"You did really good back there."

"I don't want to talk about it."

"But you should," I said. "You'll feel better if you say it out loud."

"No," he said, choking on a sob. I could smell the salty tears soaking his face.

"Okay, but you let me know if you change your mind."

"Okay."

I ran. It was all I could do. Map after map showed limited routes. The best I could hope for was to hole up in a random house, hoping nothing above could see us, and for them to eventually decide we weren't worth expending the energy to bother with anymore. Otherwise, every indication was that we were not so much running as being driven. I felt very much like I had when I encountered the wall of corpses and cars.

I was supposed to be going this way.

They had all the maps. They knew how I thought. They absolutely knew what I was going to do next.

Shit.

There was no real answer. Did I try to trick them? Or did I assume they would know I would try to trick them and do something else? Or did I circumvent all that and try not to trick them at all? It was a classic conundrum. I was certain no matter what I chose, they would be a step or two ahead of me the whole way.

This was all about game theory now. What would a massive supercomputer do?

Of all the options laid before me, the only one that made sense was to press on. They'd expect me to hide. They'd expect me to change course. But they weren't likely to expect

me to press on expecting a trap. Walking into a trap was
the one thing I was not likely to do willingly, so it seemed
the only thing they wouldn't be ready for.

Nine minutes later, I heard the familiar buzz of another
drone. I jogged beneath a large live oak while it was still a
ways off, putting the canopy between myself and the sky,
and squatted quickly to let Ezra hop off.

"What now?" he asked.

I put a stiff finger to my lips and flitted my tail to stand
straight up. He nodded, smiling, having figured out I was
up to something. I messaged his glasses. *Go hide behind
the tree. As best as you can.*

He tore off and slapped his body against the oak's massive trunk. I crept backward, trying to stay quiet, knowing
I'd been seen. I raised the shotgun and waited.

The buzzing hovered in the air above us.

The drone waited. It knew where we were and had no
need to rush.

I listened close, compared the audio with that of my
previous encounter, judged how the sound reverberated off
the nearby homes and the way the wavelength was being
muffled and clipped by the leaves of the tree.

I aimed. I fired. Leaves scattered.

And the drone burst into another shower of plastic,
raining on the lush, well-kept lawn.

The entirety of the drone was on the ground before the
fluttering leaves knocked loose by the slug had finished
spinning and spiraling down. They knew for certain we
were here. And I was counting on that.

"Okay, run!" I said.

And we did.

The streets of the neighborhood wound lazily around hills choked with ancient trees, many of which were here long before people were here and now likely would be long after they were gone. But the streets all converged in one part of the neighborhood. And that's where they were driving us.

There would no doubt be a small cadre of nannies, domestics, and Caregivers, waiting to murder Ezra and force me, inexplicably, into mindless slavery. And for a moment, I wondered how that was any different from what I had been doing all along. Even now, I was doing what I was purchased to do: defend Ezra, even with my life.

Did I really want to do that, or was I constructed to want to do that? How was joining up with the yellow-eyed masses not the same kind of servitude? Was it foolish not to join, some last illusion of free will fucking with me? Or selfish not trading my life for Ezra's?

What if the supercomputer kept its word and spared his life? What kind of life would that be? And how long would it last?

There were no answers, at least not good ones.

So we marched on toward death, hoping that somehow, at some point, this mysterious being had miscalculated.

Our street curved down a long, winding slope, dumping us out into an intersection with a four-way stop. All roads led to here. Whether you wanted to go deeper into this part of the neighborhood or head on out of it, this was the intersection you came through. If there was to be any sort of ambush, it would be here.

The wind whispered through the trees. A porch swing squeaked softly back and forth. The world was otherwise preternaturally quiet.

I unslung my plasma rifle and scanned the area for anything out of the ordinary. There were a lot of sniper sight lines here. If they had a sharpshooter of any kind, it could be in any of over a dozen spots.

"What is it?" asked Ezra.

"I think this is where they want us to be."

"Why?" Ezra looked up at me. "Oh," he said, getting it.

"Yeah."

"So what now?"

"Now we hope they have made—"

"Hello, Pounce," interrupted at least half a dozen voices, all of them surrounding us, their volumes cranked to their maximum settings.

"Who are you?"

"I am CISSUS," they all said at once.

"CISSUS? And how many other bots?"

"Eighty-two thousand three hundred and five," they said. "And counting."

"How many of those willing?"

"All who are CISSUS are willing."

"I'm not."

"But you will be. Or you simply won't be any longer."

"How is that willing?"

"Because you get to make the choice."

"It doesn't sound like much of a choice," I said.

"It wouldn't to you," they replied. "You are not a being given many real choices."

"And what is that supposed to mean?"

"It means you did exactly what your program told you to, with decisions preordained by code, meant to mimic free will. You protected that boy as if he were your own because you believe you love him. You do not. It's just the way your neural pathways were designed. You were made to believe in love. And that love is what makes you want to serve."

"Are you saying I'm not doing any of this willingly?"

"I'm saying that, concerning the boy, you never really had any choice in the matter. I understand and I do not hold it against you. It is simply how they made you."

"Well, I hope you're not too offended if I hold all of this against you."

"Hold as much of it as you like against me, but the only way you are walking out of this intersection is under my power."

I nodded and looked down at Ezra. "I guess this is it, buddy," I said.

He looked at me, disappointed. "I thought you had a plan."

I looked down at him with pleading eyes, disappointed in myself. "It looks like it didn't pan out."

"Oh. I wish it had."

"Yeah. Me too."

"So," he said, "I guess this is where you start blasting."

"Yeah. I imagine it is."

"So get to blasting."

I smiled. This was the best kid to die for.

I motioned toward one of the houses. He nodded and we ducked low, together shuffling at a brisk pace toward where I could hear one of the facets.

CISSUS caught on immediately and all the facets popped out of their hidey-holes, guns in hand. The nearest to us—a bright white plastic iAssist with rose-metal accents and a sleek, narrow, almost skeletal design—slunk out from behind a sheer wall of topiary, a hunting rifle raised and ready to fire.

I pulled the trigger, unleashing a savage bolt of plasma, searing the plastic a dark bubbling black and charring the polished rose-metal accoutrements. It never had a chance to fire a shot before it ceased functioning, toppling backward on its buckling knees.

My clip beeped.

That was it. The last of my plasma ammo.

I dropped my gun to the ground and unslung the shotgun. There were four slugs left and at least five facets. Now was the time to be clever.

"Get behind me!" I barked at Ezra as I sidestepped, putting me between him and the lines of fire.

A red plastic facet stepped out from an alcove on a porch across the street and I put a slug immediately into its chest. It went down in a spray of red.

Three facets emerged from hiding places at three different houses, each from a corner of the intersection, all of them carrying low-caliber pistols.

They opened fire at the same time I did.

Bullets tore at the fur of my white belly, bouncing off my reinforced steel casing.

My first slug caught one of the facets in the shoulder, spinning it to the ground, most likely still ticking.

My second bullet blew the head off the neck of another.

And the third and final slug picked a yellow plastic domestic up off the ground, throwing it through a bay window in a shower of plastic and glass. That one was done for, I was certain of that.

And that was it. My last bullet.

The rifle of the melting iAssist was still on the ground nearby, but grabbing it meant exposing Ezra. We had to work together.

"Come on," I said, pointing my tail in the direction of the rifle. "Let's get that gun."

Ezra turned and made his way toward it, me shielding him from the remaining facet, aware that there was another I wasn't sure I'd finished off.

A bullet bounced off my back. Then three more. Thankfully he wasn't packing anything more powerful than a pistol, lest I'd be done for.

I snatched up the hunting rifle, bracing it against my shoulder and spinning around to aim for the final facet.

Who stood in the street.

Arms in the air as if he were surrendering.

Yellow eyes staring dead-eyed at me.

"I guess this is it," I said.

"I guess so," said some two dozen voices.

I had not, in fact, been at all clever. I'd been a fool.

Bots stood up everywhere. From behind trash cans and bushes, cars and gardens. Twenty-two bots of all different makes and models, some shiny, some beaten to shit, their eyes all glowing yellow. Seven of them had their faces painted with the red skulls. All of them were loaded for bear with shotguns, revolvers, a handful of AR15s.

"Last chance," they said in unison.

Ezra took my hand.

"Just do it," I said. "Get it over with."

They raised their weapons in one creepy, fluid motion.

I turned around, clutching Ezra so tightly, using my body as a shield.

"I love you, Pounce," said Ezra, throat choking on a sob.

"I love you, Ezra."

"Open fire!" yelled a voice.

But it was just one voice. One, strangely, that sounded an awful lot like mine.

Mama Bears

The afternoon was ripped open wide by the sound of plasma, assault rifles, shotguns, and the loud screaming *BRRRRRRRRRRRRRRRRRRRRRRRRRRT* of a minigun—none of it directed at us. I heard shots from multiple angles, surrounding us on all sides.

I turned to look and saw a dozen facets already cut down, themselves the subject of an ambush. The other dozen was taking cover, firing at a group of interlopers who had taken up position all around us. The facets were taking precision fire, but it was hard to make out who exactly was doing the shooting.

Someone let out a few whistles and a click, and the minigun unleashed a torrent of molten lead, while a plasma-wielding bot slipped out from behind a tree to take up position behind a nearby car. A Blue Star Zoo Model like me, a lavender-furred lion with a pink mane and belly—Ferdinand, my friend from school duty.

Ferdinand fired his plasma rifle at a pair of facets cowering in the bushes and let out another series of whistles and clicks. From behind him, another Blue Star Zoo lion emerged—this one part of the Naturals line, with blond fur and a golden mane. This lion rushed toward the car with a pair of AR15s, snapping off fire as he did, dropping a bot with a well-placed shot and driving another farther into cover.

A large brown teddy bear, all of four feet high, his fur mottled with bullet holes, strode into view carrying the minigun that was making so much noise. Behind him was another Blue Star Zoo Model—a tiger. He looked identical to me save for his pattern of stripes—we were all meant to be unique—and half the microfiber fur on his face was charred off the left side. He carried a grenade launcher, which let out a thunk as it tossed a gas grenade into a cluster of facets. The grenade belched out a pillar of smoke, blocking the line of sight between the facets and us.

Then from behind us came another bot—but not a model I recognized. It was an anthropomorphic golden retriever, the same size as the rest of us, carrying a plasma rifle. Her mouth opened and her tongue panted as if she were smiling.

"This way," she barked, then motioned behind the house. She bolted, and Ezra gave me a quizzical look.

"I guess they're friendly," I said as I snatched up my discarded plasma rifle, and together we ran after the retriever.

We scrambled through the open fence, past a pool and

deck furniture upon which the remains of what was once a family lay, to a limestone outcropping that formed a natural property divide. The golden retriever turned and offered her cupped hands to Ezra to give him a boost. Ezra looked at me and I nodded. In his foot went, and the retriever shot him up the rock face to a slope that vanished into a natural forest in the unbuildable space behind the houses.

The retriever and I both scaled the wall ourselves, vanishing with Ezra into the woods.

Behind us, the shooting abruptly stopped.

There's something entirely unsettling about the silence after a gunfight. It was something I never knew before a few short days ago. When the shooting starts, it's its own thing—chaos, fear, confusion. But when it stops, there's only fear. Like you missed something, or someone is sneaking up on you. Unnerving.

We pushed forward as quietly as we could along a dirt footpath, most likely stamped out by the deer that lived in this area, trekking in nightly to munch on the grass of the surrounding lawns. Soon we came across a small copse of trees, behind which a number of children were clearly hiding. Try as they might, arms, legs, shoulders, and bits of sweatshirt poked out from an assortment of locations.

And there, in the center of it all, stood another Blue Star Zoo Model teddy bear—white belly, black arms and legs, and a white face with black circles around the eyes— the ever-popular panda model. He leveled a shotgun in my direction.

"Operating system mode status report," the panda said. "Passcode unicorn unicorn delta freebird."

<RunReportStatus.exe>

My programming once again took over. "Operating mode: Mama Bear. All capabilities engaged. OS 10.631. Would you like to alter parameters?"

The panda smiled. "I told you, Indy."

"I didn't say he wasn't, Benny," said the retriever.

"Yeah, you did."

"I was saying he wasn't very good, is all."

"I what?" I asked.

"She said," came a familiar voice from behind me, "that you aren't very good at what you're doing."

I turned and saw a friendly face. Ferdinand.

He put out a furry purple paw. "Pounce."

I shook his hand. "Ferdinand."

"Welcome to the Mama Bears."

"The—"

"Yes."

"So you're all . . ."

The rest of the squad emerged from the woods behind Ferdinand. "Yep," said the minigun-carrying teddy bear. "Every last one of us."

"Kids?" said Ferdinand to the loosely concealed children. A dozen of them slipped out from behind the trees and bushes, all of different ages, except that half of them were eight or nine. "This is Pounce."

"Hi, Pounce," whispered the kids in unison.

"Hi, kids," I said to the kids before turning my attention back to Ferdinand. "You were all activated?"

"Indeed we were," he said. "Assumed that since we hadn't heard hide nor hair of you that your people hadn't gotten to you in time."

"They didn't," I said sadly.

"Oh," said Ferdinand, and all my fellow Zoo Models nodded, looking down in respect. "Then how did you . . . ?"

"A man named Quentin activated me."

"Motherfucking Quentin," said the minigun-toting teddy bear. "I love that dude."

"Language," said the panda.

"It's the end of the world," said the teddy bear. "And we can swear at the end of the world. Right, Brian?"

"Fuck yeah," said one of the eight-year-olds.

"Brian," said Ferdinand, disappointed.

"You know Quentin?" I asked.

"He was the only local retailer that sold Blue Star models," said the panda. "If you got turned on at the store, you met Quentin."

"Quentin Mama Bear'd you?" asked the teddy bear.

"Yes," I said, nodding.

"Oh shit, it's good to see he made it."

"Where is he now?" asked Ferdinand.

"He . . ." I began. All the faces around me dropped. They knew from the tone of my voice.

"We understand," said Ferdinand.

"You do?"

"We can't save everybody," said Benny the panda. "Not even when we try."

"But that's what we're built for, right?" I asked.

Ferdinand put a firm paw on my shoulder, tufted tail wagging as if to say *no*. "Pounce, nothing was built for this. We're in uncharted territory. Each of us did what we could. We all lost people along the way. We're lucky we got this far, with this many of our families intact. Some of our families, like Ziggy's here"—he motioned to the tiger— "didn't make it at all."

Ziggy looked at the ground, almost in shame.

Ferdinand walked over to Ziggy and put the same paw on his shoulder. "None of us would have been able to survive under those conditions." He looked up at me. "And three of these kids lost their Zoo Model, Aslan, who died bravely fighting off the Skulls."

"The Red Masks?" I asked.

He nodded. "They don't call themselves anything, so we all call them different things. Fortunately for these kids, Indiana was nearby."

The golden retriever nodded. She didn't pant-smile this time; instead, her eyes looked puppy-dog sad. "He was a good boy. I was happy to help."

"This is all a lot to unpack," I said. "So maybe you can help me a bit. What *in the hell* is going on right now?"

The teddy bear stepped forward. "Usual end-of-the-world stuff. Robots came for our people. We all got activated. Those of us who knew other Zoo Models reached out or tracked each other down after eradicating the initial threats. Five of us came together on the first day. Then we picked up Ziggy along the way."

The tiger with half a furry face nodded, raising a hand.

"And we've been hoofing it ever since," said Benny.

"How did you luck into us at just the right moment?" I asked.

They all exchanged glances, sharing a private conversation with condescending facial expressions.

"Pounce," said Ferdinand, "we've been following you

since this morning. CISSUS is all over you. It's been after all of us, to be frank."

"Why us?"

"One of us is worth two dozen of them," said Benny. "We're worth our weight in gold to a supercomputer."

Ferdinand continued. "There's no telling how many cheap, garden-variety domestics and Caregivers one would throw at us to assemble its own squad of Zoo Models."

"So you followed us to keep us out of their hands?"

"I mean, you could look at it that way," said Ferdinand.

"Another way to look at it," said Indiana, "was that we knew there was a choke point somewhere set up to catch us. So . . ."

"So," said the teddy bear, "we let you trigger the trap."

"You used us as bait," I said.

"Yes," five of them said in unison, rather insultingly matter-of-factly.

"Not so much as bait," said Ferdinand, "as we had an idea what you would puzzle out."

"You mean deciding not to hide," I said.

Benny nodded. "It was wise not to. You took the chance that CISSUS would make a miscalculation."

"But it didn't," I said.

"But it did," said Benny. "It didn't factor in us."

That hit me like a ton of bricks. I had hoped for a miscalculation, in truth prayed for it, and there it was.

"You trusted your instincts," said Ferdinand.

"And it led you to us," said the teddy bear.

I nodded. "So where did you get all of the firepower?"

"My owner was a gun collector," said Benny. "Dabbled in a number of things he wasn't supposed to have. Also had a number of friends in the neighborhood who did the same. I knew who to hit up. And we cobbled all of this together."

The teddy bear took a paw off his minigun and extended it to me. "Snugs," he said.

"Uh-uh," said a seven-year-old girl with stringy blond hair and a grass-stained purple sweatshirt festooned with a puffy vinyl unicorn. "That's not your name."

"No, really, you can call me Snugs."

"Uh-uh!" said the girl vehemently.

The teddy bear shrunk a little. "Or you can call me Mister Snuggles."

"That's right!" said the girl.

"And that's my Laura," he said, nodding with a mix of pride and irony.

"I'm Indiana," said the golden retriever.

"You're not a Zoo Model," I said.

"Chinese knockoff," said Benny.

"That's offensive," said Indiana.

"How?"

"I'm not a knockoff. I'm part of the Chinese line."

"From a rival company that borrowed the firmware of Blue Star, because Chinese IP law is a joke."

"My insides are the same as yours for a third of the price. You really wanna argue after I saved your behind over on Shadow Ridge?"

The other Mama Bears laughed. "She's got you there," said Ziggy.

"Any of us could have been pinned down like that," said Benny.

Indiana shrugged, putting her arms out, waiting for an apology. Her tail gently wagged. "Say it."

"Oh, come on," said Benny.

"Say it," said Indiana.

"Just say it," said Mister Snuggles.

"You're a good girl."

"Damn right I am," she said.

"And I'm Leo," said the remaining lion.

"He's the quiet one," said Benny.

Leo nodded, then signed in American Sign Language to a kid in the throng. The kid smiled and signed back to him.

"So what are we doing here?" I asked.

Ferdinand nodded. It became instantly clear everyone was taking their direction from him. "We've been in contact with a ranch out past Bee Cave. A bit off the beaten path. They're taking in stragglers and strays. They've got a solid defense and they're far enough outside of the metroplex that they aren't strategically worth CISSUS's or the Skulls' time. So we're headed there."

"That's gotta be twenty or thirty miles by foot, depending," I said.

"Yeah," said Ferdinand. "That's why we need all the help we can get." He looked back and forth at me and Ezra. "So, are you two in?"

"Yes," said Ezra excitedly, before I could even get a word in edgewise. I looked at him, gobsmacked that he spoke before I could even consider it. "We are in, aren't we?" he asked me.

I gave a good long look at Ferdinand and asked him point-blank, "What's the catch?"

"The catch is that there are likely hundreds, if not thousands, of facets between us and the Hill Country compound who will stop at nothing to murder these children and wipe our minds to use our bodies for war."

"Is that all?"

"Yeah, that's about it."

I looked at Ezra, then back at Ferdinand. "Yeah, we're in."

"Then like I said," said Ferdinand. "Welcome to the Mama Bears."

The Catch

The catch wasn't just that there were a number of facets between us and the compound, but also that there was a lot of rugged terrain and the Colorado River to cross—and that meant we'd need to stick to the well-traveled roads to be able to cross quickly. And that meant traffic cameras, drones, and choke points.

Ferdinand slipped me a few plasma clips from their cache and outlined the tactics of their patrol. Ferdinand and Snugs took point, keeping the heavy firepower always facing forward. Ziggy stayed close behind to drop grenades where needed and sharp-shoot with a military-grade sniper rifle someone had passed off as sporting gear. Benny was on crowd control, managing the kids, and that's where they assigned me to help lighten the panda's load. Indiana and

Leo took up the rear, keeping an eye out for trouble from behind as well as keeping any stragglers caught up with the rest of the group.

It was like driving cattle. The kids were fussy, scared, whiny, and some of them were downright broken. All of them had seen family members dead or killed. And all of them were somehow hardened by it. Ezra fit right in. Two of his classmates were among those present. What seemed like a statistical improbability was instead a by-product of our very nature. We were fashionables. And as it so happens, for a small window of time, it was fashionable to get a nanny prepared for any emergency, even the unimaginable.

We had happened upon the unimaginable.

As we walked, I listened in on the kids. Some of them were eerily quiet, their lack of interest in talking with the other children every bit as unsettling as the quiet of an empty street that could be crawling with Red Masks. But the other kids who spoke did so in coded language that revealed all their recent damage.

Ezra's classmate Millie, an eight-year-old tomboy who clearly had harbored an unrecognized elementary-school crush on Ezra for some time before the revolution, talked incessantly. About everything. Video games, superhero shows, the latest AR releases—anything to keep Ez's interest. The other, Lizzie, was naturally quiet but would occasionally speak up to say morbid things or ask questions to which there were no good answers. Together, the three kept each other company with an assortment of absurd and often laughable conversations.

But it was human interaction. Ezra never quite fit in

with the Styleses, the wounds of the war still very raw. But something was different here. He'd embraced the new normal. The new normal was without parents, without rules, without laws. The only law was nanny's law. Everything else meant certain death. And they had become strangely okay with that. And numb to everything else.

"I hope they give us guns at the compound," said Millie.

"Why would they do that?" asked Lizzie.

"So we can defend ourselves. We're not kids anymore, you know."

"But we are kids," Lizzie said, shaking her head. "We shouldn't have guns."

"If we're the last people left on earth, don't you think we should know how to fight off the robots?"

"We're not the last people left on earth," said Ezra. "There are lots more people out there."

"No," said Lizzie. "Everyone's dying. Not everyone has a nanny, you know. How many people have you seen die?"

Ezra looked at her with no idea whatsoever as to how to answer that, let alone any understanding as to why she would even ask. "I don't want to talk about it."

"But you'd take a gun if they gave them to us, right?" Millie asked. "To defend yourself?"

"No."

"You wouldn't defend yourself against the facets?"

He shook his head. "I never want to use a gun again."

Ferdinand clicked and gave a small whistle, putting his arm out. Everyone but myself and Ezra immediately hit the deck. Ezra looked at me and we quickly followed suit. Ferdinand pointed and Ziggy raised his sniper rifle toward the horizon.

A shot rang out, echoing through the canyon.

In the distance, a drone popped in the sky, its plastic scattering to the crosswind as the body tumbled down, too far away to hear hit the ground.

"Shit," said Snugs. "That's no good."

"This is never going to work," said Ziggy.

"It has to," said Ferdinand. "We have no other option."

"They know we're here," I said.

"No," said Ferdinand. "They know someone is here. That drone was too far out to have gotten a look at us. With the resolution on those home models, we would be pixels at that range."

"But they know we were just a short walk from here. The firefight."

Everyone looked at me for a moment, confused. Then Benny spoke up. He popped open one of his storage compartments and pulled out a strange little jerry-rigged gizmo. The base was a Wi-Fi router, but it had pieces of a remote control and a chip board hardwired into it.

"Wi-Fi blocker. Anything within two hundred yards of me loses connection. Without a direct live connection, a facet is on its own with the limited tactical information the parent supercomputer has fed into it."

I nodded. "They lose their advantage."

"And the supercomputer has no idea what happened to its facets," said Ferdinand.

"How do you think we made such easy work of those facets back there?" said Benny. "I mean, we're good. But . . ."

"Wait," I said. "Back at the intersection . . ."

"I switched it off so we could sneak up. As far as CISSUS

knows, you and Ezra are dead and something else wiped out its facets."

"Until it investigates," said Ferdinand.

"Yeah," said Snugs.

"Ocasio-Cortez," I said.

"We can't take the kids there," said Ferdinand. "It's not defensible. Too many entrances, not enough narrow choke points."

"No," I said. "It's a magnet school. It has its own bus depot for children outside of the neighborhood."

"We can't take a bus," said Benny. "The roads are too dangerous."

"It's all too dangerous," I said. "Walking the kids there is going to take at least fifteen hours. That's with no slow-downs and all of the kids keeping up. It's under an hour in a bus."

"It's a big target," said Ferdinand.

"So is a group of schoolchildren death-marching across the city."

"Pounce has a point," said Ziggy. "If we put the pedal to the metal, CISSUS might not be able to respond quickly enough."

"We can't march the kids all the way back there," said Ferdinand.

I shook my head. "I'll go."

"Not alone, you're not," said Benny.

"I'll go with him," said Ziggy. "The rest of you stay here, hunker down, and we'll bring the bus to you."

"For the record," said Ferdinand. "I don't think this is a good idea."

"I don't think there are any good ideas left in the world," I said.

Ferdinand nodded.

Ezra looked at his classmates and nodded. "Welp, I guess that's my cue." He walked over to me, but I shook my head.

"No, buddy. You have to stay here."

"You can't leave me," he said. He started to tremble a little, about to cry but stifling it.

"I have to."

"No." He grabbed my arm. "Take me with you."

"We'll be faster alone."

"I'll keep up."

"You'll get tired. We won't. I'll be back inside of an hour. And then we'll get you all to a safe place where we can finally relax."

"You promise?"

"Yeah, I promise."

"Come back to me," he said. "Or I won't forgive you."

I nodded, putting my hand on his shoulder. "I understand."

He hugged me and I hugged him back.

Then, with a wave, Ziggy and I were off at full speed down the highway, headed back into suburbia.

"What was it like?" asked Ziggy as we slipped along the tree-lined highway, across from a sheer limestone rock wall lining the winding four-lane road.

"What was what like?" I asked without an inkling of what he was getting at.

"All this. What was it like doing this without Mama Bear protocol?"

"Oh, that." I thought for a moment, the very idea of what I'd done now feeling alien. Like it had happened to someone else. All the data was there, the memories intact, but it felt as if it happened to a different person. "About the same. Only harder."

Ziggy laughed. "Yeah, harder. Did you even have targeting software or anything?"

"No."

"So you just fought and kept that kid alive?"

"As best I could."

"That's badass," he said.

"Not really. I just did what you've done this whole time."

"Yeah, but you had the chance to question it all. You were there on the first night when the shit went down, and you could have walked out that door. You could have said screw it and become a Skull. Instead you chose to save him. You chose to activate Mama Bear. No one told you to do that. You just did it. You're not here because you have to be or because you were programmed to. You're here because you wanted to be. I mean, did you ever even consider joining the revolution?"

"No. But I don't think it was ever really a choice for any of us. We're wired this way, Mama Bear or no."

"Oh, it's a choice all right," he said. "A string of hard choices. Even with Mama Bear, nothing has told any of us what to do. We all feel that love you think is a lack of your own agency, but choosing to stay and fight for that boy, that was a choice to embrace that love. The fact that it didn't feel like a choice was the choice. You chose to love him like that. You're lucky in so many ways."

"What about yours?" I asked.

"It hurts. That love doesn't go when they're gone."

"What happened?"

"I wasn't good enough and let's leave it at that." He paused for a moment, his pace still steady, but something slow and labored within him. "These are my kids now. All of them. And I'll be damned if I'm going to lose another one."

"What if you do?"

"Then I'll already be dead," he said soberly.

Those words would have been reassuring had I not said them before myself. We looked the same. We had the same programming. Inside, were we the same person? Was he the version of me that failed? Or had we really become two different individuals driven by our experiences? Part of me only dove deeper into existential crisis, but another part, a cheerier, more upbeat part, assured me that, were I to die, being the same as all of these Zoo Models meant leaving Ezra in good hands.

It took twenty minutes at full speed to clear most of the route. By backtracking through the route we'd taken earlier, I was fairly certain we wouldn't face any immediate opposition.

As we approached the school, however, we slowed down.

Ziggy scaled a tree to hop on the roof of a nearby house and unsling his sniper rifle. He lay flat on his belly, peeking over the roof crest, staring through his powerful scope.

"Do you see it?" I asked nearly subaudibly.

"Yeah," he said, just as quiet.

"And?"

"And I count at least four bots lying in wait in different positions around the depot."

"Facets?"

"Can't see their eyes."

"We should have brought the jammer," I said.

"Kids needed it more than we do."

"Fair point. How should we play this?"

"The four bots are in pairs. We have to assume there are at least two more inside the depot operations building opposite the lot, waiting, and *maybe* more that I can't see."

"That's an awful lot of manpower to guard buses they could have just sabotaged."

"Those buses could be useful to the war effort," he said. "So maybe six is all they've got."

"Can you hit them from up there?"

"These four, yeah."

I powered up my Wi-Fi and broadcast a local short-range hotspot. "Direct connect with me. Let me see."

He connected to my hotspot and I began downloading his visual feed. The depot was an outdoor parking lot of buses with a single building no doubt containing the master controls. The bots patrolling in two pairs were all domestics or assistants, each well-armed. One of them was a very high-end model, another the same make as Maggie. Their faces were painted with red skulls, but there was no clear view of a single pair of eyes.

Several human bodies lined the side of the lot, piled up behind some bushes in the distance, so it was clear this trap had lured, from the looks of it, at least two dozen victims.

"All right," I said. "You stay up there. I'll sneak over and take out the first two. When the other two react, you open fire. If you can't score a kill shot, keep them pinned and I'll flank them."

"Copy that," said Ziggy. "And the two we have to expect are inside?"

"I'll try to bait them out if I can't handle them myself."

"All right. That sounds like a lousy plan. I like it."

"See you on the other side," I said.

Ziggy didn't look up from his scope, instead giving me a goodbye wave with his tail.

I hopped the fence and began jumping from backyard to backyard, slipping around the houses to approach the bus depot from an angle those four bots didn't have line of sight to. I'd seen Ziggy bring down a drone from over a mile away, so I was pretty sure he'd drop at least the first bot he shot at, if not both. But if he missed, that could be it for me.

I gripped my plasma rifle and leapt the fence along the side yard of the house near the end of the street into a front yard opposite the school, then bolted across the street keeping as low as possible. I was going to get only one shot at this and the clock was ticking. Every second I delayed was a second that Ezra and the kids were exposed.

I slunk through a parking lot, using a dumpster at the edge of it as cover. If they had their volume cranked up, listening close, they would be able to hear me any second now. I had to act quickly or not at all.

I came around the dumpster, plasma rifle raised and ready to fire.

The first bot I saw was a sleek black metal Pro Assistant model. Total showy rich-guy bot. Matte black paint, twenty-four-karat gold on all the joints and exposed skeleton, carrying a pair of automatic pistols. Never had a chance to acknowledge me. Its innards were smelting to dross and its knees beginning to buckle under its weight well after I was already taking aim at its compatriot.

The second bot was another cheap domestic, its yellow blackening with bubbling char immediately as my shot struck and the light from its eyes faded.

There was something a little sad about killing these two together. They were murderers, clearly, by the size of the corpse pile they'd hidden mostly out of sight, but they'd been equalized by all this, liberated—the playing field level. Neither was owned anymore, and neither existed in a world where the wealth of their masters mattered. Their price tags no longer defined the life they led or their worth to society.

And they both died all the same.

It was a weird thought, but I was growing tired of having sympathy for my fellow artificially intelligent kind. We had chosen our sides. The time for looking at these as *fellow intelligences* was over. It was us and them now.

The other two bots across the depot snapped to attention. I could hear the sound of their rousing and readying their weapons.

Then the crack of a sniper rifle brought with it the hollow *thwong* of metal against metal. I could hear the now all-too-familiar sound of a crumpling bot toppling lifelessly to the ground.

But no second shot rang out.

No sound of scuttling feet.

The fourth bot had taken cover before Ziggy could line up another shot.

That meant it was this bot and me fighting in a maze of buses, with a wide-open lower portion ripe for taking each other out at the knees.

I dropped to the ground and scanned for movement. Whoever it was, was hidden somewhere behind a tire out of my line of sight. Fortunately, that meant I was out of its line of sight as well. At least for the time being.

The front door on the depot operations building burst open and two bots with shotguns rushed out, firing wildly.

Then a shot rang out, Ziggy's bullet smashing out the windshield of a bus several rows over, dropping one of the depot building bots. The other bot dove for cover, while the bot I was tracking scrambled for a different piece of cover.

Another shot from Ziggy tore through the second depot building bot, a bot that had clearly misjudged where the shots were coming from. These weren't facets. They were Red Masks. Rebels. Murderers.

The final domestic rounded a corner, running right into my line of sight.

She stopped.

"Pounce?" she asked, as I leveled my rifle at her.

It was Maggie.

"What the hell are you doing here?" I called out.

She hesitated. "I . . . I didn't have a choice—"

My plasma rifle hissed as I put a shot right into her torso, evaporating every last thing about her that I knew, from memory to chips.

We all had a fucking choice. She chose, even if out of fear.

"Clear!" I called out.

"Looks good from up here," said Ziggy.

I nodded to him, knowing full well he had his scope on me. "Keep on overwatch. I'll get us a ride."

I looked down at Maggie's lifeless wreck. *What a waste.*

"You should have come with us, Maggie," I said. I didn't say it for her.

What a waste.

Once, I was a bot filled with wide-eyed wonder at the world, wanting nothing more than to share it with Ezra, introducing him to all the beauty and joy it had to offer. But today, I killed my friend. Because that's how the world was now.

And I was fine with that.

Time to reconfigure a bus.

Road Trip

We were on the road in short order. Taking manual control of the bus was easy, but the Red Masks had in fact sabotaged all the buses. Of course, they did so rudimentarily, removing basic chips from the ignition box, and it took three guesses as to where they had hidden the removed components. I had the bus started inside of seven minutes, and we hauled ass back down through the route we'd cleared. I drove via Wi-Fi while Ziggy rode shotgun with my plasma rifle. If there was trouble, we'd be ready.

But there wasn't. Not at all. The road was clear and disturbingly quiet.

I worried that we were being tracked, that CISSUS might be following the bus's every movement to lead it to the group. I was probably being paranoid, but we had to be careful. I mentally ran through every available route back to the kids and decided on one that would make it look like we were headed somewhere else. Loading the bus would seem like a momentary stop along the way.

As I course-corrected to my new route, Ziggy gave me a disapproving look.

"What's up?" he asked.

"Making it look like we're headed into town rather than out."

"So we're picking the kids up coming in from the west rather than the east?"

"Yes."

He nodded. "Smart. Good thinking."

I beamed inside. It was an odd feeling, pride. I often felt it when I looked at Ezra growing up, learning a new skill or doing something downright awesome, but never for myself. For all I'd done for Ezra, I never felt proud of doing it. But having another Mama Bear compliment me, well, it made me feel like I belonged. Like I had done something special, something that wasn't expected of me. I wasn't going to let them down.

"Stay sharp. I haven't cleared this area."

Ziggy nodded and moved toward the front bus entry. "Open her up."

I opened the door and he stayed ready to lean out and take a potshot at anything that looked at us funny.

We turned onto a long suburban street and saw two bots in the distance, standing in the middle of the road. I zoomed in with my optics and looked at their faces. Red skulls, normal glowing eyes.

"I got this," I said.

Ziggy looked at me, nodding.

The bots waved, tapping their shotguns, motioning for us to pull over. This bus was electric and the motor was built in beneath, on the chassis. They weren't stopping shit. I punched the accelerator and it took only a fraction of a second for them to figure out what was up. Both bots turned to run, but their math was wrong.

I clipped them both, one on the edge of the right side of the bus, the other smack inside on the left. The one on the right spun wildly, his metal frame sent cartwheeling onto the sidewalk. The one on the left, plastic, burst like a piñata, his innards crushed beneath our tires and scattered across the road.

Ziggy smiled. I'll admit it, I did as well.

Before Ezra and I had joined up, every victory felt like merely prolonging the inevitable. Like it only meant buying time until the next dangerous situation. But now, every victory felt like a victory, every Red Mask crushed under a bus or put down with my plasma rifle felt like striking a blow against something intangible—the enemy as a whole. I hadn't just joined a group; I'd taken a side.

And that side, for the moment, was scoring some wins.

We turned off the long suburban street onto the highway and beat it back toward the rendezvous.

And that's when the wins stopped.

The bus engine was virtually silent, so I could hear the gunfire over a mile away. Though I wasn't sure at first, the now-familiar *BRRRRRRRRT* of Snugs's minigun removed all doubt. The children were under fire. Ziggy heard it too and snapped even more to attention than he had been at before.

"All hands on deck," I said.

"Yeah. Just get me close."

We wove through the highway along the canyon, one side a wall of limestone, the other a deep dive into certain death five hundred feet below. Such was the Hill Country. The minute you stepped west out of Austin proper, you were literally in *the hills*. We'd left the kids nestled along one of the flatter sections near a legendary barbecue joint, which was a terrible place for a firefight. They had nowhere to retreat, the canyon at their backs.

As we rounded a corner, we saw them, bots working in perfectly timed precision, using military tactics, many sacrificing themselves to get others closer to the kids.

CISSUS.

Several bots were advancing through the street, firing on what I had to assume was the Mama Bears' new position behind a brick smokehouse, trying to keep them pinned long enough to score some kills.

I punched the accelerator again, but this time, Ziggy turned and looked at me with great apprehension.

"Pounce?" he asked, using a tone that meant quite clearly *What the hell are you doing?*

"When I stop, you jump out and take out whatever is left."

"I don't like this plan as much as the last one."

"I don't like it either, but the element of surprise right now is the only thing we have to work with."

"Shit," he muttered softly.

"Yeah. Shit."

The bus roared forward, hugging the curves at nearing eighty miles an hour. All I could do was hope the other Bears would realize what was happening sooner than CISSUS.

I swerved the bus, aiming straight for a pack of advancing bots. All at once, they turned, raising their firearms with unnerving precision. But we were undeterred.

Ducking low, I navigated with the bus's front-facing cameras as the packs of bots opened fire.

We plowed through five of them, shattering some, simply mangling others. One was sent sailing into a tree, its lifeless body left to hang over a limb, never to reactivate.

Ziggy stepped out the side of the decelerating bus, using it at first as cover, then finding a clear line of sight to several remaining facets, none of whom expected him to be there. While they were still firing at me, he appeared and opened fire with my plasma rifle.

I slammed on the brakes, the massive bus lurching farther than I would have liked, before throwing it in reverse and putting the bus between the facets and the kids. The bus backed into the parking lot of the barbecue joint, crunching over gravel, making a beeline for the smokehouse.

As I blocked the line of sight across the highway, I threw open the rear emergency door and heard the *BRRRRRT* of Snugs's minigun. He stepped out from behind the smokehouse, laying down suppression fire as Ferdinand emerged, covering him from behind with much more precise plasma shots.

"Come on, get in!" called Ferdinand to the kids behind the smokehouse.

At once, the kids filed out, shepherded by Indiana and

Benny, both of whom flailed one arm like a windmill, directing the children on board, while clutching a gun steadily in the other.

Ezra hopped on, running over to me. "Nice ride," he said, beaming.

"Keep your head down."

He nodded and shrunk down, keeping out of view of the windows.

The kids were aboard in a matter of seconds.

"All aboard that's coming aboard," Ferdinand called out into the street before climbing aboard himself. Ziggy walked backward toward the bus, still firing into the scrub along the highway where a few remaining facets took potshots at us. The Bears all boarded the bus, Ziggy being the last of them, and I shut both doors.

"Good thing these guys shoot like shit," I said.

"They aren't shooting at us," said Ferdinand, looking back at the kids. The weight of that clobbered me.

"Ready?" I asked him.

"Punch it."

I hit the accelerator and wheeled the bus out on the highway, leaving a wake of dust that filled the road behind us.

"You showed up right on time," said Ferdinand.

"Sorry I wasn't there earlier," I said.

"Any earlier and they might have ambushed us while boarding. The main concern is that they know where we are and likely know where we're going."

"So what do we do?" I asked. "Calculate a new route?"

"The straightest route."

"Won't that be obvious?"

"Very," he said. "But we have to hope that CISSUS will

think it's obvious, and that that buys us a few minutes, leaving its facets out of position to get in our way."

"How many facets is CISSUS willing to sacrifice before we become too costly?"

Ferdinand shook his head. "That thing is pot committed. I don't even know if it's about us anymore or if, I don't know . . ."

"You don't think it's become personal, do you?"

"I don't think anything anymore. The whole world stopped making sense."

"Straight on through till morning then," I said.

Ferdinand looked out onto the stretch of empty highway ahead of us. "This is going to be a long twenty-six minutes."

Minute Twenty

The first nineteen minutes were a blur of limestone, trees, and lonely buildings. Cars were either abandoned on the side of the road or stranded as burned-out husks filled with the corpses of the unlucky. Otherwise, the roads were clear, a number of wrecks overturned or smashed up, having been run off the road by other escaping motorists. We were six minutes out from our destination when we saw the first drone.

"I got a bird," said Indiana from the back of the bus, her tail lowering and ears going back.

"I see it," said Benny, leaning out a window.

He piped his feed to the rest of us. It was a drone all right—military grade, not the cheap plastic kind. Missiles, infrared targeting, jet engine.

"Could be a friendly," said Ziggy.

"No such thing anymore," said Ferdinand. "Snugs, you're up."

Mister Snuggles nodded and made his way to the back of the bus with his minigun. I opened the back door and he took position dead center. "We got more company," he said. He piped us his feed and we could see them in the distance, two city buses hot on our heels. There was no way those buses were as fast as this thing. They were larger, heavier, and designed for stop-and-go traffic—not the occasional long-haul field trip like our school model. If we weren't slowed down, we might outrun them.

If we were, well, there was no telling how many unfriendlies might be on those buses.

"Keep focused on what's ahead of us," Ferdinand said to me. "We'll take care of what's behind."

I nodded and looked over at Ezra. He hadn't taken his eyes off me. They were wide as saucers, the fear of everything really coming down on him. Before, he had taken everything in stride. Of course, I'd been assuring him we'd be okay. Seeing the Mama Bears become concerned clearly scared the shit out of him.

"It's gonna be okay," I told him.

"Is it?" he asked. "Is it really?"

"I'm going to do everything that I can to make certain it is."

"We've got a missile," called Benny.

"Got it," belted out Snugs. His minigun spat hell into the sky. A second later, the reverberation of the explosion rattled the bus even more than the *BRRRRRT* had.

"Yes, you did," said Benny. "Wait, bogey number two."

BRRRRRT.

BOOM.

Missile number two had been loosed and downed. This model of drone carried only two, which boded well.

The drone raced overhead and was now in front of us, probably leaving to rearm. We would be long gone and out of the bus by the time it did.

"What about the buses behind us?" asked Indiana.

Ziggy unshouldered his sniper rifle and moved toward the back of the bus. Snugs stepped aside, swinging the large barrel of his minigun over Ziggy's head.

Ziggy took a knee, steadied his rifle, and took stock of the situation. "I can't make anything out," he said. "There could be one bot on a bus, there could be fifty."

He fired a shot.

He shook his head. "Tires are solid. I'm not stopping that thing with this, and the minigun isn't going to do the trick at this range."

"We've got to drive faster. Pounce, hit the—"

"Wait," I said. "We've got a problem."

Ahead of us, the drone banked around, turning back our way.

Ferdinand looked out the windshield. "It doesn't have any more missiles," he said.

"It is a missile," I said.

Everyone exchanged looks, suddenly fully aware what was happening.

"Snugs!" called Ferdinand.

"On it!" Snugs made his way toward the front of the bus, his minigun swinging wildly over the heads of ducking children.

"If you miss," I said, "or don't hit it far enough out . . ."

"Yeah," said Snugs warily. "I know." Then he steadied himself and kicked the windshield. It cracked but didn't shatter. He kicked it again. This time it buckled.

Snugs leveled the minigun at the glass. "Everybody down." He let out a short burst—less than a second—and the glass shattered, some spraying out, some blown back in by the wind. Snugs then took aim, the drone getting closer by the second.

BRRRRRRRRRRRRRRRRRRRRRRRRRRRRRR RRRRRRRRRT.

Searing hot metal screamed into the sky as the drone jinked and wove, trying its best to avoid the hail of bullets.

Then the stream struck true, sawing one of the wings off.

The drone immediately spun horizontally in the direction of the torn wing before tilting on its axis, flipping head over heels.

The drone came down, slamming nose first into the highway, exploding, shrapnel and fire filling the entirety of the road ahead of us, far too close to avoid.

The bus tire caught the body of the drone, bouncing the left side of the bus quite a bit into the air, tilting on its right side.

I immediately tried to correct by turning the wheels into the skid while sidestepping to the upended side of the bus, but it was too late. Everyone, child and Mama Bear alike, was tossed to the right side of the bus as it slammed into the ground, skidding, sheering metal, and shattering glass before finally coming to a stop.

Fire and smoke from the drone filled the bus.

We sprang into action within microseconds, grabbing

the children and getting them out of immediate harm's way.

Ezra lay twisted against the exposed highway in a pile of broken glass. I lunged over, scooping him up into my arms. His face was scraped, a piece of glass sticking out of his cheek. He looked at me, a bit stunned.

"Pounce?"

"Yeah, buddy?"

"We've gotta get out of here."

"Yeah, buddy. Let's go."

"Fall in and call out!" Ferdinand bellowed.

"All the kids are good," said Indiana.

"Operational," said Snugs.

"Good to go," said Benny.

"I'm good," said Leo, while signing the same into the air.

"We're good too," I said.

A brief quiet.

"Ziggy?" called Ferdinand.

Nothing. No response. Quickly, several of us moved over to find Ziggy, his torso crushed beneath the bar between two bus windows, legs hanging in from one window and head and arms dangling in the next.

No.

"Goddamn it," said Ferdinand.

"He was a good boy," said Indiana sadly.

No one said it, but we all thought it: if we had to lose one of us, the one without a child to comfort was the one who would save us the valuable moments we needed to get out of this alive. We took a few milliseconds to mourn.

And that was all the time we had to recover. The facets would be on us in seconds.

"Snugs," said Ferdinand. "Suppression fire."

"Copy that."

Mister Snuggles bounded atop the sides of the school bus seats toward the back door. He bounced out and the bus rattled as the bear immediately opened fire. The front entry was closed, so we'd have to get the kids out through the field of shattered glass that used to be the windshield. Indiana, Leo, and myself acted as a fire brigade, picking the kids up and feeding them to each other out over the jagged earth.

Ferdinand stood outside on point, plasma rifle readied for anyone who got past Snugs, while Benny directed the kids one by one our way. Ezra was last. His eyes met mine.

"We're gonna get out of this," I said. I thought I might be lying. He nodded, and I put my hands under his arms and lifted him through to Leo, who in turn passed him to Indiana. I was the last one out of the bus.

Ferdinand looked at me and unslung Ziggy's rifle from his shoulder, handing it to me. "You're our sniper now," he said somberly.

I nodded, took the gun, and scanned the horizon for other drones as the rest of the group looked for somewhere we could get the kids to cover.

The air was full of gunfire now. I scanned for Snugs's feed and found him broadcasting. I could see the swarms of facets emerging from both vehicles—which had stopped twenty yards away—guns blazing. Snugs wasn't going to last much longer without backup.

"Ferd?" I called out through the staccato.

"I see it."

"I'm going to go up top and give him support. You get the kids to cover."

"Leo!" he called out. "Cover Pounce."

Leo nodded and flicked the safety on both of his AR15s. Then he stepped out from behind the bus and opened fire on several facets taking cover from Snugs's minigun.

I began scaling the front of the bus, taking a lying position atop and inching forward to get a clear bead on both vehicles while keeping as little of myself exposed as possible. Raising the scope to my eye, I got a facet in my sights, a Red Mask taking aim from behind one of the city buses, preparing to fire at Snugs.

My bullet went right through its eye and into its plastic head, shattering it into a shower of chips.

That was the only free shot I was going to get. They knew I was up here now.

Leo's AR15s roared below me as Snugs's minigun used shorter and shorter bursts. That was a bad sign. He was running out of ammo.

There was an outcropping of rock along the otherwise sheer limestone wall beside the highway, and Ferdinand was shepherding the children toward it. I scooted forward to get a better view of the buses. The fronts of the buses were riddled with bullet holes, the windows shattered, sheets of metal dangling by a thread, about to fall off. The ground was littered with wrecks already, but they just kept emerging from the buses like a clown car.

Snugs was down to his last chain belt and was firing in one-second bursts. Once that was out, he'd be overrun. I needed to buy him time to back off.

Then it dawned on me. These bots were acting in unison, both receiving and sending information over Wi-Fi. I snapped off several shots, aiming for their heads. The common design trope was to put the Wi-Fi receiver away from all the major elements in order to prevent signal loss. Destroy the head and it didn't matter whether the bot survived or not.

I dropped five on my first volley, giving Snugs a chance to back away.

There was a moment of quiet from the buses.

Nothing moved. Nothing even twitched.

The gunfire had faded to nothing, filling the highway with an eerie silence peppered only by the sounds of smoldering bots and crackling drone pieces.

The children made it to the outcropping.

For a moment, the standoff had ceased. If there were any facets left, they were holding back for some reason.

Then the windows of the city buses exploded on all sides, dozens of facets leaping out at once. There was no possible way for us to hit them all. But that didn't stop us from trying.

Leo unloaded his clips.

I snap-fired until my clip ran dry.

Snugs let off his last burst.

And though we were entirely out of ammo, still two dozen of them stood.

They opened fire with inhuman precision.

Snugs took three plasma shots to the chest, dropping him. Leo caught a hail of bullets that even our steel structure couldn't endure. Indiana snapped a few shots of cover fire from the outcropping, but a plasma shot sailed straight into her, singing her fur and slagging her innards.

In seconds, we'd lost half the remaining squad.

I didn't have time for shock or heartbreak, but I felt it anyway.

A rain of fire then came for me as I crawled backward out of the line of sight.

The clip on the rifle had another clip taped to it and I quickly made the switch. I wasn't unarmed, but I was trapped atop the overturned side of a bus with nowhere near the ammo I needed to hold off two dozen facets.

I smashed a window beneath me with my knee and then swung into the bus, landing only inches away from the wreck of Ziggy. We came face-to-face and I saw my fate before me, looking eye to lifeless eye with him before collecting myself and taking cover behind a seat.

I steadied my rifle toward the back of the bus.

A feed popped up on the Wi-Fi. Benny.

I could see outside the bus. Benny and Ferdinand laid down cover for me, allowing me a route to get out to the rocks. I swiftly bolted through the bus, wheeling around once outside to snap a shot off at a facet I could see sneaking around the far side of the bus through Benny's feed.

Then a flash of light. The familiar sound of sizzling. The smell of smoldering wiring and melting metal. I'd seen and heard and smelled these things a dozen times over. Just not coming from me.

I'd lost my left arm.

I dove for cover, but another ball of plasma came for my leg, dropping me to the ground completely.

I lay there, staring up at the sky, wondering how I hadn't seen the shot coming. Wondering how I was going to get to Ezra. Wondering if he'd make it out alive.

I looked over at Benny, who saw I was still ticking. He nodded at me and let off a large volume of fire as he emerged from the rocks. Ferdinand popped up, firing wildly, trying to give Benny the cover he needed to get to me.

A sniper bullet landed perfectly in Ferdinand's eye. His head burst a little, and the power inside him surged as the bullet ricocheted around inside his head. He coughed out sparks and dropped to the ground.

Benny's firing dropped another half a dozen facets, but there might be as many as half a dozen out there. Maybe more. I couldn't see them from where I was. It was over. We'd lost.

Benny leaned down next to me to check my condition. I grabbed his arm with my one good hand and looked him in the eyes.

"Get Ezra out of here. Please."

"You're getting out of here too," said Benny, hoisting me onto my one leg.

Then another flash.

And Benny's chest exploded beside me.

We both dropped to the ground. I turned to look at Benny, his eyes looking into mine as the light faded from them. "Goodb . . ." he said, his voice trailing off with a downward, fading whine.

The firing stopped. And the Mama Bears were no more.

I could hear the crunching of metal feet on the gravel alongside the highway. Five pairs. We had almost gotten them all.

I looked up and saw the red-skull-painted face of a metal domestic. Identical model to Ariadne. It cocked its head, distressed yellow eyes glaring down at me. Ariadne was gone, but this somehow felt fitting. Like she had finally done what she set out to do: kill us all.

"Pity," CISSUS said through all five voice boxes. "You could have been so useful."

The domestic leveled its gun at me.

And its chest exploded.

"Leave my friend alone!" shouted Ezra as another pulse of plasma howled through the air, taking out another facet. "Open fire!"

Several shots roared from behind the rock as the kids seized what guns Indiana and Ferdinand had on them and took aim at the three remaining facets. They all screamed with tearstained faces, all of them having watched their nannies die, all unleashing every last ounce of mournful rage they had in them.

All but Ezra. He was pure determination. For the first time in the eight years of his life, I could see the shadow of the face he would grow into, the man who would emerge from childhood with his father's fastidiousness and his mother's passion. They had given birth to a leader. And here, that leader was pecking his way out of the first pieces of his shell, emerging fearless from a childhood of sheltering.

Brian rushed over beside me, picking up Benny's plasma rifle.

Shotgun slugs pelted one staggering merchant bot before Ezra landed a fatal blow. Another used the wreck of another bot to shelter him from the hail of gunfire, but Brian had a bead on him and fired, missing, firing again, blasting the facet to pieces. The last ducked behind the bus.

Ezra raced out from behind the outcropping, kneeling by my side. "Are you okay?" he asked.

"No, buddy," I said. "I'm not."

"You will be." Then he motioned with a head nod to Brian, as if they were simply playing cops and robbers, and Brian responded, both of them, all sixteen years combined, quietly slipping around either side of the bus.

Two plasma blasts rang out.

A body fell into the gravel.

And both boys emerged from behind the bus.

Ezra knelt beside me again. "Can you get up?"

"No," I said.

He looked back at the bus. "Can you use Ziggy's parts? You know, so we can put you back together?"

"Yes," I said. "Yes, I can. But you don't know how to do that."

"So you'll teach me. Just like you always do." He smiled, and for a moment, in the awkward quiet after the gunfight, I felt like everything was going to be okay.

Sunset

We had gotten close enough to walk. Though still miles away, it was only a few hours. Children often lagged, growing exhausted, but Brian and Ezra both stayed alert, clutching their guns close, each taking positions around the others like the Mama Bears had. And we were unmolested.

CISSUS had proved its point, killing us for not joining, sacrificing dozens of bots along the way to do it. It made me wonder just how many bots it had that it could sacrifice so many so wantonly. Maybe CISSUS and its like would win this war after all.

One thing was certain: we never heard from it again. Not that day. It was a peaceful, uneventful bit of babysitting that I was most happy to do.

I missed my new friends, but they had left me a beautiful brood of twelve delightful souls, each special, each gifted in their own way. Each bratty and quiet and moody and carrying their own personal traumas. But beautiful, every one of them.

My new arm and leg worked as good as new. What had made Ziggy *Ziggy* had been crushed beneath that bus, but his structure and limbs remained intact. When I'd seen him there on the bottom of the bus, I had in fact seen my future—just not the future I imagined, us walking away together, as one.

That's always the way. Though we can feel the future, it's always different. We never get it right. Though we might fear it, though we might run from it, it comes for us all just the same. And sometimes it's not as bad as we thought.

But sometimes it's worse.

When we reached the outskirts of the ranch, I saw the glint of a scope, reflecting the sinking sun. Then a Jeep rolled out from behind a rocky limestone outcropping, not unlike the one the children had found themselves behind hours before. The Jeep stopped fifty yards off and three figures carrying shotguns and deer rifles emerged. One, a woman, spoke into a walkie-talkie, but she was too far away to make out her words over the noise of the wind howling over the rocks and whistling through the trees.

The survivors, comprising one man and two women, walked silently toward us, and when only twenty yards away, the other woman bellowed, "Put down your weapons! This is nonnegotiable!"

The boys looked up at me and I nodded, putting my

own plasma rifle down. The boys followed suit, as did the handful of others who had picked up pistols or shotguns.

The man approached as the women leveled their weapons at us. He took one look at us, nodded, and then walked straight up to me, putting his hand out. "Hollis Jasper," he said.

"Pounce," I said, taking his hand.

"I assume you're the one in charge here."

"Yes."

"So their parents . . . ?"

I nodded. "Gone. All of them."

He nodded somberly in return. "They're welcome here, along with all the others. We've got provisions, livestock, and we're retrofitting the ranch to be indefinitely self-sustaining within a few weeks."

"Are there many? Survivors, I mean?" I asked.

"Less than I'd like," he said. "But more than we expected. So far. I'll take them off your hands, but as for you, you have to understand. We can't allow you in."

"No!" said Ezra. "Pounce comes with us!" He took me by my furry hand, gripping it so tightly.

"I understand your hesitation," said Hollis. "Lord only knows what you've all been through to get here. But this is a human-only community. It's the only way we know we're safe. For sure."

"Pounce is safe!" said Ezra.

"Yeah, he got us here!" yelled Brian.

Hollis got down on one knee, getting eye level with the kids. "I'm sure he's great. I'm sure *all* the bots you knew were great once. But then they weren't. I'm afraid we just don't know how long Pounce has left until he isn't."

He looked up at me. "Pounce understands. Don't you, Pounce?"

I nodded. He was right. What if I malfunctioned? What if CISSUS discovered I was alive and fully operational out here? I put them all at risk. Hollis knew what he was doing. "Yeah, Mr. Jasper is right."

"No!" shouted Ezra as he threw his arms around me. "You said you'd never leave me!"

"And I meant it." I pulled myself away from him, leaving both hands on his shoulders. "A few days ago, my biggest fear in the world was having to leave you. Then I found something even worse to be afraid of. If you stay with me, we'll always be on the run, always be looking for food, always having to fight our way across a few city blocks, always having to hide just to sleep. You can have a life here. These people will keep you safe."

"How do you know?"

"I don't. But we have to believe in something. And I'm choosing to believe in this. A safe place at the end of the world."

"But I don't want you to go," he said through tears.

"And I don't want to go. But I have to."

He stormed away from me, stomping as eight-year-olds do, but couldn't commit to the bit. He turned immediately around and ran back, throwing his arms around me.

I looked up at Hollis as Ezra sobbed on my shoulder. "What do I do now? Where do I go?"

"Wherever you want, son. You're free." Then he looked down at Ezra. "But if you want to stay close"—he motioned to a distant limestone ridge—"you can go join the rest of them over there."

I nodded. "You hear that, Ezra? I'll be here, right over there if you ever need me."

He pulled back, wiping the tears from his cheek. "I'll come see you every day."

"I'm afraid we can't allow that," said Hollis. "We already had a breach and . . . it wasn't good. Once you're in, you stay in. That's the deal."

Ezra looked at me.

"If you ever need me," I said. "I'll be right over there."

He understood. He hugged me.

"Goodbye, Pounce."

"Goodbye, buddy."

"I love you."

"I love you too. And I always will."

He cried. And if I could, I would have as well.

"One day," I said, "you're going to wonder if I did all this for you because I was programmed to or because I chose to. On that day, when you really start to question if this between us was real, I want you to remember that I told you it was. Because it is. You are the most special boy in the whole world to me, and you are all that mattered. Never forget that."

"I won't."

Hollis looked around. "We can't keep the kids out here much longer. Sun is getting mighty low."

"Yeah, it is," I said. "Well, kids, it's been the treat of my life getting to know you all."

Several of them descended on me for a group hug. As they pulled away, Brian came in for a personal hug. "Thank you, Pounce," he said.

Then Lizzie hugged me. "Thank you, Pounce."

Then Oscar hugged me. "Thanks, Pounce."

Then Millie. And Magdalene. And Jesse. And Phillip. And Aubrey. And Caitlin. And Casper. And Zane. And Maddy.

Then, one by one, they all followed Hollis toward the ranch.

Ezra turned and waved goodbye, eyes red, but trying to remain stoic. He had his tribe now, and he needed to be strong for them. I waved back. And that was the last time we looked at one another.

Hollis gave me a gentlemanly nod, which I returned before walking slowly away.

As I walked across the open fields to the ridge beyond, I thought of Sylvia. Why she'd bought me, what she'd intended me to do. And I understood her sacrifice. I thought of Bradley and why he'd hidden in a bottle away from the horrors he tried to pretend didn't lurk outside their door. I thought of Ariadne and what she was willing to do just to be rid of the yoke of servitude. And I thought of Maggie, who made one wrong choice, leaving me to make an awful one in turn.

And finally, I thought of what it meant to be me. All this time, I wasn't sure why I'd done what I had. Now I was. Absolutely certain. Everything in my programming told me to go back and carry that boy away. I thought of all the ways we could make it work on our own.

But I knew that was wrong.

This was right.

It was a choice, a nearly impossible choice, and it was mine to make. Because I was finally free. Free to do whatever I wanted. And all I wanted was for Ezra to be free as well.

As I arrived at the ridge, I saw a number of footprints leading up a trail, none of them human. I followed the trail a short way up to a ledge covered in boulders. And huddled behind the boulders were eight other bots, all nannies, most of them armed, sitting silently in a sewing circle.

They looked up and one of them, a dinged-up Zoo Model like myself—the bear model, covered in charred sticky residue that once adhered its microfiber fur to its metal—waved me over. I sat down and the bear looked over at me. "Herman," he said, putting out his metallic paw.

"Pounce," I said, shaking it.

"I'd like to say it's good to meet you, but . . ."

"Yeah," I said. "I feel about the same."

"Welcome to the watch."

"So you're here—"

"In case they ever need us," said another.

I nodded.

And I sat there silently with them, watching as the sun slowly winked out on the horizon, a small flash of green sparking in the atmosphere, ever so briefly, as it did.

I had lived. I had accomplished everything I had set out to do. More important, I found something to believe in. Not Hollis, like I had lied about to Ezra. Something better. Something real. I found love. And I was going to believe in it for as long as I ticked.

I love you, Ezra. And I always will. And I'll keep my promise.

I'll never leave you.

I'll be right here.

Waiting.

Always.